THE Show

N. G. SANDERS

GETTING ON IT IS MURDER!

AND THEN THERE WERE MORE

A TRILOGY OF STAND-ALONE NOVELS

Front Cover by Rolff Images & Covers

Printed by CreateSpace and Amazon KDP
Printed in the United States of America
Available from Amazon.com and other retail outlets

First Printing Edition, 2020

For my parents

Scribbled notes on the cast of the Divine Leader show

(An early list describing seven of the assembled housemates, later submitted as Exhibit 2A in court)

Alice

This aspiring celebrity chef will raise the spirits in the house by keeping everyone well fed.

Tim

This Zen master has his own YouTube fitness and wellbeing channel. Tim will keep everyone in shape after Alice's treats.

Phil

With a set of perfect abs, the rock-hard former-soldier turned personal trainer will assist Tim in his efforts.

Harvey

A mature student and former local radio DJ, noisy by nature and will have no reservations asking personal questions of the other housemates.

Jenny

This model from Essex is no one's bimbo, running her own PR company. A widower estranged from her stepdaughter.

Rachel

The baby of the group. An agreeable person to go with the disagreeable people so far on this list.

Dale

The rebel without a cause who will break all the house rules in a heartbeat. A musician who busks on the streets of London.

PART ONE

Lights, Camera, Action!

Chapter One

Tia was the last contestant to enter the house. Her knuckles turned white as she gripped a suitcase weighing a microgram less than the twenty kilos the rules stipulated, the fingers of her free hand crossed for luck.

An electronic pulsing sounded as the door clanged shut, sealing her off from the rest of the world.

I'm on TV! I've done it! I'm on mainstream, prime-time TV.

There must be more than a million people watching me right now.

The exhilaration of finally fulfilling this goal felt all-encompassing in its significance. As if the world Tia had occupied for the previous twenty-nine years had ceased to exist.

Tia took a sharp intake of breath, trying not to look as nervous as she felt. Her dress started to feel too short and her make-up too thin as she made her way down the stairwell in high heels.

Tia tried not to think of all the cameras on her.

It proved an impossible task as she looked straight into one, her nerves making her feel clumsy and self-conscious.

A tall guy in skinny jeans and a fitted black jacket waited for her at the bottom of the stairwell.

"I'll be a gentleman," the kickboxer-thin guy said to her, taking the suitcase from Tia and introducing himself as Harvey.

"I'm Tia," she replied.

"As in the drink?"

"Sorry, you what?"

"Surely someone must have called you Tia Maria before?"

"Oh right," Tia rolled her eyes and grinned. "When I was a kid."

Even with the weight of her suitcase, Harvey walked in a natural, confident way as he spoke. "Are you the last?"

"I believe so."

He smiled, "trust me, there's no reason to be nervous. We're all in the same boat."

Tia nodded.

Everywhere Tia looked the decor was a sterile, futuristic white and chrome effect that some overpaid sci-fi fanboy designer must have thought was tech chic but felt as far removed from homely as could be. The harsh lighting was unsettling with its bars of fluorescent glow, washing out the colour in their clothing.

A chorus of hellos greeted Tia as she entered the main living area where the other housemates were seated on two massive, L-shaped sofas. They all stood up in unison the moment they saw Tia.

"Nice to meet you, everyone," Tia said, barely recognizing her voice.

Harvey promptly introduced Tia. "I think it's better if we all go sit down and say a little about ourselves again. Give Tia a chance to settle in."

"Now for the most important question," Harvey said. "Red or white?"

Grinning, he held up two plastic flutes.

Taking consideration of the fact that she was on live television, and not wanting red wine teeth, she opted for the fizzing glass of white she assumed was Prosecco but turned out to be champagne.

"Champers," Harvey confirmed. "Classy lady."

Tia's first task was to remember all their names. Then to work out who her allies were, as well as her frenemies, and her competition for eviction.

They bonded over the one thing they all had in common: how much they despised their meaningless jobs. Three of them were currently between occupations.

"I'm a mature student," Harvey said with a wry smile. "It covers a multitude of sins."

Alice, seldom out of the kitchen, was the aspiring celebrity chef. Alice had the sort of self-assurance that only a private-school education brings, and had never had to work full-time for a living because of the financially privileged position of her parents.

The other non-worker was Dale, a busker who was unabashed by his situation.

"So, Dale," Tia asked. "What is it you do for a living?"

"As little as possible," he replied, breaking into a song titled, "I do nothing all day long, babe."

After being pushed to clear this detail up, he said with a smile that he got the "benefit of the doubt".

Dale's comment led to a debate on the fairness of the benefits system, and the work ethic of those who claimed it. The discussion was initiated and fuelled by Alice, who was annoyed at Dale's laid-back attitude to being out of work.

The conversation remained intense and opinionated for the next two hours.

11:13 p.m.

Tia agreed to do some washing-up, snatching up glasses, mugs and cups. To her surprise, Dale volunteered to help with the drying.

Dale had that grungy look, with stylistically tousled hair, designer stubble, baggy combats and a Nirvana T-shirt that would no doubt be getting pungent by the end of the first week because Tia could tell that he wasn't going to change it.

The tattoo on his forearm Tia recognized as a Kurt Cobain quote: *everyone laughs at me because I'm different, I laugh at them because they are all the same.*

Coming from Cobain, a naturally rebellious bad boy, the words seemed insightful, but written on Dale's flesh they came across as defensive; reduced to mere self-justification for being a loner who didn't fit in.

Verdict on Dale: A loner but capable of making people laugh. Possible ally, but hard to read at times.

Yawning at each other, but even more hungry than they were tired, they were about to eat in the kitchen when Phil started up another debate. Tia sensed the type of argument developing where a man genuinely thinks he is being objective in his viewpoint and not subjective.

"So," Phil said, gesturing at Tim and Rachel snuggling up together on a lounge chair. "What's your take on infidelity? Is it the ultimate betrayal as society would have us believe?"

"What?" Rachel said, sounding more confused than irritated by Phil's comment.

"Cheating," Phil said. "What's your view on it? Is it the ultimate shame, or is it about unexpressed desires?"

"I know what infidelity is," Rachel said. "You don't need to spell it out for me. And I don't appreciate what you're insinuating."

Phil threw his hands up in despair. "I'm not insinuating anything, it's just you said you had a boyfriend. And Tim has a girlfriend."

"I don't," Tim said.

"I heard you talking about a Sadie?" Phil said.

"That's my cat," Tim replied, looking perplexed. As if Phil were crazy.

Dale and Jenny couldn't help but snigger.

"Oh, Phil!" Jenny burst out into uncontrollable laughter. "You ass."

Phil smiled. "Okay, bad example, but hear me out. I've got a point."

"And what is your point?" Tia waded in, which everyone laughed at, including Tia herself. "Do you even have one?"

"Other than you're a natural-born *cheater*," Alice said.

"Hey," Harvey mocked, "put that shovel down, mate. Soon you'll have dug yourself so deep we won't be able to find you when you get nominated for eviction."

Phil threw a cushion at Harvey, bouncing it off Harvey's forehead.

"Are you married?" Tia asked the question on everybody's lips. Phil wore a gym glove over his left hand so no one could tell if he wore a ring or not.

"Divorced," Phil said.

"Figures." Tia rolled her eyes and everybody laughed. "Big surprise."

"I was married," Jenny said. "It was horrible. I lost more than my name; I lost my whole identity. I even had to talk 'posh like this' for him," she went on, sounding like Eliza Doolittle post elocution lessons. "Everything became about him. It wasn't until we… separated that I realized how much he'd taken over my life."

"He was…" Jenny broke off. "Oh, it doesn't matter who he was. It's all in the past now."

Tia put her hand on hers as a show of support.

"I mean," Jenny said. "For a start, he would never have let me go on a show like this."

Tia debated internally about how much personal information she should give out this early. Not wanting to say too much, but not wanting to say too little either. But she felt so strongly about the subject that she felt compelled to say something.

"My ex," Tia said, stopping herself in time. She had almost said her ex-husband. The last thing Tia wanted was to give them details of her disastrous marriage. "I caught him with another woman."

"I'm sorry," Rachel said as if she knew the worst of it.

"Saw him with a woman just like me," Tia said. "That's what made the betrayal all the worse. She looked so much like me. Maybe five or six years younger."

She looked carefree, Tia wanted to say. *How I would appear if I were unburdened of my soul.*

Tia continued the story, censoring it, doing the self-editing in her mind before speaking to keep the tone light and avoiding painting herself as a victim.

The ease at which Tia had adapted to being on television surprised her. She made a few observational jokes about the rather formal interviewing process to seek some common ground and received some knowing laughter from everyone. She no longer lingered on the thought that the world was watching her.

She began to feel more likeable to the group and the audience because of it.

Tia felt that her nerves had gone; reality TV had transitioned into, well, reality.

Chapter Two

Immersed in conversation, they had forgotten to eat anything more substantial than the snacks Alice had rustled up. They agreed that they ought to eat something before they turned in. Tia hadn't had a bite since breakfast.

Alice cooked a pretty impressive gourmet meal, given the scraps they had found in the kitchen.

They stayed up till two-thirty in the morning getting to know each other. It reminded Tia of her first night in university halls.

The upstairs consisted of three rooms: the boys' bedroom, the girls' bedroom and a communal bathroom. The girls' room appeared cramped (and was) compared to the boys' because it was smaller and had to accommodate four as opposed to three because Dale had made the living room sofa his bed. His sleeping arrangements became yet another point of contention with Jenny, because of his lax body hygiene "and she had to sit there".

Jenny took up most of the girls' dresser space with an assortment of moisturizer creams, make-up bags, self-tanning products, hair sprays, body scrubs and cleansers. Anything Avon, the Body Shop or Clairol had in their catalogue basically, which had the effect of making the room appear even more cluttered. It only served to heighten Tia's anxiety that this was not her own space.

3:32 a.m.

Tia's sleep was skittish because of a mattress which felt firmer than a bloody tombstone. It was also the adrenalin rush of having fulfilled a lifelong dream of being on prime-time television that kept her awake. Fed up with dividing her time between ceiling watching and rolling on her side, Tia went downstairs to make hot cocoa.

"Yo!" announced a still-awake Dale from the shadows. "Can't sleep?"

"Afraid not," Tia said. "Want some cocoa?"

"No," Dale said in a tone which suggested a non-alcoholic drink offended him.

She chatted about life in general while Dale focused on his guitar-playing mother as she waited for her cocoa to cool. Somehow, she couldn't remember how exactly, they got onto star signs.

"I don't know if I'd say I believe in them," Tia said. "But I find it interesting that others do. And that they plan their whole lives around them."

"My Ma did," Dale said. "She wouldn't go a week without checking them out in the paper. She swore by them."

"Are they accurate? I mean, does the advice help her to shape her future in any positive way?"

"I guess they did in a way," Dale said, smiling. "It's only three lines of print, right?"

"You say did?"

"She's dead."

"I'm sorry," Tia said.

"Don't be; it was a long time ago. Ma was a Cancer, and she died of lung cancer. So I guess you could say they at least got that part right."

Not knowing how to respond to this, Tia changed the subject.

What could you say to that?

Dale was unwilling to move on from the subject of his departed mother as he pulled the last can of beer from a six-pack the Divine Leader had left for them to celebrate the first night in the house.

"Again, I'm sorry."

"For what?"

"I mean, how awful for you," Tia said. "At such a young age, you must have struggled to cope."

Dale shrugged, taking a swig of beer. "Shit happens, and we adapt to it."

Tia changed the subject for a second time to his guitar playing to avoid the awkward silence and also to wake Dale from his introverted stare, which was starting to freak her out.

Dale picked up his guitar and started to play before Tia shushed him, pointing to the bedroom to indicate the others sleeping. "We don't want to be made outcasts on the first night, now do we?"

"Shit, man, forgot," Dale said, putting a hand to his forehead. "My body clock's all over the place."

"No worries. Mine is too."

The combination of the living room darkness, Dale's conversation turning even more freaky, and his lighting up a spliff after he'd drained his can of beer, persuaded Tia that it was time to depart.

When she succumbed to sleep, she dreamed of Richard. He would be watching this in their Islington flat, cheering her on and seeing everything from her side.

The fame itch scratched, Tia felt that she could move forward in her relationship. Richard had always been able to calm her. That was his special gift, that and a hundred other things.

When Tia was with Richard, she forgot all about her ex-husband, and the witnessing of his brutal murder which set her free.

Chapter Three

7:46 a.m.

The vain four – Jenny, Harvey, Alice and Phil – monopolised the bathroom all morning, using up all the hot water in the process.

The others, sick of waiting, breakfasted instead.

Tia had always fancied herself as something of an amateur psychologist. It was what had attracted her to the *Divine Leader* show as a viewer. You could, for instance, tell a lot about someone by what they had for breakfast. Rachel and Dale opted for a bowl of Coco Pops, a child's choice. Tim had a meagre portion of dried apricots and an apple to cleanse his body. Tia had buttered toast and black coffee, the practical choice, which spoke of the hectic morning routine of a London commuter.

When the others emerged from their beauty regimes, they breakfasted too. Harvey, reeking of Brylcreem, opted for a full English breakfast (cooked by an obliging Alice).

Having only just turned forty and thin as a rake, Harvey was still at an age where he could afford to be less concerned about cholesterol than taste. Jenny nibbled mouse-like at rice cakes she'd packed in her case out of an almost fanatical fear of gaining even an excess ounce on her flawless figure. A concern Tia, like most women, could relate to and one that had been a factor in her own choice of only thinly spreading butter on her toast. Alice snacked on scraps of ingredients around the kitchen as she played mother and prepared Harvey's fry-up; revealing someone (like a devoted mother) too caught up in nervous energy to enjoy her food and indeed her own existence with others around.

Phil, the quiet one this morning, ate porridge in a daze. Others whispered of his lack of sociability, but Tia just thought that he wasn't a morning person.

5:37 a.m.

Dale woke the house playing, as irony would have it, *The Sound of Silence*. Dale's spaced-out state indicated the irony was unintended. When asked why the hell he was playing his guitar at five in the morning again, he shrugged and said, "Forgot." When Tia saw that he was too stoned for her grating words to have any effect, she went back to bed like the rest of the house.

How the hell he'd been able to sneak in his weed when she hadn't even been able to get her mobile phone into the house was beyond her. She didn't want to think about where he'd hidden it.

Having already awoken and seen that it was twenty to six, Tia wriggled out of bed, deciding to shower while the water was still hot. As she lathered her greasy hair with shampoo, Tia sensed someone other than a watching camera looking on.

When Tia heard a noise, she wiped the soapiness from her eyes, and looked out, just in time to see the supposedly locked door swing shut.

"Hello?"

She stepped out of the stall to peer out of the bathroom door. Tia dismissed it with a shrug and went back to showering when no one was in the hallway.

She'd been in such a hurry to get into the bathroom while it was free (with the boiler charged with hot water) that she must not have clicked the sign saying "do not enter" all the way across. She giggled to herself; someone got an eyeful. No doubt one of the guys as they'd fled, too embarrassed to apologise. She had her money on Dale.

Or Tim.

When she got into bed, she heard a voice whisper, "Tia?"

"Yes?"

It took Tia a moment to work out that it was Rachel talking in the darkness. Her tone was anxious.

"I've got something to ask you," Rachel said.

"Go ahead."

"I was in the shower earlier, when I felt someone was watching me."

Freaked out by this, Tia headed straight for the Diary Room to demand that the Divine Leader say if someone was perving on them, but the Divine Leader wasn't answering. The Diary Room appeared to be suffering a power cut as the screen didn't come on, and the red light on the camera had stopped winking intermittently.

Chapter Four

Day ??

8:14 a.m.

Tia and Jenny were the early risers this morning. Dale, miraculously, was asleep on the sofa. She thought that perhaps he was faking it, having been the one watching her in the shower. But without the Divine Leader's co-operation, she had no proof, and Tia didn't want to leap to any false conclusions.

She asked Jenny if she'd noticed anyone watching her in the shower and she shook her head. Tia suspected that lost in her own world, Jenny wasn't even listening to her.

Jenny, wearing an almost knee-length Minnie Mouse T-shirt, sipped a mug of black coffee. The Disney T-shirt a sign of her innate desire to appear more youthful than her thirty-plus years.

Screwing up her face in disgust, Jenny scraped egg remnants off a dirty plate and washed it for one of her rice cakes. Tia had tried one of the rice cakes yesterday. Never again; she might as well have eaten a page of a newspaper for breakfast.

Tia loved to exercise, cardio and free weights, so she could afford the extra calories.

"Tia?" Jenny whispered.

"Uh-huh," Tia said, reading her book.

"Is it me, or is Dale a bit of a loser?"

"It's you," Tia said, making a point of looking up at her.

"Well, excuse me for speaking my mind," Jenny said. "I won't make that mistake again."

"Okay, whatever. I'm trying to read here."

Jenny, who either didn't hear Tia's comment or chose to ignore it, went on. "It's just there's something, you know, *off* about him. When I came down last night, after the annoying-as-hell guitar playing, I could have sworn I heard him talking to himself. I don't know about you, but I'm hoping that he gets voted out this week. I mean, what were they thinking putting a geeky guy like that in a show like this in the first place?"

"We're not having this conversation," Tia said, this time backing it up with the sort of stern look that was sometimes necessary to get your point across to someone like Jenny.

She was now sure that it wasn't Dale who'd been watching her shower. She couldn't put her finger on it exactly, but…

"I'm just saying –"

"I know what you're insinuating," Tia said, "but I don't agree. He's not a loser."

Harvey entered the kitchen, yawned, stretched, farted. "Morning all."

"You're disgusting," Jenny said.

"Well good morning yourself, gorgeous."

Harvey laughed when Jenny stuck her tongue out at him. "Morning, Tia. Sleep well?"

"About as well as can be expected under the circumstances."

"I know what you mean," Harvey said. "I'm probably going to be sleeping for a week when all this is over."

"You sleep all day anyway," Jenny muttered under her breath. "This is a young person's show."

"And what's got your goat this morning?"

Jenny rolled her eyes. "It's things like saying 'got your goat' that makes you sound old."

"Well, excuse me for breathing."

"And that looks ridiculous on you, by the way," Jenny added, referring to Harvey's burgundy silk dressing gown.

"It's the Hefner look. It's back. Get with the programme, honey."

Tia didn't catch Jenny's response, as Tim and Rachel entered the kitchen together.

"Morning!" Tim and Rachel said in chorus.

"Tim was just telling me about Indonesia," Rachel said. "And about –"

"Oh, was he," Alice interrupted as she came in, clutching her hands to her chest in mock excitement. "Why don't you just go right ahead and marry him then?"

Alice ran a finger along the stainless-steel worktop, tut-tutting at the griminess of the stove. "I won't cook for any of you if you don't clear up after yourselves. I refuse to work in a fucking messy kitchen," she said, before cracking an egg on the basin. "And Harvey, you can make your own breakfast this morning. It won't kill you to do something around here."

"Cereal for me then," Harvey said with a wink. "Just so we're clear on this, Alice, the late-night sexual favours will stop now too."

Alice looked as if a week-old kipper had been thrust under her nose and the table laughed loud enough to wake Dale.

"Where's Phil?" Harvey asked Tim.

"Still in bed," Tim said.

"Really?" Alice said. "What the hell was he doing last night anyway?"

"Don't ask," Rachel said. "I think he was feeling a bit rough. He was outside all night."

"He wasn't feeling rough." Harvey laughed his long, wheezy chuckle. It was the laugh of an old tramp with yellow teeth and a brown-paper-bagged bottle in his hand. "He was staying where there are no cameras."

Tim started laughing at the boys' in-joke.

"What's so funny?" a puzzled Rachel asked Harvey. "I don't get it."

"Well," Harvey said. "You know what Phil's favourite movie is…"

"No," Rachel said.

"Actually," Harvey said, "it's better if you go outside and see for yourself."

7:02 a.m.

When Harvey doubled over with laughter, the others couldn't resist going outside to see what was so funny.

Using only a garden trowel, Phil had managed to dig a tunnel as deep as a coffin under the wire fence around the garden. Phil skipped around outside the wire, doing a celebratory jig for his audience.

"*The Great Escape*, okay," Rachel said between laughs. "Now I get it."

It was funny enough even for Dale to laugh, spitting his coffee back into his mug in the process, which didn't score him any more points with Alice or Jenny.

"Please come back inside the perimeter fence, or you'll be disqualified outright," the voice of Jenny said, not unlike the emotionless drone of the Divine Leader. "Come back or we'll all have to do a forfeit, you idiot."

Jenny's whining, of course, only made them laugh even harder.

There was no condemnation from the Divine Leader, which surprised them. The fact that there was a further, outer wire fence still to penetrate was perhaps why the Divine Leader chose to ignore Phil's escapades, Tia thought.

The smells of the fried bread and bacon they'd received amongst yesterday's supplies for Tim having completed his half of the morning task filled the kitchen, as Harvey proved himself a surprisingly adept chef. The Divine Leader had changed its mind and allowed Tim to share the food with them this time. This was so that Tim wouldn't be cast out from the group unfairly because of his earlier excellence, Tia thought.

The Divine Leader was doing its best to be fair; it was just that they hadn't heard from the Divine Leader for hours.

1:08 p.m.

"I've been told by a reliable source that you're not really a fitness instructor," Tia began, washing mugs in the kitchen while Phil dried them. Her tone sounded accusing, and so she smiled disarmingly. She passed another mug to Phil, who wiped and neatly stacked the mugs one by one on the kitchen draining board.

"I've been rumbled," Phil said with a wolfish grin. "It wouldn't by chance have been Harvey who gave me away, would it?"

"Might have been."

"But you're sworn to secrecy, right?" Phil laughed before his stare became deadly serious, the plastic nicotine replacement e-cigarette that had been bobbing in his mouth as he spoke as if set in concrete now. "The truth is I'm in the SAS. That's what all the secrecy is about. My mission, and it's been accepted I might add, is to escape the house without detection from the Divine Loser's cameras. I don't know exactly why; it's all on a need-to-know basis."

"Cut the bullshit, Phil. What do you do for a living? But you are in the armed forces, aren't you?"

"I could tell you that, but…"

"You'd have to kill me, right?"

"No, the truth is I'm the executive producer in disguise."

She playfully threw the kitchen cloth at him. "Oh, shut up. You're not going to tell me, are you?"

Phil shook his head. "Nope. I prefer being the man of mystery. Yeah, baby, yeah."

Phil bared his upper teeth to make himself look goofy like Austin Powers.

"You're more like Johnny English," Tia said.

"Oh, sod off," Phil said, laughing. His face became serious. "Although we've only been here a couple of days, it feels like a year," Phil confessed. "It's starting to feel like a Club 18–30 holiday that will never end; although you're probably too young to remember what that is."

His eyes softened as he looked down and then back at Tia. She wasn't expecting him to show her his vulnerable side, but this was what Phil was doing.

"I'm still finding it difficult to adjust. Being cooped up in here with strangers day and night is weird for me," he said.

"I know what you mean," Tia whispered.

They were subconsciously leaning into each other, Phil gazing into her eyes when Harvey came in and broke the spell.

5:16 p.m.

Out for a walk, Tia saw Jenny and Alice were still outside, bathing in the late-afternoon sun, which was getting weaker by the minute. Dale was playing his guitar, smoking a joint and just being Dale.

Tia returned to chat with the others. Over coffee, the five house members who had taken part in Tim's yoga class spoke mostly about travelling: the other common topic uniting them.

Tim was engaging and informative on the topic of Indonesia, Tibet and Vietnam; his favourite touring spots. When he spoke, he had the knack of captivating the imagination, no doubt due to how differently he seemed to view life from the rest of them.

If Tia was single and not so sure that Rachel was smitten with him, she might have made a play for him herself. It may also have had something to do with the fact that Tim reminded her of a young Sting, who, along with Michael Bublé, had monopolized her thoughts during her early teens with his seductive voice and sensual lyrics.

Although he was about the same age as Tia – okay, a couple of years younger – Tim seemed like an older man. Tia had always preferred to date older men. At least the ones who looked after themselves.

Rachel had admitted to Tia she also found Phil sexually appealing, but this might have been her sex-starved hormones making her feel like a teenager again. There was something about their caged-in existence that was bestial, something which brought out the raw nuances of sexuality. She could almost smell that musky man smell on the soap in the shower, and if Tim had walked in on her the other night, she would have wanted to invite him into the shower stall with her. "But that could just be me turning into a slut," she had told Tia with a smile. "What do you think?"

Tia didn't smile back.

Of course, it might not have been Tim, Tia thought. *And if it was, he spied on me too, remember? Which wasn't at all sexy, it was damned creepy.*

Why was Rachel so keen to move on from the incident? Why dismiss this serious breach of privacy so quickly? *Does she know something I don't?*

Tia's wandering thoughts came back to the conversation as she stopped looking at Rachel and the way Rachel was looking at Tim. Phil described the Australian outback, which had some of the most jaw-dropping scenery, but at a price – it also had some of the deadliest creatures known to mankind lurking there.

Harvey said he could rough it like Phil, but preferred to live it up in a five-star hotel, preferably in Vegas. Harvey told them about how he'd played a few hands of low-limit poker and tried not to look like the chump he was, but still blew half his spending money within an hour of sitting down; the Australian outback wasn't the only place where deadly predators resided.

He also told them all a cliché of a story about how he got so pissed once he nearly married a prostitute in a hired Elvis suit. "Only in Vegas," Harvey said with a smile.

This surprised Tia as she had Harvey down as gay, and a few of the others looked confused by his talk of women too.

When asked her favourite holiday destination, Tia said she had to be boring and go for Paris. The food, the nightlife and the art galleries made it a completely different world in her eyes.

Phil said he loathed Paris as he detested all French people. He concluded it would be the ideal destination for him too, but only if he were a post-apocalyptic traveller, which got a laugh from the table.

Rachel, a little nervous when she first started talking, said that she loved Italy, particularly the Amalfi Coast. Rachel and two friends had driven it in a week, stopping overnight in a guest house in a different town, each one hanging on to the cliff's edge as if for dear life.

That topic exhausted, they were once again stuck for conversation. Other than travel, the only other common interest they shared right now was who was going to be evicted from the house. So they spoke about that for a time, and then about the actual location, they were staying at, speculating where in the UK the secret location might be.

"Why in the hell did they decide to build this place?" Harvey said. "A friggin' life-size doll's house, in the middle of nowhere?"

"That's the whole point," Phil said. "Where we are is a mystery."

"I was led to believe," Rachel said, "it was because in the last *Divine Leader* series a bunch of thugs nearly burned the house down. They had people interfering with the camera crew working –"

"But there's no camera crew here," Harvey said, looking irritated. "I haven't seen a single camera operator here so far, have you? It's all computer-operated probably, cheapskate bastards."

"I've seen some camera guys around, one or two," Tim said. "There's a crew camped outside the walls, I think. But I haven't seen or heard anything of them since yesterday morning."

"You just know that's going to be edited out," Phil said, smiling.

"And what's the deal with that, exactly?" Harvey said. "They cut the sound whenever someone swears? Sound like a cushy job to you?"

"Yeah, you've seen it on TV," Tia said. "They cut the audio and it sounds like a hairdryer has been turned on. Then they return once the swearing or 'inappropriate' conversation for daytime television ceases."

"Don't you just fucking hate that fucking shit," Dale sang, playing his guitar. "What? Occasionally, one or two fucking swear words get through," he said rather than sang this time.

"They do not," Tia said. "They loop it back, so it's not exactly live. Five minutes or so delay. Then they know to block out the swearing."

"So, strictly speaking, it's not live?" Harvey said. "There's some time-lapse? Couldn't they get sued by saying it's live then?"

"Who cares about the legality of it, you boring old sod," Alice said.

"It's also to stop guys like that YouTube prankster from gatecrashing the live show," Tia said. "He turned up at eviction time, didn't you see it?"

Rachel grinned then shrugged. "I was also told they had people coming home from pubs and clubs congregating outside and cheering, and chanting loud enough to wake up the contestants, and loud enough for it to be heard on camera."

"Not on this show, honey," Harvey said. "Weren't you listening? We're in the middle of nowhere."

"I heard about what Rachel mentioned," Tia said. "Some drunken louts got into the lot and smashed the whole studio up. They had to go off the air for three hours until the police finished their enquiries and they could repair the damage. That's why we were brought out here by helicopter and blindfolded."

"No, honey," Harvey replied. "*That* was for TV."

Phil leaned back in his chair, tapping on the wall with his knuckles. "I'm not surprised; this place is made of friggin' cardboard. One strong wind and we've had it, lol. Stupid bastards, though," he added. "Smashing up a place with a hundred cameras in it; it's one of the dumbest criminal acts I've ever heard of. They were all caught."

"I'm guessing the crowd outside were flown here too?" Tia said.

"There were," Harvey answered. "There was this big thing on the radio that fifty lucky winners would be flown to the secret location to make up the live audience on the opening night. It's just them and us out here."

"Getting to see us in the flesh, lucky devils; not exactly a lottery win." Phil laughed at his own joke as he got up from the sofa. "More coffee, anyone? Tea? Okay, suit yourself. Cheap round."

"I'm going to do some t'ai chi before the ordeal of eviction time," the previously silent Tim put in. "I didn't sleep too well last night and I'm starting to feel a bit on edge about this. Catch you later."

A chorus of goodbyes, and then there were only four lost souls worried about eviction.

"They've refilled your hole, by the way," Harvey said to Phil as he returned from the kitchen with his coffee. "Must have done it last night. Probably had a covert team, working in black overalls so as not to be seen."

"What?" Phil said.

"I'm pulling your leg, you plonker," Harvey said. "No one's done anything about it. You could tunnel right the way out of here for all they care."

They all laughed at this.

"Oh, so that was what *that* was," Rachel said. "You digging again. I got up in the middle of the night to get a glass of water and I could hear a lot of commotion. I was only half awake so I didn't investigate. I thought that it was either some nocturnal animal or Dale."

"Not much difference," Phil said, now that Dale was outside smoking. "What is it with that guy, anyway? He fascinates me. They must have picked him for the Norman Bates factor. What's he doing now, sitting in the garden perving on Jenny in her bikini?"

"Leave him alone, he's alright," Tia said, nearly mentioning the shower incident but refraining from doing so at the last second. They would only blame Dale.

"No, I'm not knocking him," Phil said. "If it wasn't for him, I'd already had my bags packed for tonight. He's going, bet you any amount of money."

"Fifty quid," Harvey said.

Phil shook on it. "You're on."

"There's no way the public's going to evict you," Rachel said, looking at Phil. "For entertainment value alone, you've got the edge on everyone else. No, if anyone goes –"

"Let's talk about something else, shall we?" Tia said.

"What do you think the soundtrack to this programme's going to be like?" Phil asked. "Some thumping dance tune, something clubby?"

"I've heard it," Harvey said.

"How?" Phil said, sipping his tea.

"Exec producer's a friend of a friend."

"No shit. Any good?"

"Not really," Harvey said. "It sounds like gentle, lapping ocean waves and then it explodes into some thumping dance music that's catchy but also so annoying."

"Gonna give us a rendition then?" Phil said.

"I only heard it once," Harvey said. "So I couldn't if I tried."

"Oh, go on," Phil said. "You boring bastard, try."

Harvey shook his head, "I can't, mate."

"Spoilsport," Rachel said.

Harvey spread his hands wide in surrender before lying down on a free sofa and putting on his silk eye mask. "I'm taking a nap if you don't mind. The sofa's more comfortable than the bed. Dale's right about that."

8:51 p.m.

They gathered in the living room in front of the plasma screen, waiting for the Divine Leader to appear and collate their eviction votes.

Tia started to feel nervous. She didn't want to be the first to be voted out. She still didn't know who she was going to vote against.

Only Dale and Tim were yet to come inside and gather around the screen. Tim was practising t'ai chi in the freezing garden by moonlight while Dale smoked a joint.

Harvey nodded in Tim's direction. "Think he's going?"

"Who, Tim? Well," Phil said, leaning in and lowering his voice. "He did get all of his questions right the other day. Including the inspiration for the *Divine Leader* show coming from George Orwell's novel, *Nineteen Eighty-Four*. I mean, who knows that kind of stuff? No one likes a know-it-all, that's all I'm saying."

"Tim's not a know-it-all," Rachel protested.

"Look at him," Phil said, observing Tim with the others. Tim swept his right hand around his hip in slow motion as if he was drawing a sword while standing completely balanced on one leg. "If that's not a know-it-all then I don't know what is. He's going."

"You said Dale was going earlier," Harvey said. "You put money on it, mate."

"I've changed my mind."

During the day the programme's logo served as a screensaver. A logo someone had been paid a handsome sum to come up with. It was a strange world, Tia mused. Nurses and teachers were on strike because of their ridiculously low pay, and someone could be paid a million quid for coming up with a design as simple as an awakening eye.

The Divine Leader did not appear at nine, nor even by a quarter past. By half nine they no longer thought it was a deliberate ploy to make them wait. The Divine Leader wasn't answering any of their questions, even in the Diary Room. They hadn't been updated by the Divine Leader for sixteen hours. The joke in the house had been that the Divine Leader was running a glorified bed and breakfast.

"Something's up," Tim said as he came in, running a hand through his thinning blonde hair and staring at the blank television screen with piercing eyes the colour of freezing water.

Phil pressed a couple of buttons and nothing happened just like nothing had happened half an hour ago. Turning it completely off and then on again only produced a shrill sound of static, before the screen returned to the awakening eye logo screensaver.

The overhead lighting flickered.

"Oops, technical problems," Harvey said, smiling. "Hello, Divine Leader."

"Yo, Divine Loser!" Phil said.

Some nervous laughter startled Tia. It came from Dale, who'd emerged from smoking by the pool.

Dale looked confused. "What the fuck is going on?"

The lights went out on them completely.

Chapter Five

"Be quiet," Tim shouted out, causing more laughter. Only Tim remained disciplined enough to keep a straight face through this.

He looked deeply concerned.

They could only make out each other's faces by the flames of Tia and Dale's lighters. After a few moments, the emergency lighting kicked in, providing them with a dim light not much brighter than the lighter flames. It reminded Tia of her favourite movie, *The Beach*. They were suddenly lost souls in a forgotten civilization. To suggest this was some kind of paradise was a bit of stretch, though.

None of the guys was as good-looking as Leonardo DiCaprio. Nowhere near. He'd played a character called Richard, of course. Not unlike her Richard in personality and looks. At least, Tia always thought so. Perhaps she flattered Richard by the comparison, but that was what love did to you, made you see the best in each other. Leaving tonight wouldn't be so bad if Richard was waiting outside those perimeter gates to take her home.

"I'm not joking. I think we've been left here," Tim said as Tia's attention snapped back into the here and now and she rejoined the debate.

"Shut up," Alice said. "It's a test. It's all just a big test."

"To prove what exactly?" Tim said.

"I don't know, but it's an experiment," Alice said. "The whole fucking show's a social experiment, 'genius'."

"I agree with Tim," Jenny said. "There's no point to any of this. The show's not that extreme. You have to ask yourself if you've ever seen anything like this on the show before."

"And that's the whole point, 'genius number two'," Phil responded, backing Alice up.

Harvey came back with the ridiculous torch on his keyring. Jenny remarked that it was probably about as big as his knob, which elicited a giggle from Alice.

"When the power comes back on," Tia said, "I'll make us some hot drinks."

"*If* the power comes back on," Harvey pointed out.

It didn't.

??:?? p.m.

Sod the lot of you, Tia thought, finding her way by touch alone in the near darkness.

Tia had decided to go to bed as there was nothing else to do. She had fallen out with the others in a big way. An argument about health and safety in the house had broken out when she took a steak knife from the kitchen with her when she showered (the water in the cylinder was still hot at least). Harvey and Alice were the most worried about this, and even Dale seemed to break his television persona to voice his discontent.

Tim and Phil agreed that something needed to be done about it.

Jenny had played devil's advocate and explained that someone was watching the women shower, which inevitably made the men defensive. It hadn't scored Jenny any points either, as the group maintained that Tia's adoption of a weapon was a clear violation of the house rules. Jenny took their side after careful consideration and so Tia was left on her own, trying not to cry.

Tia's breath came in ragged stitches, deeply disturbed by the turn of events.

Why couldn't they see it her way? Somebody was watching her, even when she showered.

Now she had to shower in darkness.

They didn't know what had gone on with her ex-husband.

Why couldn't they trust her with the knife when she showered? She hadn't been in the least bit aggressive so far. Couldn't they see that?

Didn't they know her well enough by now to know she would only use it if attacked?

They're making me out to be a criminal.

The house had become a hostile place, with Tia feeling like the outsider.

A room full of strangers again, just like that. Tia subjected to weary faces looking upon her with distrust in their eyes.

She witnessed Dale and Alice break off their conversation like conspirators when she entered the kitchen, leaving the room abruptly shortly afterwards. They were making a point by keeping their distance.

A distressed Tia couldn't sleep, and so she read her book by torchlight: *Rosemary's Baby.*

She had reached the part where the handsome young doctor had sold Rosemary out. Doctor Hill, the last person Rosemary felt she could trust. Everyone was treating Rosemary like a mentally ill patient when she only wanted what was best for her body and her baby. Something the male figures in Rosemary's life insisted they had more knowledge and control over than she did.

After an age, Tia fell into a deep, dreamless sleep, as though, like Rosemary, she had been drugged.

1:27 a.m.

What's going on?

Tia awoke to find none of the other women in their beds. Venturing downstairs, she found Phil sitting on a sun lounger by the pool.

"You okay?" Tia said.

"Not really," Phil replied, looking shaken as he pulled his Nike hoodie up and massaged his temples. "I think I'm going to throw up."

Tia knew what he meant. She had a nauseating feeling in her gut with the anxiety of not knowing what was going on here. Sitting in the darkness, illuminated only by a faint moon, the only thing to do was to go back to bed and draw the covers up over herself and think of something pleasant.

She had used this tactic as a child when her stepfather came into her room. It was a case of hanging on until morning.

Phil, as if reading her mind, asked Tia with sudden aggression, "So are you going to tell us why you think you must carry a knife every time you go for a shower or into the bathroom? I mean, what happened to you?"

Tia thought of how she had clasped the knife as the hot water bled down her body, how she couldn't let it go. To her surprise, she looked down and saw she was clutching a knife, the smallest blade in the pyramid rack of kitchen steak knives. She quickly concealed it by sitting on her hands, hoping the others couldn't see it in the near darkness.

Tia started talking as the other housemates sat down to listen. One word tumbling into another. It was a release for her, and she was glad the others had joined them. Tia spoke of a Halloween night two years ago. It seemed to be the only appropriate place to start.

An evening her husband David had started in fancy dress and had transformed into a real-life monster by the end of it. A monster residing behind the closed doors of their home.

A night Tia had tried so hard to push back into the recesses of her memory. A night she thought she'd never mention again.

3:16 a.m.

Tia couldn't sleep and decided to go outside for a smoke to calm herself down.

She tiptoed down the stairs and ever so carefully slid open the patio doors so that she didn't wake any of the others. Tia snuck out onto the decking, sitting down at the closest table and chairs with an ashtray. At that moment she heard two people splashing around in the water.

Jenny and Dale were in the hot tub together in their swimwear. Tia had had no idea they were close. Not an inkling. At no point had they given the others any indication. Tia was under the impression they hated each other's guts - avoiding each other at every opportunity.

Jenny had referred to Dale as a creep, a geek – even a perv if memory served.

This was a sly move Tia hadn't foreseen.

Maybe it was all part of their game plan.

A game plan to advance further in this *Divine Leader* contest as a secret alliance.

"As far as I'm concerned," Dale said, "her boyfriend's right, she's a fucking headcase."

It took a moment for Tia to realize that Dale was talking about her. And it took all of Tia's restraint for her to bite down and not vocally defend herself against these accusations.

Dale shook his head. "No wonder we can't sleep tonight. I mean, how messed up was her story?"

Tia elected to stay in the shadows, watching on.

"I do feel sorry for her," Jenny said. "Don't get me wrong. Any woman would after what she's been through with her ex. But we're taking a risk with her being here, let me tell you. She zones out like all the time. I've seen her staring at that screen and the *Divine Leader* logo as though she's a junkie. Spaced out, like."

"She's far too unpredictable," Dale said. "She picks up a knife without warning. It's not what I signed up for when I agreed to come on this programme, I'll tell you that much."

They're talking about me.

Tia felt sickened by what Jenny and Dale had said and then enraged. They were working to eliminate her, that's what it sounded like to her.

Tia had shared an intimate part of her life, only to have it thrown back in her face by these two.

She felt violated. She felt worse now that she'd shared that part of her life.

This betrayal of trust was a disgrace.

They both held beer bottles, taking indulgent swigs. As far as Tia knew they were all out of booze. The other housemates wouldn't be too happy to learn that these two had stashed away their private supply of alcohol.

It started to make sense. No wonder Dale was kipping out on the sofa and sleeping in, with Jenny going back for a mid-afternoon siesta herself.

Well, the rest of the house would hear about the liquor and the late-night rendezvous. Tia wasn't above using it as ammunition to play these two at their own game. She wouldn't feel the least bit guilty either, especially seeing as these two had played them all for fools.

The bubbles in the hot tub were dissolving as Jenny glanced in Tia's direction. Tia was worried that she'd been spotted. After a moment, it became obvious she hadn't been seen, with Jenny taking the opportunity to lean across Dale to restart the jet supply.

"I can't believe this thing still works," Jenny said.

"It's about the only thing that fucking does," Dale replied. "What a joke."

As Jenny leaned across Dale, he slapped her bikini-clad bottom playfully. "This is the real show they've been waiting for," Dale said. "I know I have."

"Oi, cheeky," Jenny said, laughing. "Keep your hands to yourself."

They kissed, the hot tub bubbles fizzing back into action.

Tia finished her cigarette. The anger dissipating in favour of exhaustion, she drifted off to sleep as soon as her head hit the pillow.

Again, as if she had been drugged.

8:17 a.m.

The first thing Tia heard when she awoke in the morning was Harvey's excited voice.

"Phil's been tunnelling under the walls all night," Harvey enthusiastically informed them, his hair windswept. He clutched a large dish with dirt in it. "We've got to find out what went down last night. I've been helping him; we're nearly past the second perimeter fence. Another hour and we'll be outside the complex, I reckon."

"How did you sleep last night, any better?" Rachel asked, yawning and turning over to face Tia and Jenny. Tia propped herself up on her side to see that Jenny was still snoozing with her eye mask on; no surprise there.

Tia focused on Rachel instead of the tilted view of Harvey jabbering away in the hallway outside their bedroom.

"Not bad, actually," Tia lied, yawning. "Still feel dead tired, though."

Rachel replied with a yawn of her own. "I was freaked out by the power going out, so I didn't sleep that well."

Rachel yawned again before her eyes lit up. "By the way, the guys now understand your point of view regarding the shower intrusion and the need to have a knife with you in there."

Thank God! Tia nodded. "I take it the power's back on now?"

"Good question, I don't know."

The power wasn't back on, they discovered, bar a trickle of hot water from the boiler. They sat down for a meagre breakfast, watching Harvey disappear and reappear under the garden wall to assist Phil.

Tia was eager to find out what had gone down outside the complex last night, deeply concerned that they had been left to their own devices.

"Sorry for being such a bitch to you last night," Alice said to Tia. Tia waved it off, but the apology surprised her. Alice hadn't behaved any differently towards her last night than at any other time.

"It's the atmosphere of this place that makes you feel so tired," Alice grumbled. "Being watched like a bug under a glass you'd think your primal senses, or whatever, would be more alert. But no, you feel whacked out all the time."

The trundling steps on the stairs announced Tim, once again with Rachel.

"What's the deal with those two anyway?" Alice said. "They always seem to come down together, as if they've been waiting for each other."

"Don't, I think it's sweet," Tia said.

Sweeter than Dale and Jenny's sleazy romance anyway.

Tia decided she'd wait until the right moment before she exposed Dale and Jenny and the sordid little game of deceit they were playing.

Harvey stood in front of them, all his previous childlike enthusiasm at tunnelling out of the compound lost.

"What's up?" Tim said, spotting him first.

Harvey dropped the bowl he'd been digging with, his face working in a hundred different directions and as pallid as the overcast sky outside.

"Oh my God," Alice said, watching Harvey shaking with fear. "He's having some kind of seizure."

"Stop it, you're freaking me out," Tia said. "What is it?"

Harvey ran past them to the kitchen sink where he threw up.

Chapter Six

Dale was floating, lying face down in the pool.

"Only Dale could drown in less than three feet of water. Christ," Phil said, running a hand through his hair.

"He must have been high," Tim said.

"You don't say," Phil replied sarcastically.

"What do you think this means for the show?" Alice said, looking more annoyed than upset.

"You mean the prize money?" Phil said in the same tone.

"Stop it!" Rachel walked to the pool's edge. "Think about his family watching this."

Tia made a point of looking at Jenny's reaction. Jenny looked shocked rather than remorseful.

"Of course they won't air this," Jenny said. "And besides, he said that he had no family. Right, Tia?"

Tia ignored Jenny. She wanted to help Phil and Tim drag Dale's body out of the pool, but they told her to stay back and not get in their way.

Dale's lifeless face remained perfectly serene, so calm and unmoving it freaked Tia out. She only caught a glimpse of him as she was standing behind Alice and Rachel, trying to peer over them. It was almost as if they were trying to crowd her out on the small patch of AstroTurf where they were lying him down.

"Look at his shoulder," Phil said. "There's something carved there."

On Dale's hairless upper back, carved with what looked like a knife incision, were two pinky-white capital letters: a D and an L.

"Divine Leader," Harvey said, stating the obvious. "How fucked up would you have to be to engrave that onto yourself?"

"More likely stands for 'Desperate Loser'," Alice added. "Now he's fucked it up for all of us."

The electronic ping of a power surge sounded as the lights in the house came back on with a flicker and then held their illumination. The neon pink and sky-blue *Divine Leader* eye on the wall next to them glowed again.

Harvey's complexion was as pale as the glass in the patio doors, and only a shade more colourful than Dale's corpse, as he re-emerged from the bathroom moments later.

"I'm afraid there's something else."

The plasma screen was back on.

A few words displayed onscreen like a TV game show quiz board. Only this was no quiz board. The heading was, "Guess who?"

Chilling in its simplicity; an evil little game to punish the guilty.

The top line read:

DEALER

Next to it a smiling image of Dale.

Below it, six more entries with question marks next to them.

Three further entries were titled 'TBA' with double question marks.

The full board read:

DEALER – Dale

HIT AND RUN DRIVER?

CELEBRITY KILLER?

LEECH?

MURDERER?

BULLY?

VOYEUR AND STALKER?

TBA?? 13 hours 54 mins until revealed

TBA?? 13 hours 59 mins until revealed

TBA?? 14 hours 4 mins until revealed

WINNER AND SURVIVOR??

After a few seconds, a right-facing triangle appeared, covering the photo of Dale's smiling face.

A play button.

Phil leaned forward and touched it.

A female voice startled them all, as the image of a middle-aged woman appeared on the screen in a recording.

"I recognize her," Rachel said.

"She was on the audition panel," said Tia.

"Shush," Alice said.

Finding it difficult to talk, the woman held a photo up to the camera.

"This is my daughter Melissa – was, I should say.

"You see, Melissa, or Mel to her friends, is no longer with us.

"Our little honeybee was so cruelly taken from us.

"Oh God, she was beautiful. So photogenic. But she was also so kind and loving.

"Mel died of an overdose three days shy of her twenty-first birthday. The coroner said ecstasy Mel had taken at a music festival killed her.

"We later found that she'd been given it by somebody we did not know was her boyfriend. We had never even met him.

"His name was Dale, a man-boy in his mid-twenties. A university dropout, who busked a little on the street and went to auditions, but mostly he made his living by claiming benefits and selling drugs to young people. Vulnerable young girls like my Mel.

"It was my husband Bill who did the detective work to find out about Dale. He and I are no longer together; he couldn't accept that the charges were dropped against Dale through a lack of evidence. His source wouldn't testify, which frustrated the hell out of him. The police did all they could but the CPS wouldn't prosecute.

"Mel, our only child, was Bill's whole world like she was mine.

"When Bill and I separated, I followed Dale, stalked him you could say. Dale was even worse than I had suspected. Not only did he sell drugs, he also preyed on vulnerable young girls, sexually harassing them.

"I found that I couldn't sleep at night, knowing somebody like that was out and about. Partying, going to auditions, full of youth and hope himself while my Mel is lying six feet under, rotting away.

"I asked Bill to kill him. Get it over with; be a man.

"That's when we parted company.

"I became a drunk, a recluse; not getting out of bed for months."

She cut off for a second, looking off-camera at somebody. A smile crept across her face for the first time.

"It wasn't until I met the Divine Leader by chance that I got my life back on track.

"The Divine Leader promised me revenge.

"And now I see that I will have it. Not only revenge but justice. That's important, you see.

"Finally, my Mel will have justice."

The middle-aged woman smiled triumphantly again as the video abruptly cut off, as though it was going to cut to revealing content not intended for the housemates.

"The labels on the board are for each of us," Phil said, leaving the room. "Jesus, what company I'm in."

"I'm not," Tia said.

"You're not what?" Rachel said.

"I'm not on it," Tia blurted out. "I'm none of these things."

"Me neither," Harvey said.

"Nor me," said Alice.

"I couldn't be any of those things if I lived to be a thousand years old," Rachel said.

"They've made a mistake," Tim said. "A horrible mistake."

"Not with me."

Tia was amazed to find that it was Jenny confessing. Tia could see the determination on her face as she bravely spoke up.

"I'm on the board, sort of," Jenny said. "If you didn't know me, that is."

There was a stunned silence.

"My married name was Kane," Jenny said.

"As in the magician?" Harvey asked.

"He would have hated that description," Jenny said, "but yes, that's right."

"But his death was an accident," Rachel said to the room more than to Jenny, in obvious defence of her friend.

"I remember that too," said Alice.

"Trust me, it was no accident," Jenny said.

The room took in her expression, the fire behind her eyes. There was a defiance and strength in Jenny that had been unseen thus far; a depth too. It was as though another actor had stepped into the room, and Jenny had left. None of them believed now that Vincent Kane's death – the supposed tragedy in the news a few years back – was an accident.

PART TWO

THE BOARD OF SHAME

Chapter Seven

Five years earlier...

Jenny's Story

I

Jenny appreciated that catching somebody in a lie is not always as easy as we would like to think. While people care about what the world thinks of them, they will lie without breaking a sweat or raising an eyebrow. And they will happily lie to themselves and everybody close to them. The problem is, without truth, you can't have a relationship that matters. But what they don't know won't hurt them, right?

Now You See Me, the title of her husband's imminent autobiography, Jenny had never found to be an uplifting statement. If Vincent could manipulate millions into focusing on what he wanted them to see at any given moment, what hope did she have of ever finding him again?

And the scarier question for Jenny: did she want to find her husband again?

"But that's my point, Larry. Don't you see?" Vincent insisted, refilling his glass with red wine. "Without danger, there's little point in doing the illusion at all. The audience responds to a challenge, to pressure, to risk. Houdini and all the greats knew this."

"Their stage presence, you mean?" Larry said.

"No, no," Vincent Kane said. "They were showmen, not stage performers."

"There's a difference?"

"A crucial difference," Vincent said. "This is what is wrong with the world of magic today; not enough showmen to go around. Too many charlatans, performing bland variations of old tricks, too reliant on the theatre of modern production: dry-ice smoke machines, pumping techno beats and all that crap to distract from their mediocrity."

"Ah, a purist," Larry commented in his trashy Queens accent. Virtually every sentence he'd spoken so far this evening was a throwaway or a cliché, or both. "Only I don't think our insurance guys are going to be too happy to hear you talking like that."

"Insurance has no place in magic," Vincent said. "No place in life even. Without risk, there is no life. Life, by its very definition, is a triumph against the odds. What is a miracle if not a triumph over the ordinary?" He looked at Jenny with disdain. "The fucking ordinary that's all around us."

"If you don't mind," Larry said, buttering a roll, "I'll quote you on that when I speak to the producers. They respond to passion."

Vincent didn't answer. Jenny could tell her husband was barely tolerating this brash American's ignorance, recognizing the necessity of having this man onside to be a success in the States.

Vincent was preaching again, but Jenny wasn't listening any more as she switched her attention to Courtney, and watched her stepdaughter pick at her starter.

God, she's getting thin. At sixteen, Courtney was at an impressionable age. She made a promise to herself to watch her more closely from now on; eating disorders seemed to be as common as spots amongst teenage girls these days.

Larry's wife, Peggy-Sue (not named after the Buddy Holly song, she insisted firmly on first acquaintance; far too young for that, thank you) finally spoke, commending the quality of the salad dish. The over-the-top manner in which Peggy-Sue acted was almost Stepfordesque. She could think of nothing to say in response, nodding. Courtney made wide eyes at her mother as if to say, *Is she for real?* Well, the answer to that was most of her wasn't.

She smiled at them again, her eyes struggling to move past years of Botox that made her resemble a puppet. Jenny couldn't pin down how old Peggy-Sue was, anything from forty-five to sixty-five, which lent her a mystique her personality could not.

Thankfully, Larry and Peggy-Sue didn't pick up on the looks mother and daughter were giving each other. Vincent did, though, and the knitted bushy brows and hooded eyes she had once found attractive told Jenny that he would have words to say about it later.

"I have to hand it to you," Larry said, already grinning with the compliment he was about to give. "This is one of the fanciest restaurants I've dined at."

"One of the most expensive, anyway," Vincent said. "Though the service recently leaves a lot to be desired." His remark aimed at a waiter hovering at the table next to them. "It was great. Once."

Forty-five minutes later, the main course arrived. It was not worth the wait. Jenny found the chicken a little rubbery and the sauce too sweet and spicy but chewed it without complaint. Courtney, meanwhile, looked thoroughly unimpressed by the lobster, having done little but rearrange the snaking twines of lettuce on her plate.

Just eat it for God's sake, Courtney, Jenny thought, communicating as much to her stepdaughter with a long look. They had learned to converse this way to accommodate Vincent, who loathed "woman's talk" at the dinner table. Courtney, however, was taking no notice. She'd inherited her stubbornness from her father, and more than a sprinkling of his petulant attitude.

"Maybe the girl's not that hungry, is all," Larry said. "Let me know if I can help you out. I could eat a horse, as you Brits are so fond of saying."

Vincent ignored him, his eyes boring into his daughter's. "You chose the most expensive dish on the menu. You can damn well eat it."

"My Ronda's at that age," Larry said. "She'll hardly eat a thing either."

"Stay out of it, Larry," Vince snapped, not taking his eyes off Courtney to look at him when he spoke.

There was a long, heavy silence before Courtney sighed, picked up her knife and fork and started eating. Everyone at the table apart from Vincent wore their gratitude for her doing so on their faces.

II

Larry and Vincent discussed the finer details and the business end of the arrangements for Vincent's forthcoming American tour. The much-hyped tour intended to make him a household name in the States overnight. Jenny started to relax, thinking that, for once, everything was going to work out.

It was over post-dessert coffee that it happened. More specifically, when Larry produced a silver cigar case from his top pocket. Vincent, in turn, provided the cigarette lighter. As he did so, Jenny gave an involuntary shudder and knocked over her wine glass. Vincent looked at Jenny for a long second, and Jenny looked back at him with the vulnerability of a child; the wine left to spill out onto the tablecloth as if from a gaping wound. It took Peggy-Sue's intervention with a napkin to stop it trickling over the table's edge and onto Jenny's dress. Jenny broke out of her stupor and helped Peggy-Sue mop it up, apologizing three times in quick succession.

Another moment of paralysis struck Jenny, as she realized she'd lapsed and spoken in her native Essex accent and not the posh one six months of paid elocution lessons had honed.

"Accidents happen," Larry said, appealing to Vincent more than anyone else.

After a pause, Vincent's face relaxed. He smiled a sardonic grin. "Of course they do."

"Here. Have another glass," Peggy-Sue said, leaning over to pour Jenny some more wine.

"She's had enough already," Vincent said.

"Yes," Jenny said. "He's right, better not. I do feel a little bit tipsy. Sorry, everyone."

"Rubbish," Peggy-Sue said. "You've only had the one glass, hon; and most of that is on my napkin."

Peggy-Sue dropped the subject when Larry glared at her.

"She only needs a sniff of the stuff to get her drunk," Vincent said, putting a close to the matter. "Trust me, she's had enough."

While Larry stuffed cheese and biscuits (his second dessert) into his mouth between sentences they discussed at length how Vincent's

America tour would be nothing like the fiasco of two years ago when attendances had been disastrous.

"This time we've got a marketing team who've done their homework," Larry said with confidence. "The location, the dates. Trust me, we'll sell out the venues twice over. Easy."

Vincent Kane, "the brand", was better known in America two years on. That was the "bottom line" Larry kept alluding to.

Vincent Kane's more daring acts had even landed him on the cover of *Time* magazine. Larry repeated that they would not have any problems filling the auditoriums this time around, with the most expensive marketing budget he'd ever encountered allocated to the tour; he'd stake his mortgage on it. Jenny got the impression he may well have done.

Larry assured him that they would not be dealing with small-time managers and cowboy promoters this time either. He wrapped up his hard sell with a few more of his clichés which had him and Peggy-Sue smiling in unison.

Her husband's fears about the forthcoming American tour eased, Jenny hoped this would put him in good spirits. Of course, she only hoped. However, she knew Vincent's moods well enough to remain silent during the cab ride back to their Kensington home.

Complete silence was not a good sign as they dropped Courtney off on the way for a sleepover.

Back in their house, she slipped out of her Prada dress at the first opportunity, hanging it in her wardrobe and putting on a long-sleeved blouse. (All her blouses and dresses were long-sleeved; she owned no summer dresses). She knew the oversized Jackie O sunglasses would not be necessary this time as she would be required to be seen in public later that week for his opening performance at the Playhouse Theatre. That part of her flesh would remain untouched, but there was still plenty of skin not on show for her husband to bruise.

Jenny was startled when he whispered in her ear, creeping up behind her while she was removing her earrings. She could only make out half of his face in the soft light of their bedroom, the other half an unreadable silhouette. He raised the flame of his cigarette lighter, bringing it within an inch of her face.

"Is this what startled you, darling," he purred with menace. "Maybe you'd like to tell the whole world about our private life?"

"I didn't mean to, I swear. It's just," she said, feeling the flame warm her earlobe.

"Just what?" Vincent said.

A burn on her ear with an imminent public appearance might be a nuisance to explain; he withdrew the flame.

Taking a step back from the mirror, his face in total darkness, she couldn't see his lips move as he said, "take your clothes off."

She could have said, "Vincent, please don't do this," or "Darling, I beg you not to," or even "Keep your fucking hands off me, you creep," but she didn't. There seemed little point in doing so. It would only delay the inevitable, maybe rile him up even more. To do so tonight would just be making it worse. There was a time, in the distant past – a memory which made a mockery of the fact that they had been together a mere eight years – when she had been brave enough to threaten divorce. Or even to go to the police. Jenny had been only a little older than Courtney was now when she got married. She had freedom and a spirit back then. That Jenny had been forever broken, as remote to her now as the voice of her dead mother. Her mother would have been disgusted by her weakness. But her mother had never encountered a man like Vincent.

His eyes were almost entirely black, and shining with a horrendous appetite as he moved towards her.

A ripping of fabric sounded, followed by a pitter-patter on the carpet like hail as he ripped the buttons of her blouse. He unfastened her bra with the hook of a coat hanger, gently heated by the flame of the Zippo lighter. She stood as lifeless as a store mannequin as he went about the task of removing her stockings. His muffled grunts were either anger from the difficulty of removing the clinging lacy undergarments or arousal. She doubted whether he knew himself because the two emotions were inseparable for Vincent.

Jenny stood in the half-light, a solitary tear running down her cheek.

III

"This is a fucking shambles!" Vincent Kane roared. "We have a performance to give in two nights' time, people." As if on cue, a light fell from the overhead scaffolding, landing in a detonation of glass.

"Amateurs, I'm working with fucking amateurs," He stormed off the stage set to take a seat in the auditorium next to Larry.

"Problems?" Larry said.

"Where do I begin?"

"Never mind, I'm sure it'll all go right on the night."

"It's precisely that type of thinking which keeps these morons in employment. What is it you want? Can't you see I'm working?"

"Gee," Larry said. "If this is how you treat your friends, I'd hate to be your enemy. Anyway, I am the bearer of good news. Everything's set to go my end. I managed to get Madison, baby. *Madison Square Garden. Fourth of July.* Now tell me if that hasn't lifted your spirits. Did I not tell you that I'd deliver the goods?"

"Yes, well done, Larry," Vincent said, voicing it loud enough for the onstage crew to hear. "I'm glad someone around here knows what they're doing."

In one corner of the stage, dancers in skin-tight silver leotards practised a choreographed routine. In the opposite corner, a stagehand swept up the glass, unable to take his eyes off the growling caged lion behind him. Larry grinned, gesturing at the stage. "I thought you said you didn't need all the, quote, 'theatre of modern production' in your act."

"I never said I didn't need it," Vincent said. "Simply that I don't *rely* on it the way most illusionists do these days. Anyhow, are you staying on for the performance?"

"Wouldn't miss it for the world," Larry said, demolishing a Snickers bar.

"Good, I'm trying out a new illusion in my act," Vincent announced. "Something which will be the main feature of my US tour. I've been toying with it for months now, perfecting it. It requires me to lie strapped to a turning wheel while my feet and hands are bound. I'll also be wearing a neck clamp. Six swords will fall at eight-second intervals."

"Okay," Larry said, attempting to visualize the finer details of the act. "How does that work exactly?"

"The first will miss my right hand by a whisker," Vincent said, "as I jimmy the lock and pull my arm free. Another sword will descend upon my left arm, the third my left leg, the fourth my right leg, the fifth will miss my head as I unfasten the neck clamp, before I remove my body from the plummeting sixth blade which will fall in the space my torso will have occupied a split second earlier. In many ways, it is my most daring stunt yet, and will be the most thrilling, breath-taking sixty seconds ever witnessed in the world of magic."

"Sounds a blast," Larry said, slapping Vincent on the back. "You'll have the audience gasping. Providing you get out of the way of those falling swords, of course. If not, they'll be gasping for another reason."

"Yes, well, like I said –"

Larry turned to see what had caused Vincent to break off mid-sentence. The dancers were on a break, his sixteen-year-old daughter among them, being chatted up by one of the male dancers. She was revelling in the attention, loving the opportunity to flirt. Vincent stormed over.

"So, you think that my name sounds ridiculous?" the young Canadian dancer quipped, placing a hand on Courtney's shoulder. "With a name like Courtney Kane, I don't think you have a leg to stand on in that department."

Jenny, watching her daughter's dance practice from a balcony above, saw the whole thing. She called out but found that her voice wouldn't carry.

"What's your problem, man?" the young dancer said, spilling the bottled water he was sipping as the illusionist shoved him aside. "We were only talking."

"It looked like you were doing more than talking to me," Vincent said.

"Daddy no," Courtney pleaded. "We were practising the routine in a fun way, that's all. Please don't embarrass me."

Vincent silenced her with a slap to her face, hard enough to leave a red mark. She ran off crying.

"Hey!" the dancer protested. "She didn't do anything other than share a joke, you prick."

The dancer matched Vincent's six-two and had more muscle on his frame than the slender illusionist. Kane's aura of professional and social superiority made that fact irrelevant - like a superior officer interrogating a soldier. Vincent Kane looked as though he was revelling in putting the young dancer in the subordinate role.

"How old are you?" Vincent said.

"What's that got to do with it?"

"Just answer the question."

"Twenty-two."

"And how old do you think my daughter is?"

"Whatever, man," he said, rolling his eyes.

"I'll tell you how old she is: she's sixteen. A child."

"I didn't know there was a legal age for sharing a joke with somebody."

The stage director, an effeminate man hugging a clipboard, came over. "Philip, please apologize to Mr Kane. No? Okay, then you're fired. Get your things and leave. I'll get security to escort you from the premises. I did warn you about this." He snapped his fingers. "Now, come on. Back to work everybody. Show's over."

"No problem, your show sucks anyway." The young dancer turned to the illusionist, jabbing a finger in his chest. "Soon you're going to lose your precious little girl to someone, and there's not a damned thing you can do about it."

Vincent socked him in the jaw, hard enough to make him slump into the first-row seats. There was a murmur of disbelief from the crowd of dancers, technicians and stage workers. When the dancer rose, his steps were uncertain, and when he tried to throw a quick right in retaliation, he fell to the ground. Larry grabbed Vincent as he attempted to wade in with a kick to his exposed kidneys, and the dancer was eventually led away by security.

Jenny left her balcony seat to check on Courtney. She found her in the toilets, her face puffy with tears. "I was only talking to him, Mum, I swear."

"I know, darling," Jenny said, smothering her with a hug.

"Why does he have to act like that?" Courtney said. "It's not as if I'm a bad daughter, is it?"

"He doesn't see things straight sometimes, but he does love you. He's just overprotective. He has trouble showing his emotions."

"I do everything he asks me to do. Even…"

Her stepdaughter's words made Jenny feel as if an elevator had plunged deep into her stomach. For a moment she thought she was going to be sick, before choking back bile. "What things?"

"Even," Courtney said, after a long pause. "You know, things… to please him."

A thousand sordid memories of the past eight years went through her mind; a kaleidoscope of perversions.

Jenny never considered for a moment that he could do those same unspeakable things to his daughter. She gripped her stepdaughter's upper arms hard enough for her nails to dig in. "Listen to me, Courtney. Has he ever –"

"Get off me! Now you're hurting me!" Courtney sobbed, throwing her stepmother off. She retreated to a cubicle and tried to lock herself in, but Jenny wedged her foot in the door.

"I'm sorry, darling," Jenny said. "Forgive me, I didn't mean to hurt you."

Courtney fought to close the cubicle door for a moment, before giving up and collapsing to the floor.

"I'm sorry," Jenny said. "But what things? Come on, please tell me. What things?"

Courtney said nothing else, but her silence confirmed everything Jenny had feared more than words could ever have. She felt nauseated, failing as a mother in the most elementary way, failing to protect her only daughter. All those times she thought she was acting brave covering for him for Courtney's sake. And all the time he had been abusing his daughter.

They sat for a long time looking at the spotlessly clean, whiter than white, porcelain floor tiling; not saying anything, but saying everything in the ensuing silence.

IV

Saturday night.

The lights dimmed.

A packed auditorium waited with anticipation for the great Vincent Kane, wondering what dramatic entrance he would think of this time. A thick broth of smoke poured off the stage. A clap of thunderclouds was heard over the state-of-the-art Dolby surround sound system. The dancers made silhouettes on a flaming backdrop, their forms remaining as still as corpses.

An explosion of searing white light brought the dancers to life, like the breaking of a magic spell. Clad in silver and tiger-stripe leotards moulded to their bodies, Kane's daughter among them, the dancers gave a twirling display of the graceful, fluid agility only extremely youthful bodies know, but soon forget.

Meanwhile, Kane was cursing backstage, the last touches of make-up brushed onto his right temple.

"No André," Vincent said, "I don't refer to them as assistants as that would imply that they assisted me in some way, that's why I called him a stagehand. If he takes offence, that's his problem. What are you doing? Let me see. Fine, just make double sure nothing runs into my eyes when I sweat, that's all I'm concerned about."

Vincent signed a couple of programmes for relatives of the make-up artist before his eyes fell on his wife. "What are you doing here? I'm on in two minutes."

"Ninety seconds," the stage director amended.

"I came to wish you luck, darling," Jenny said.

"Luck, ha! I sincerely hope that doesn't come into it," Vincent said. "Anyway, there's not enough time. Just sit down over there and keep out of the way."

Jenny obediently sat in the corner. The make-up artists and the rest of the backstage crew in the dressing room gave her sympathetic looks.

"Marks, where the hell are you?" Vincent shouted. "Marks?"

"Yeah?" Marks said, sipping an energy drink from a can.

"You fixed that pulley?" Vincent said.

"Yes, sir. No problems there."

"Good," Vincent said. "Checked the harness release?"

"Yes."

"The hydraulics? If the cage door doesn't open the moment I gesture towards it, you'll be looking for a new job. Understand?"

"Yes," Marks said. "All checked and double-checked. It's all computerized, sir. Nothing to worry about."

"I don't have to worry. You do."

The stage director couldn't resist giving Marks a look of disdain, as if he were a disgraced pupil, before addressing Vincent.

"You don't have faith in anyone's ability other than your own," he said with a smile. "An admirable trait."

"In light of what has gone on so far this past week, with good bloody reason," Vincent responded.

The stage director ignored the implication and indicated it was time for Vincent to climb into the cage and make his entrance. High over the heads of the audience, the illusionist made a steady descent to the stage, his backstage crew members eagerly watching his performance on the dressing-room monitor. Other than the stage director, who was barking orders, they were more relaxed than Jenny would have anticipated. She had got into the habit of watching from the auditorium, as it was only during those early days when Vincent had required her to be backstage helping. She remembered it fondly: the small production team rushing like mad to prepare for the next act. These people, despite his protestations of incompetence, were consummate professionals.

Unfortunately, their lack of activity made it more difficult for her to do what she had planned without being noticed. A make-up artist struck up a conversation with her, and Jenny wished she would go away and leave her the opportunity to do what she had to do.

Eventually, the make-up artist left her alone long enough for Jenny to slip away. Jenny needed to avoid detection heading into his dressing room.

His dressing room was as tidy and as impersonal as a budget hotel suite. On the table, under a lit mirror, sat his flask, the one he always kept some form of glucose drink or Protein Shake in, sipping it between acts to keep his energy levels up. She opened the top and found it to be three-quarters full – which equated to about half a litre. Jenny took out the small envelope containing the fine powder of crushed, fast-acting barbiturate tablets she had bought from the pharmacist.

Jenny had paid for them in cash; one less way she could be traced. She mixed the powder into the drink with her finger. She shook it around until it dissolved satisfactorily into the pink liquid, hoping that the tablets were as tasteless as the label claimed. The liquid turning from a deep rose colour to a pale, almost fleshy pink, and contained bubbles like a milkshake. The fluid was inside the flask, of course, but he would notice if it tasted peculiar to him, but there was nothing she could do about that. It was a far from perfect plan anyway.

For one, there were no guarantees that 'fast-acting' barbiturate tablets would enter his bloodstream in time for his new act. Conversely, maybe the dosage was too high, and he would abandon the daring new illusion straight away if he felt unwell.

The numerous flaws in her plan overwhelmed Jenny. A nagging internal monologue informed her that her plan stank of something out of an episode of *Midsomer Murders* and that the harsh repercussions of trying such a thing for real would come crashing around her. At this point, Jenny was more worried about looking foolish and being caught out by her husband than by the authorities. Although her husband was not a likeable man, Jenny felt she would be the only plausible suspect in an investigation.

She had broken her routine and been present backstage for the first time in years, and perhaps she'd been spotted entering his private dressing room. The mounting self-doubts were proving more insoluble than the tablets.

Summoning strength from somewhere deep within herself she managed to turn off the treacherous voice in her head telling her to stop now and pour the contents of the flask down the sink. Listening to that voice had led her nowhere these past eight years. It was too late to pull out now, and maybe, just maybe, it might all work out the way she had pictured it in her mind.

"Oh, there you are." The voice of a female technician startled her as Jenny shut the dressing room door. "You're as anxious as we are about the new illusion, I see," the technician continued.

Jenny nodded with a smile and rejoined the others.

"Here, come and sit down," said the woman who had caught her coming out of her husband's dressing room. She put an arm around Jenny. "You look as white as a sheet, my love. Can I get you anything? Tea? Coffee? No? Perhaps something stronger?"

Jenny shook her head.

"You needn't worry," the technician said.

"He's practised it at least two dozen times this week without even the slightest mishap," the stage director said confidently.

"Yeah, you might say that he's done it to death," quipped the man they referred to as Marks.

"You're not funny, you know, Marks," the stage director said.

"Oh, lighten up, Steven," Marks said. "You're not helping her, or anybody else for that matter, by being so goddamn serious all the time."

"It's called being a professional," Vincent Kane said, taking pleasure in catching them out. "Maybe you ought to try it yourself sometime." The illusionist mopped his shiny brow with the back of his hand. Marks, momentarily out of sight to everyone except Jenny, gave the stage director the finger.

"Everything in place?" Kane said.

"Sure," Marks said. "Still up for this, Maestro? We could always substitute it with the disappearing, reappearing cage trick; it's all set up. We could save this as the *pièce de résistance* for the US tour."

"Marks has a point, you know," the stage director said timidly, unable to avoid lowering his gaze.

The illusionist didn't bother with a reply, disappearing into his dressing room. He re-emerged with the flask in his hand. Jenny forced herself to look away, her eyes subconsciously drawn to the flask. Her husband, who had caught the look, mistook it for fear. "Don't worry, darling," Vincent said. "I'll be back soon enough. Be a long time before you get your greedy mitts on any inheritance money, I'm afraid."

"What an awful thing to say," said a female technician, but Vincent laughed it off.

Drink it, Jenny willed, mentally clenching. *Just drink the goddamned stuff.*

Vincent put the flask down as the rest of the crew fussed around him, the illusionist verbally pushing them away as if they were street beggars. He picked it up again, raising it to his lips but put it down for a second and gave Marks his usual last-minute interrogation when the SFX supervisor came back from checking the equipment.

"Do me a favour and oversee the rechecks, will you?" Vincent said, performing his usual idiosyncratic gesture of drawing circles with the flask he held. "Let the audience wait a few more minutes. Builds more tension that way. It also lets them know that I'll throw out a performance when I'm good and ready."

They could hear the bellowing voice of the event co-ordinator warming up the crowd as they waited for the maintenance crew to carry out the final equipment checks. "And now, ladies and gentlemen, you're about to take part in history. As you will witness the most dangerous, the most daring and, without question, the most unique trick ever performed in the world of magic. Sixty feet above him are six dangling swords…"

The announcer went on to describe the act in meandering detail as they waited for the go-ahead from the equipment crew when Marks returned. Vincent raised the flask to his lips, taking a gulping swallow. He looked questioningly at the flask for a moment. Then looked at his wife. Jenny was sure he suspected until he took a second swig. He disappeared down the tunnel leading to the stage, taking his third and fourth sips.

V

The equipment delays they were having, Jenny at first saw as a blessing; the drugs would have sufficient time to work their way into his bloodstream. But the longer the delay went on, the more nervous she got. She looked at the doll-sized version of her husband on the fourteen-inch monitor for signs of grogginess. His complexion was an unhealthy grey-green, but that was merely the picture contrast and the stage lighting. He was strapped to the circular table, just shy of full stretch in a star shape. All five constraints were locked in place now. If he'd had an apple on his head, Jenny thought, he would have looked like a knife thrower's assistant at the circus, although his table was horizontal instead of vertical.

"This is going to astound you, ladies and gentlemen," the event announcer boomed. "Make you question your very eyes." When he finished, he came backstage, loosening the collar of his tux. "If you want me to go out there again, I want a raise."

"Not much longer, Johnny. Five minutes tops," the stage director said.

It took another quarter of an hour.

Time passed not so much as fifteen minutes for Jenny but nine hundred sluggish, ticking seconds where she was glued to the monitor, watching for signs of wooziness in her husband. She expected him to pass out at any moment.

"Don't worry; he's in good hands," a backstage crew member tried to reassure her. Her soothing voice radiated confidence and instilled calm amongst the rest of the crew. Jenny thought that perhaps she was employed as a calming influence, brought in for times like this. "It's better this way," she went on. "Like an aeroplane taking off, you want to be sure that everything is functioning as it should be before you commit to taking action."

The first sword fell. A glittering silver stalactite glowing incandescently, a spreading white-hot V shape as it caught the studio lights. Kane grappled with the lock, jimmying it with the uncurled safety pin he held in his hand. He jimmied it in the nick of time as the blade missed his right forearm by a fraction of an inch. The audience instinctively gasped as though an avalanche of ice-cold water had soaked them.

Jenny and the rest of the backstage crew watched the monitor intently.

"That was a little too close," Marks said. "I don't like the look of this. His timing's out. If he's behind now…"

"Shut up, Marks," the stage director said. "I told you, you're not funny."

"No joke," Marks said. "Are you blind? He's behind."

The stage director gave Jenny a tight grin and said, "He's a showman, after all. He likes to cut it down to the wire, so to speak; like he said, building suspense and all that."

The second sword fell.

"I'm not sure he's in full control of this," Marks said.

The second blade caught the light again, like reflected flash photography on their monitor.

It missed. Just.

But it was close enough to pin the shirt cuff of the illusionist's left sleeve to the table. Because of the fuzziness in picture definition on the small monitor, they couldn't see this.

The illusionist writhed like a fish on a hook before ripping his sleeve and freeing his arm.

"He's behind," Marks said. "I don't like the look of this. I'm going to –"

"Shut up and stay where you are," the stage director said. "Marks, if you don't simmer down you're fired."

The third blade fell, catching the light as it plunged into the illusionist's inner left thigh, causing a volcanic eruption of crimson from his trouser leg, greeted with a gasp from the majority of onlookers. The audience, a blur of tuxedos and ball gowns, looked on, angst evident in their faces. Some wrung their hands; others bobbed and weaved like a boxer on the ropes. Others drew themselves up to their full height or dampened programmes with their upper lips. An impression in the air, over and above the five senses, that this was no act.

"Oh my God," the stage director said. "Shut your damned machine off. Now."

"There's no way to shut it down," Marks said. "Other than going up there. That's what I've been trying to tell you."

"Go!"

"It's too late now – we decided to forgo the computerized override," Marks said, his face drained of all colour. "Your decision, remember? I'll have to key in the shut-down code."

"Fuck."

The fourth blade descended. Vincent Kane grappled with the next constraint, pulling at the neck clamp, having already given up on his right leg. The blade sank deep into the flesh at mid-thigh level as he howled with pain.

With a metallic ka-ching sound, the fifth blade dropped.

The illusionist pulled at his neck like a man trying to rip off a mask. The black metal bar came up as he released it, Vincent shifting his head a fraction so that the only flesh the sword bit into was a thin slice of his left ear.

A few members of the audience were clambering up the steps of the auditorium; some turned away, unable to watch. Others hoped it was still part of the act, an illusion, and the blood was fake like in the movies; but the vast majority remained seated, numbed by the sheer horror of what they were witnessing.

The cries of pain were all too real.

Backstage the reactions were similar. The only people making a sound were a man who was hysterically wailing and the stage director barking out instructions. A scrambling member of the technical crew had reached the swirling overhead structure, but the sixth sword had already fallen by the time he shut it down manually.

That final sword landed six inches below the illusionist's solar plexus and an inch above the thick waistband of his tuxedo. It divided his intestines, his last moments in this world an agonizing scream. He was denied even that, as choking blood welled up from his mouth to give him a blood-goatee before he cried out.

The curtain descended on the stage. Only those backstage were privy to the horror show that was still spinning on the horizontal turntable. On it was the illusionist, three blades around him, three blades in him so that he resembled a life-size voodoo doll.

The closely spaced silver swords looked like crosses to Jenny, giving her husband's body the grisly appearance of a flesh graveyard. Blood was still being thrown everywhere by the revolving turntable, like raspberries in a blender. The scene was gorier than anything her mind had imagined.

So much blood.

Jenny found that she didn't have to fake her shock. Her world was spinning too as another darker curtain mercifully descended over her vision as Jenny fainted.

Chapter Eight

Present day...

??:?? p.m.

For the first time, Tia felt sorry for Jenny. She knew the ordeal all too well. Jenny was in tears, having fought hard to hold them back to tell her story.

Rachel put a consoling arm around her, and Jenny nodded her gratitude before going on.

"The worst part is that I hardly saw Courtney again after that," Jenny said. "She went off to college. It can only mean that she must have found out and she hates me. Hates me enough to volunteer me for this hell house. That's what hurts."

Shortly after the sun went down as if by clockwork, the electrical power cut off again.

A chorus of groans rang out from the housemates.

Tia was with the three men in the living room at the time, laid out on the sofa reading, right in the middle of reading the final act of *Rosemary's Baby*, the eerie climax creeping closer and making her skin crawl. Was it all in Rosemary's head or did she have the spawn of the Devil growing inside her? Not until she gave birth would she know for sure.

Tia had read the same page for the past half-hour, her mind skipping, unable to concentrate beyond the labels on that board.

One, in particular, bothered her.

Voyeur.

It wasn't the worst of the crimes on the board, but it creeped Tia out. It confirmed that one of these three men seated a few feet away had watched her shower naked.

The fifty-inch 8K plasma screen switched off again, coolly casting their reflections like a black mirror. As distant and unfeeling in its hypnotic gaze as outer space; alien and unfathomable.

The screen jumped into life again.

The board of shame back for all to see.

The hideous labels that allegedly fitted each one of them.

Tim and Harvey left the room to go outside, uncomfortable with the board's reappearance.

Tia decided to go to bed. She found the other three female housemates sitting on Jenny's bed, a torch in the middle of them as though they were telling stories around a campfire.

All three looked up when Tia came in and sat on her bed. The conversation immediately stopped, and their body language became rigid, giving Tia the unpleasant impression that they had been talking about her.

"I noticed you had to get up in the middle of the night," Alice said. "What were you doing?"

"Having a ciggy," Tia said. "I couldn't sleep."

"The fact remains," Alice said. "You were the only one to leave the bedroom last night, and Dale turned up dead in the morning."

Tia glared at Jenny. "Is that right?"

"Sorry," Jenny said. "I don't follow."

"I saw you," Tia said, her breath short with anger and excitement. "I saw the two of you in that Jacuzzi. You were kissing him."

Jenny looked at the other two women with a puzzled expression, as if Tia was mad. "I suppose by *him* you're referring to Dale?" Jenny said. "Are you fucking kidding me? That reprobate? I wouldn't touch him with a bargepole, let alone snog him. You're mistaken."

Alice and Rachel looked at Jenny.

"Oh, come on," Jenny said. "You're going to take her word for it, are you? I mean, look at him and look at me. He should be so fucking lucky." Jenny laughed a high-pitched cackle, for a moment oblivious to the fact that the person she was referring to was no longer alive. "I'm sorry," she said. "I didn't mean to laugh at the dead – it's the stress of it all."

Rachel looked at Tia uneasily.

"Is it possible," Rachel said with nauseating care, "that you were mistaken?"

"Too right, she was mistaken," Jenny said. "I mean, come on. Dale and me?"

"It was dark last night," Rachel said, ignoring Jenny. Rachel tried to keep her voice level and kind, addressing Tia as if she were a child. "Are you sure –"

Tia felt so angry she started to shake.

Jenny is lying because Dale has been outed as drug-dealing scum, and they don't believe me. It's on their faces. Oh my God, they don't believe me, and I'm starting to sound nuts.

Tia couldn't hold in her frustration and anger any longer. "Of course I'm fucking sure!" she screamed, leaving the bedroom, almost falling down the stairs to the living area.

Tia didn't need to look back to see Jenny's smug face. She could feel it her eyes brightened with the victory.

"What's all the fuss?" Harvey said when Tia stumbled into the half-light of the living room area. "Are you alright?"

"No, I'm not," was all Tia could say in reply as she sat on the sofa, as far away from the others as possible, hugging her knees.

Tia continued to ignore Harvey, so he gave up, throwing his hands up in an expression of theatrical hopelessness to the others.

Tia couldn't face Harvey giving her the "Jen and Dale, are you sure?" treatment like the others had.

Tia's boyfriend Richard didn't always believe her and liked to put her down. It was an ongoing theme of their relationship.

At times, Tia felt so unhappy it hurt her deep down in her bones. She had woken up last month in the middle of the night shaking all over and breathing heavily, her hands making tight fists. It was like morphing into a werewolf. Only she didn't change; she only stayed the same, keeping the frustration of her life inside rather than letting it out.

Her inner scream reduced to a whistling tea kettle.

It was the lying that got to her. Tia had to lie to Richard about the number of auditions she attended in a week. He didn't support her dreams of becoming an actress. He didn't say it outright, he wasn't abusive (like David was, not even close), he wasn't aggressive about it (like David was), but it was in the put-downs.

Put-downs have an accumulative effect on a relationship. Maybe they are even the worst type of abuse because the pain is slow and invisible until one day, there is a vice of resentment that grips your whole body.

No one leaves a long-term relationship because of put-downs: sticks and stones and all that.

She couldn't leave Richard. Whenever she entertained it, he did something so sweet and thoughtful, bringing back that feeling of love like a surprise, as if he knew that it would keep her by his side.

David had done that too. It must be a sixth sense men have to keep you from straying.

Dreams were her only escape, something pure. That's why she acted, to become the person she wanted to be, deep in her bones. Only, with fear now taking over her every thought, Tia could no longer participate in this justice reality television show; if that was what it was.

After a minute or two, a restless Tia went outside for a smoke.

She had intended to ration her cigarettes as she was down to her last five.

PART THREE
SWITCHING GENRES

Chapter Nine

Tia still felt on edge from the accusations. Isolated from the group, she sat down on a sun lounger watching yet another argument unfold in the house.

Occasionally, someone would glance at Tia sitting outside on her own. She was glad to be out of it.

The gaudy all-seeing *Divine Leader* eye watched her like an unfeeling neon god whilst cameras overhead observed her.

Closer still, a stalker, killer and other unpunished criminals watched her.

"We've found a fire exit in the garden," Tim said, startling Tia by sliding back the patio door. "But it's locked and bolted from the outside, and secured with a chain."

The others joined Tim and Tia outside.

"We're not to leave the complex, remember?" Alice said. "Or we'll forfeit the money."

"Really," Phil said, trying to keep his temper under control. "That's what you're taking from this? Look, Alice, there's a dead body over there, and no one has done so much as contact us about it."

They couldn't help but look at the corpse of Dale, his form mummified by the sheet taken from his bed.

"Plus there's that fucking board," Phil persisted. "This is not your run-of-the-mill *Divine Leader* show, that's for sure. What more do you need to happen before that sinks into your thick skull? We're not on fucking television; we're on trial."

"If we're not on television," Alice muttered under her breath, "then why are there cameras?"

Tia had to admit Alice had a fair point. One which Phil couldn't answer.

"Alright, Phil," Jenny said. "There's no need to shout at her. She's in shock. Like the rest of us."

Jenny, suddenly besties with Alice, consoled her with a hug.

Phil didn't bother answering, let alone apologizing as he strode off purposely towards the end of the garden.

"Typical," Jenny muttered, commenting on Phil's lack of an apology.

Phil hoisted himself up to the top of the garden wall, peering over.

"What can you see?" Tim asked.

Phil dropped back down, shaking his head. "Barbed wire. A lot of it."

Phil attempted to climb the wall anyway, tackling the barbed wire with his gloved left hand, when Harvey shouted, "Wait!"

Phil froze for a second, before dropping athletically down.

"Wait!" Harvey shouted again. "For God's sake. Please wait."

Harvey was having difficulty getting his words out but eventually strung a sentence together. "They've upped the ante," he said. "The screen now says, if you leave the complex you'll be shot on sight."

All seven of them went into the living room to witness the updated board for themselves. It indeed reflected the threat Harvey had mentioned of being shot for leaving the complex.

"They can't do this," Rachel said. "It's a violation of my human rights."

"Shot on sight," Phil scoffed. "It's overkill. I never saw anyone with a firearm when I was outside the perimeter."

"Care to test that theory?" Jenny said. And, after a pause, "Thought not."

Phil left the group seemingly in disgust.

"He's all talk," Jenny said to the others after he'd departed. "He's not going to get us out of here."

Tia felt dizzy all of a sudden, sitting down hard on the sofa. Her vertigo was spiralling out of control and directly mirroring her reality.

None of the others noticed her discomfort. They were too busy concerning themselves with their fate on that plasma screen.

"Who do you think is watching us?" Tia heard Tim say, as she left the living-room area to get some fresh air. "I mean, is this even going out to the general viewing public at home?"

"Oh, my God!" Jenny said. "You don't think it's one of those Dark Web things, do you? One of those sicko pay-per-view channels."

Tia stopped listening to watch Phil.

Tia watched on in silent horror as, without warning, Phil ducked down into one of the tunnels he'd dug at the back of the garden complex leading to a section of the trellised outer wall to climb.

Tia anxiously dug her fingernails into her hand, waiting for a gunshot to ring out.

Silence.

A minute or two later, a barbed wire wall behind Tia started to vibrate and then move. Tia retreated. No more than fifteen feet wide at the most, the wall with a trellis slid back with a slow, mechanical burring noise that was loud enough for the others to come filtering out of the living room.

The concealed front entrance peeled back to show Phil's handsome, weathered features.

"Still in one piece," Phil grinned. "Who dares wins and all that. It would seem that their threat was an empty one."

Tia recognized that although Phil was smiling, he wasn't amused. Not this time. The smile didn't touch his eyes. He was angry.

Tia learned that Phil had released the front entrance barrier by activating an outside switch; leaving the complex proved as simple as that.

Although unchallenged, Tia still felt on edge about leaving the house, biting her lip hard enough to make it bleed and taste of copper. She was not as confident as Phil and some of the others that the Divine Leader's threat was an idle one, remaining fearful of gunfire breaking out at any moment.

Tia subconsciously kept her head down, staying low to the ground. She was the last to emerge as the housemates came out on to a raised dais, like a fashion catwalk, where their presenter host had introduced them to the cheering and jeering crowd only days ago.

Amazingly, the crowds of people on the platforms below and the terracing above were still there, only motionless and silent, and she realized with a shock that they consisted entirely of mannequins. The type you'd see in a department store, only they were a mix of races, had a wide variety of imperfect clothes on, with a range of radically different haircuts, some with glasses and wearing hoodies, others in smarter jackets. Some possessed padded bellies and double chins to make them appear more lifelike. A great deal of work had gone into the deception.

Seeing them again now it was difficult to understand how they'd ever mistaken them for human beings but in the darkness and the euphoria of being on live television they had.

It almost seemed like a joke. On the side Tia was standing, there appeared to be as many individual loudspeakers nestled in the crowd as mannequins, and they'd still missed it. These had been producing the cheering, clapping, booing and catcalling. All the sounds that had duped them into believing this to be a crowd of punters wanting to be on TV were nothing more than an audience of inanimate plastic.

On reflection, however, it seemed far from a joke.

Tia felt a chill go down her back as if invisible hands were playing an icy flute on her spine. Looking around at the faces of the others, she was not alone in this sentiment.

*

The grounds surrounding the outer perimeter fence of the *Divine Leader* house consisted of the helipad they'd landed on (when arriving blindfolded in the helicopter that had brought them here). Past the helipad, a sloping lawn ended in a sheer cliff with a perilous-looking trail path winding behind the house and leading down to a beach.

A giant insect as big as a football stood in their way for a moment, like a prison sentinel blocking their escape. This alien creature possessed thick black frog legs, buzzing as it lingered at head height. They were close enough to see the camera sitting dead in the middle of what they now recognized to be a drone, four rotor blades spinning in unison to keep it in flight.

Tia was close enough to read the word ETHEL written in a white stencil font across its base.

Phil reached down for a large stone and, without warning, hurled it at the drone. "Piss off!" he yelled.

The drone took a glancing blow. A hit which rocked its flight for a second, but didn't bring it down as Phil intended. The strike considered enough of a warning for the drone to take off in a hurry though. They watched it disappear over the treetops and out of view.

Leaving the woods, they started down the trail.

The spiralling path led down to a deserted beach, the water choppy enough to engulf the alcoves under the cliff, where seawater crashed against the rocks in a fizzing explosion of white foam fireworks.

Crossing the small beach led them to further woodland which covered no more than an acre. Bizarrely, they came across a tennis court. The neglected court had become overgrown with nature. The court had a rusty ten-foot mesh perimeter fence around it and lacked a net. Its hard surface was covered in a carpet of green moss, obscuring all the court's markings except for a white L in one of the corners.

"Anyone for tennis?" Harvey said.

"What's a tennis court doing out here?" Jenny asked, in a tone which suggested it somehow offended her.

No one could answer.

A search of the woods behind the tennis court kept them close to the cliff's edge.

Following the cliff around they kept the sea on their left-hand side. Phil, taking the lead, made sure they covered every square foot in their search.

They came around full-circle after no more than ten minutes of walking.

"Oh my God," Tim said, out of breath through anxiety rather than exercise. "We're on an island."

*

Nothing else of note stood on this island except for an old, dilapidated church.

Seagulls watched them from its roof; a raven cawed eerily in the distance. The church was Gothic in style, with Norman arches and pointed windows. Its front windows smashed into jagged edges, and illegible graffiti scrawled across its walls in ugly black spray paint. The charcoal-coloured sky above the church matched its mood perfectly.

If Tim Burton had made an island for a film set this would be it, Tia thought. The only thing out of place was the modern *Divine Leader* house, possessing a zen Swedish open-plan vibe. It gave the island a split personality, breaking out in all directions.

The seven-strong group moved around to the front entrance of the church where a radio set lay, smashed to smithereens.

Proceeding with caution, they went inside. Tim led the way, brushing past Tia as he produced a knife from his sock. Tia immediately recognized it as a small steak knife from the kitchen.

Inside, the smell of damp was almost overpowering. Birds fluttered in the rafters, and the wooden floorboards groaned in protest at its ungodly new visitors.

"This place is falling apart," Tim's voice echoed as if it had come from the altar and not right in front of Tia.

Phil put an arm across Tim's chest, moving to pass him and looking at the floor as though the boards beneath him contained a secret.

"Stay still, please," Phil said to the group. "I don't like the look of this."

Each cautious footstep greeted with a protesting creak that made everyone wince, except Phil who strode on with confidence. The wooden flooring held, but Phil prevented the others from following with a wave of his hand, not wanting to test the rotting floor with additional weight.

Numerous holes in the church's roof provided sufficient light with which to see.

"Careful," Tim said.

Phil nodded. He was standing in the middle of a wide nave, with pews on either side of him. They were of the old-fashioned Puritan type, with doors on the end of each row.

The stuffy, ancient smell of the church filled Tia's nostrils.

"It's fine." Phil motioned the others to come forward, the nave flooring sound.

"Looks like there's no one here," Rachel said. She had barely uttered the first syllable when Tia spotted a figure strung up on the altar.

From a distance, they'd mistaken it for a crucified Jesus.

"Oh, God!" Alice screamed.

It was the show's presenter, Helen Westling.

She was the presenting host who'd ushered each of them into *the Divine Leader* house on their very first night.

"I never rated her," Harvey said matter-of-factly, ignoring his callousness. "She was lucky to get the *Divine Leader* gig after what she did, even though no one deserves what's happened to her."

"I didn't like the way she treated me," Jenny said. "She wanted to get me into the house as quickly as possible. I agree that nobody deserves *this*, though."

"Perhaps she did," Rachel said. "I mean, not that she deserved this. Of course, she didn't. I mean that she did something bad. Really bad. Didn't you read about it? What comes around goes around and all that."

"What did she do?" Tim asked, speaking for the majority of the group and looking puzzled.

"Don't you know?" Harvey said with a tut-tut tone in his voice. "Obviously you don't watch the news or read the papers. Well, dear old Helen was in a hit and run. In Coventry, I think it was."

"Birmingham," Rachel corrected him.

"Who cares?" Harvey said. "Anyway, she didn't stop. She was pissed and driving a hundred miles an hour in her boyfriend's sports car. Porsche, I think."

Rachel nodded this time, and Harvey continued.

"She didn't even do jail time," Harvey said. "To cut a long story short, the police dropped the ball, and a fancy lawyer got her off. There was a real stink surrounding it. The whole time I was with her, I kept thinking *Don't mention it, Harvey, whatever you do, don't mention the elephant in the room.* You know? Not on live television. It made our interaction awkward and made me look a bit wooden. I wish I'd been oblivious to it like you lot, I can tell you."

Moving closer to the TV presenter's corpse, they saw that her face and neck were almost overwhelmed with thick, purple veins, like a sea of little snakes, breaking through her alabaster skin.

Behind her, on the wall, in sprawling writing, perhaps painted in her blood, were two gigantic letters.

DL

"Divine Leader again," Harvey said.

"I've heard 'Divine Leader' mentioned in an entirely different context than the TV show," Phil said, with a finality in his voice. "Way back in the past this was." Tia noticed that Phil's expression was one of grim inevitability.

They all looked around at Phil, but he didn't say any more.

"Help me get her down," Tim said, tugging at her feet.

Phil assisted in getting the body down from where it hung, pulling down the dead TV presenter's polo neck to reveal a metal collar.

"What is that thing, a neck brace?" Harvey said. "After her accident?"

Phil shook his head. "It's made out of steel. I've seen this before too. Years ago. It's fitted with two needles pressing into the skin. One for the poison, one for the antidote. It's operated by remote. If you try to remove it, then it pricks the skin around your neck and the poison kicks in. It's fatal within seconds."

Phil waved at the ceiling. "Smile, everyone!"

They all looked up to see yet another TV camera.

"Putting a camera here shows they planned on us finding Helen's corpse," Phil said, removing the gym glove he wore at all times.

Tia gasped. Phil had an artificial hand made out of metal. Phil used it to clamp his iron grip between the brace and the TV presenter's neck. After an exertion of concentrated pressure, it snapped open. Phil inspected it closely for several seconds.

"You said you'd seen this before," Tia said, confused.

"When I was in Germany, yes. The military used it. There were two initials on the one I saw: GF. *Göttlich Führer*. Divine Leader in German."

"Go on," Tim said when Phil cut off abruptly.

"That's all I'm saying for now," Phil said with a smile.

"What?" Alice said. "For God's sake, just tell us - this is no time for one of your games."

"Oh, this is no game," Phil said. "As I say, I've seen this before. Or rather the aftermath of it. I'm keeping my cards close to my chest. And if you're so keen for everything to be disclosed - why don't you go first, Alice?"

"I don't know what you're talking about," Alice said.

"Oh, I think you do." Phil looked around at the others. "I think we all do. We've all done something we're not proud of; that's why we're here, unfortunately."

"Not me," Tia said.

"Nor me," Harvey added. "The idiots have cocked up. I've never even harmed a fly, for Christ's sake."

"Just tell the whole story will you, Phil?" Jenny said. "I for one am already suspicious of you because you're the only one that's been sneaking out of the complex at night."

Phil maintained his silence, and so, with no assailant on this tiny island, the only logical conclusion was that one of them had killed Dale and carved "DL" on the flesh of his back. The same person who'd tortured Helen Westling to death.

Suspicion was palpable in the air. Tia couldn't help but look at Jenny, who returned her stare.

PART FOUR

STRANGERS ON AN ISLAND

Chapter Ten

After they had recovered their composure, they left the church as a united group to explore the rest of the island. It didn't take long as the island was comprised mainly of trees and rock.

Sea surrounded them without even a hint of land in its all-encompassing, taut and sunless horizon.

There was only one more building left to investigate if you could call it such. An outhouse, barely more than a shed, that was located close to the house and the mock audience of freakily still mannequins.

As they approached, the mannequins shot into life for the briefest of seconds, clapping, cheering, booing and whistling; a realistic crowd cacophony. The sound system sent out a final shrill blast of static before dying down again.

"Christ!" Harvey said. "I think I need to change my shorts after that."

"This seems like a lovely island to vacation on," Tia said sarcastically.

"Yeah, if you're Hannibal Lecter," Alice added. "Or Jigsaw."

The door to the outhouse building was stiff, but between them, they managed to push it open. The person inside, seated at a desk, seemed as startled as they were in a dark room lit only by multiple TV monitors.

"And ta-da: there's our elusive cameraman," Harvey announced. "What do you have to say for yourself? Film anything good did you, mate?"

The cameraman remained seated uneasily behind what was more of a control panel than a desk. A control panel hooked up to multiple monitors showing the house and its surrounding grounds. He did not answer Harvey's question.

Nor the others which followed.

But as soon as Tia concluded he was going to say nothing, he blurted out a torrent of passionate words clipped into short sentences in a foreign language. His speech became nothing more than a frantic tirade, and his eyes widened like golf balls in his bald head.

"That's just great," Alice said. "The guy doesn't even speak English. I mean, who can't speak English these days?"

Harvey nudged past Tia in an attempt to grab him. "I'm not buying that. Trust me he's going to understand."

As soon as Harvey did so, the guy produced a handgun; drawing it like a gunslinger. Harvey immediately stopped dead in his tracks, throwing his hands up.

The cameraman started up another tirade, punctuating each sentence by pointing the gun at somebody else until Phil shocked them all by responding in a machine-gun blast of words in the same foreign tongue. Visibly calming, the cameraman put his gun away, sitting back down.

"Back off, Harvey, that's it," Phil said. "It's okay. He's a prisoner here like us."

Tia nodded her agreement. "Look at his neck: he's got one of those braces clamped around his neck like Helen Westling. He's Russian, isn't he?"

Phil nodded. "He's telling us how he got here," he said. "Everyone shut up, and I'll translate for you."

Peter's Story: Lost

Peter awoke to bright, intense light.

Peter's first thought was that he was lying in the scorching sand of a desert. The sunlight high in the cloudless sky, torturing his dry eyes whenever he opened them, his eyelids simultaneously smooth and rough to the touch like sandpaper.

The gentle sound of lapping waves told Peter he was lying on a beach.

His eyes settled enough for him to stare at a taut horizon where the sea met a gunmetal sky. The white-hot sun formed flecks of gold on the waves that hurt his vision like a searing path to the afterlife.

Peter stood unsteadily for a moment, facing the sea, his head throbbing though he didn't think he'd been drinking last night.

Peter couldn't be sure of this though, or anything else for that matter, because he didn't remember last night and couldn't remember how he'd got here.

Peter's right ankle felt sore, and when he examined it closely, he saw it was damaged, perhaps even broken.

Peter felt something tug him back as he leaned forward, clawing him down onto the hot sandy floor as he attempted to walk.

It took Peter a moment to recognize he was fixed in place by a harness of some kind. When he looked directly behind him, Peter realized the harness was attached to a parachute.

The parachute felt heavy because it was wet, half of it still floating in the sea.

He'd landed in the water and crawled his way to the safety of the shore.

That could be the only logical conclusion, though again, he could not remember any of it.

Peter felt so weak that it took him a moment to shrug himself out of the parachute harness and unclip the straps.

Once free, he took stock of his situation.

Something had attached itself to his neck, something not part of the harness made out of metal, steel maybe. It felt sore against his skin, but every time he attempted to remove the metal collar, he felt like passing out, so he left it on.

Peter had no idea how he'd got here beyond the parachute attached to him. He believed he'd perhaps received a concussion; the only detail he could remember about himself was his name: Peter.

No second name came after this revelation, though Peter tried to mentally clasp hold of it the same way the metal collar gripped his neck.

Peter What?

Peter ... I've no idea.

One sentence kept reverberating in his head: "The sinner must repent by watching other sinners."

Peter hadn't a clue what that meant, and frustratingly, it was the only detail he could recall.

From the Bible, perhaps? The Old Testament? Most of the Old Testament was about sin.

The shrill beeping on the device attached to his wrist startled him, and he cursed out loud.

Peter looked dumbly down at an updating digital map accompanied by a glowing red dot. The dot appeared to be over the skull-shaped cliff he was facing. It was certainly no smartwatch, lacking face or shoulder buttons to press. It contained only a scrolling map with this moving red dot and in the top-right-hand corner a timer; a timer counting down.

It read 52:33, changing to 52:32 as he viewed it. By the time he finished looking at the interface in detail, the countdown was 52 minutes exactly.

52 minutes from what?

Trying to fathom out the riddle of this countdown made Peter's headache feel worse, so he concentrated on his breathing, slowing it down and emptying his mind while sitting in the sand.

The shoreline stretched a mere fifty metres, curving out of sight and giving way to rocks in both directions.

After a time, Peter walked along the beach looking for an easy route up the cliff, hobbling at first and then walking more freely.

Nothing came back to him other than a name. A name that was not his own.

Karen.

No, Karina; that was it.

The name welled up emotions from deep within himself, but he had no clue as to why. He cared for this Karina.

Perhaps Karina was his wife.

Girlfriend.

Sister.

Mother.

Auntie?

The more he thought about it, the more elusive and frustrating it was for him.

Peter decided to let his thoughts go blank.

After a few minutes of walking in the gentle surf under a baking hot sun (almost exactly ten minutes – as the counter now read 41 minutes …) Peter decided to head inland.

Peter battled his way up a cliff until he started to see green forestry. He gripped a stray vine to ease his ascent over the last few feet of the clifftop.

Peter had to rest his beaten-up body, the climb sapping his energy levels.

Peter slid the leather army boots he'd carried around his neck back on to his feet. It hurt his ankle like hell to do so. It was necessary pain as he had to ensure that he didn't injure the soles of his feet on the brambles and thick thorns.

As the counter dipped below 30 minutes, Peter found himself immersed in woodland.

It was still hot, even under the shade of the trees. Tasting salt on his lips, Peter removed his sweaty black T-shirt and tied it around his waist.

Peter spotted a large house and believed he had found his way back to civilization.

Isolated properties always reminded Peter of Edward Hopper paintings. Hopper captured the lonely mood with eerie precision in his works.

I'm a loner. Is that it?

Why would I think that? And why do I remember Edward Hopper paintings but not my own fucking full name?

Peter walked through an open gate and past a small swimming pool leading to a raised Jacuzzi on AstroTurf. He knocked a few times on the glass of the patio doors without reply, before realizing there were no locks on the doors.

Cameras greeted Peter indoors as they had outside the property. The myriad of cameras staring at him, Peter at first mistook for security CCTV, but there were far too many of them for that to be the case. Closer inspection of the cameras revealed they were high-definition. They were the variety used on reality television shows rather than the grainy, low-grade picture quality of security cameras.

"Hello?" Peter called out. "Anybody home?"

Guess not.

The interior proved as generic as the grounds outside. The spotless house was like a show home, to be displayed and admired rather than to live in it. The upstairs consisted of two large bedrooms, both containing four single beds, all eight of them made up.

Peter lay down on one of the beds, gathering his racing thoughts.

How bizarre is this? I've found my way onto a reality TV set - I should know, I worked on one for years. I'm a cameraman and a damned good one too.

A neon eye watched him in whichever room he visited in this house, the eye situated next to the plasma screen on the wall in the living room revealed that he was, in fact, inside a *Divine Leader* house.

Surreal as that felt.

The eyeball insignia unsettled Peter as it reminded him of the Illuminati, something to be feared rather than respected.

Peter explored downstairs, walking over to an open-plan kitchen and spotting a space-age silver fridge. Mercifully, still and sparkling bottled water sat on the top shelf in plentiful supply.

There was no food to be found.

Nothing tastes better than water to a thirsty man, Peter thought, as he gulped down the refreshingly cool liquid.

Peter moved on, exploring each room in the house.

Peter whistled for a time but didn't recognize the tune.

Like nearly everything else, it eluded his memory.

It seemed, like so many other details, hauntingly familiar. Peter made an effort to let his curiosity remain dormant. It would no doubt all come back to him in time …

Time.

Sixteen minutes …

The sentence about sinners floated back to Peter. He deliberately tried to incorporate logic rather than memory to solve this riddle.

I've sinned; that has to be why I'm here.

Something stirred inside Peter and faded again like an elusive inner image fading to black as though it were the end of a movie.

"Forget it, Peter," he said to himself sternly. "It'll come back to you when you least expect it. That's how memory works. You can't force it."

Talking out loud familiarized Peter with his own voice. He hoped that by providing greater stimulation to his brain, he might salvage his failing memory.

The timer continued counting down – it seemed to speed up every time he checked it – and Peter reluctantly left the comfort of the house to follow the red dot on the map displayed on his wristwatch. He talked to himself in a monologue, hobbling further until he ended up standing on a flat, winding dirt track.

His neck brace beeped loudly, startling him. He cursed the wretched device clamped around his neck, strangling his skin like an electronic python. The damned thing would not budge no matter how hard he tried – it seemed surgically welded to his flesh.

A vision from nowhere hit Peter. A strong one.

A blonde girl, early to mid-twenties, tall, easy on the eye. No, not just easy on the eye; stunning. Her freckled, unlined face broke into a sweet smile, lips parting to reveal perfect white-picket-fence teeth through which she spoke Peter's name lightly whilst laughing.

The mood changed in a blink; she looked worried as Peter forced her to the ground. Another man stood there, behind Peter, watching from the shadows.

Why am I doing that? Why am I holding her down?

Another vision, another victim. Same age, equally as stunning.

The young girl completely helpless, writhing under Peter's bulk as she gave up fighting back.

Another memory came to him, similar circumstances. This time it was a brunette five or six years younger than the last victim.

She was in that same dark back room, a camera recording her struggle. And a heavy-breathing watcher in the shadows who could barely contain his excitement.

Peter tried to force more memories, but nothing further came. Mercifully, the unsavoury memory faded until it was completely gone as if censored by some mind-control gadget.

Gadget, Peter said to himself. *Now that's familiar.* The elusive sense of déjà vu again passing over the word "gadget" for Peter; like a gentle breeze in the night that couldn't be heard or felt but was there because you sensed it.

I'm a gadget man.

Or, at least, Peter had been.

Once.

Peter could sense that he was fond of the word. He'd worked for a TV station in Moscow. His colleagues affectionately referred to him as "the gadget". That's right.

"Gadget means a small mechanical device or tool, especially an ingenious or novel one," Peter said robotically, remembering its precise dictionary definition.

I'm losing it, I'm going crazy, he began to despair. *Or I will if I don't see someone soon. Or if this dirt track doesn't lead anywhere.*

The counter on Peter's wristband read four minutes.

Four minutes from what exactly?

"I'll keep walking," Peter thought. "Walking and talking to myself and getting one hell of a suntan. What else can I do?"

Peter didn't answer himself this time. Instead, he breathed a sigh and stayed silent. Peter was starting to panic.

Panic like one of his victims.

From up here, Peter could only make out sea, stretching as far as the eye could see in all directions. And after all, the first prisons were built on islands.

Desperation slowly replaced anticipation, though Peter did not know why.

At least not yet.

The dirt track on this uninhabited island ended at a small wooden shed.

The device on Peter's wrist stopped beeping; the countdown disappeared altogether.

Peter let out a long sigh. He'd reached his destination.

Inside the shed, a control panel stood alongside multiple screens and monitors dominating all four walls.

As soon as he sat down, a message popped up on a screen. Peter pressed the play button.

The message which followed would explain everything to Peter.

Chapter Eleven

Peter broke off from his story as he swivelled in the control panel hot seat, his eyes searching for something. He pressed another button on the panel.

"He's going to play it for us," Phil translated. "The recording."

A message in Russian came on, delivered by an unnaturally enhanced voice – the sort of deep, rasping baritone of a movie trailer narrator, or a killer phoning the housebound, taunted victim in teen slasher movies. Its distortion lent the voice an otherworldly quality.

Phil took a deep breath before translating the message.

Hello Peter, nice of you to drop by.

Welcome to your punishment. Your day of reckoning, if you will. You will finally pay for your crimes on this island through ensuring that other unpunished criminals pay their debt to society.

There's a video to remind you of what you did. The serum pumping into your bloodstream will provide you with the impetus to keep going. The only drawback is that it will rob you of your long-term memory.

It will also keep your depraved sex drive in check - the one which fuels your crimes.

These measures ensure you will remain in here and keep everything going to plan instead of having your own little fun and games with the housemates.

Follow my instructions, and I guarantee you will stay alive. You have enough food and water in here to comfortably sustain good health for a month. If you play along, I promise you'll be a free man at the end of it.

Your job is simple: to fire the communication updates into the house. It's all set to a schedule, laid out in full in the laminated folder under your desk. This schedule will keep the show going for the housemates, including the games, the nominations and the forfeits. The delivery of food and drink as a reward you will supply via the hatch at the back of the kitchen area. That's all you have to do. Don't talk to any of the housemates, even if they spot you.

One of the first updates you will implement kills the power to the house. The purpose at this stage is to unsettle them and create an atmosphere of abandonment.

After a few hours have passed, you can start up the generator and give them electricity and heating again.

When this has completed, play video three – it describes some procedures you will need to learn. Starting with how to apply make-up in case you have to appear to be dead to the housemates.

Phil stopped his translation and looked around at the others.

"I guess we need to play tape three," Harvey said.

Peter clutched his neck; his face was starting to turn a deep crimson.

He spoke an English word for the first time: "Go!" he shouted.

Peter raised the pistol in their direction and shouted some more quick-fire Russian.

Phil shot into life. "He says if we don't go now the poison will be released into his system until it's fatal. We're not supposed to see that tape."

When Peter fired a warning shot over their heads, shattering a monitor screen on the wall, they made for the door like sheep spilling out of a pen. Tia, first out of the door and sprinting through the woods, felt the adrenalin rush through her system in a fight-or-flight response.

PART FIVE

PLOT TWIST

Chapter Twelve

Tia nervously finished her cigarette, daintily stubbing it out on the sand with her toe like a Cuban dance move before lighting another, seconds later - her last one.

At least this is one way to give up smoking, Tia thought without amusement.

The wind blew a refreshing breeze, but the natural windbreak of the skull-shaped cliff towering above protected her from it.

"Mind if I bum a light?"

The voice startled her, but Tia saw it was Phil. She liked Phil.

He held out his hands like a magician to show there was nothing in them as he approached her. "The others are freaking out. We've been looking everywhere for you."

"As if they care," Tia said.

"I care," Phil replied.

Tia found she could raise a smile, a faint one but still a smile. Phil smiled back, or at least the corners of his mouth curled up in a way that Tia found cute.

"Here," he said, handing her a pack of Benson & Hedges. "You said you were almost out."

"Thank you," Tia said, exhaling in relief more than anything. "Are you sure?"

"Keep it," Phil said. "It's no problem."

His lips parted into one of his wolfish smiles. "It comes at a price, though."

Tia was at first puzzled and then shocked.

"Oh…" He worked out the miscommunication from Tia's expression. "God no, I don't mean that kind of a price. Come on, what do you take me for?"

Her smile was one of relief as she took an indulgent drag of her cigarette, knowing it wouldn't be her last smoke, thanks to Phil.

"I mean you have to tell me your story, that's all," Phil said, taking a long drag of his cigarette after Tia had obligingly lit it for him. "Only first, I have to ask you: have you ever read it?"

"Read what?" Tia replied.

"*And Then There Were None*, of course."

"Actually, I have. I was made to read it in school."

"Who was your favourite character?" Phil said. "I mean, who did you most want to survive?"

"Vera, I guess," Tia said. "Although she let a boy drown, she was so tortured by her crime. It destroyed her whole life. I also felt sorry for the doctor."

"Armstrong?"

"Yes, that's his name. I had an ex who was an alcoholic. Things can easily spiral out of control and he was made to work all hours caring for his patients."

"That's interesting."

"What about you?"

"Well, I used to like Lombard," Phil said with a smile. "I played him when I was a young actor; years ago, this was. A small production, little more than a school play really. Society celebrates youthful playfulness in men, even when it's less than, well, ethical. But as I've got older, I tend to empathise with Emily Brent."

"Really?" Tia said. "I think, along with that sociopath Anthony, she's everyone's least favourite. I mean, just look at the way she ordered the servants about and her general coldness."

"Ah, but you see," Phil said, "society made her that way. She was unable to have children and dismissed as a spinster - such a horrible, disgusting word. She was cast aside by society. Seeing that young girl being so frivolous about her pregnancy must have been cruel on her. When you think about it, she didn't murder anyone. She was singled out, as they all were, by a privileged upper-class white judge who decided that they deserved their fate."

"I never really looked at it that way," Tia said.

Their cigarettes were winking like the eyes of an awakening demon.

They watched grey waves break into whitecaps, taking in the mesmeric sea, keeping them there like an unassailable prison wall constructed by God.

Or the Devil.

"God, listen to yourself, Phil!", he said, chucking a pebble into the sea, attempting to skim it across the surface. "You're a real charmer. Not that our situation isn't depressing enough."

"No," Tia said. "It's helping."

Another long silence ensued, but not an uncomfortable one as they continued to look at the sea, Tia thinking about it being their prison sentinel rather than enjoying its natural flowing beauty.

Phil stopped tossing pebbles into the sea for a moment. "So, who do you think is doing this?"

"I honestly don't know," Tia said. "I'm so frightened I can't even think straight."

"If it's any consolation," Phil looked down at the sand and then at the horizon, "I am too."

"It's not," Tia said.

Phil looked back at her.

"I was rather hoping you were going to look after me."

Phil smiled. "I will if you tell me what you did. Come on, fess up. It's just the two of us, the others don't need to know."

Tia looked up at the cliff face at yet another installed camera, covering them both in its view. She shook her head.

"I don't know what to tell you," Tia said. "Perhaps I'm Emily Brent."

Phil smiled. "That's an interesting way of putting it. Although I think you're a bit sexier."

They kissed for a moment, which seemed to surprise them both. The raw passion in the kiss spoke of ravenous desire.

Or desperation for an alliance.

Less than a minute later, the two of them were climbing back up to the house, keeping their distance from each other.

Tia reflected that Phil, all of a sudden, seemed a completely different person.

She wasn't entirely at ease with his probing questions into her past either while his cryptic responses to her enquiries about him stacked up. His elusive demeanour unsettled her.

Snapping back to reality, Tia also remembered that the entries on that hideous board had included voyeur and stalker.

Safety in numbers, as the saying went. Survival rule number one for Tia had to be that she was not left alone with anyone.

Phil included.

Chapter Thirteen

On returning to the *Divine Leader* house, Tia overheard Tim and Rachel arguing in the kitchen. She settled in a niche behind the wall designed to conceal a camera. The tight space was dark enough for Tia to remain an undetected eavesdropper.

"I don't understand," Tim said, making an effort to keep his voice low and even. "Why do you need to know the details? What good will it do?"

"Because," Rachel replied, unable to keep the vulnerability out of her voice. "I like you."

Tim bowed his head.

A prolonged silence followed before Tim started to speak.

It was immediately clear to Tia that this was going to be his confession. A confession to a real-life murder.

Tim's Story: Murder on the Menu

I: THE STARTER

Tim agreed to meet up with a work colleague of Wendy's. It was only supposed to be drinks, but now it was a full-on meal.

Pete Avery was his name; some smug, superficially popular bastard from sales. Mid-thirties, tall, career-focused, gym-goer, drove an Audi.

So here they were, the three of them waiting for the maître d' to show them to a table.

The restaurant was French. One of those posh, over-priced eateries half a mile from Brindleyplace. Avery's choice no doubt, as Frankie & Benny's or Nando's was more Wendy's style. Tim couldn't remember a restaurant where she had failed to produce a discount voucher or plucked a code from a website on her iPhone.

"Table for three," Pete said, taking the words out of Tim's mouth.

Ushered to Table 43, Pete joked (if you could call it that), "How fitting, table 4-3, for three."

"Pete's good with numbers," Wendy said.

"Getting extravagant purchase orders signed off, maybe," Pete said. "Calculating client commission, definitely. An indulgent expense or two that needs to be hidden, every time." Pete sniggered with Wendy at their in-joke, a gag that Tim wasn't privy to, not working for their company.

Tim was glad to see a sweating Pete was nervous; Wendy even more so.

Wendy began to sit next to Pete, before instead parking her ample-sized butt beside Tim, making Pete the apex of the triangle.

The waiter hovered for the drinks order, and Tim nearly slipped up by conversing in French. Thankfully, he pulled out in time, and bighead Avery jumped in, as Tim suspected he would. A flashy geezer like Avery never missed a chance to show off. Tim guessed it was a sales thing that came with the territory.

They were sitting outside, not inside: Tim's choice. It was cold and wet, but they were seated under a canopy. Tim would have liked to light up, just for the extra irritation factor. Tim promised Wendy he'd quit. He knew how much Wendy detested the smell, but patting his pockets, he realized he'd left his ciggies at home. Damn. Not to worry though there were plenty of other ways to get on her nerves, and Tim intended to explore every one of them before the evening was over.

COURSE II: MAIN COURSE

This little meeting had been pitched to Tim like so: "I've become quite friendly with this guy I've been assigned to work with. You've got to meet him, Tim, he's a riot."

And he was, that was the annoying thing. Pete had the gift of the gab, and effortless charm. A part of Tim was finding it difficult to hate Pete completely.

That image playing like a movie in his head again stopped any such weaknesses - the one he censored from everybody else. He tried to shut it out for a moment: to control it.

"Are you alright?" Pete said, suddenly serious.

"Okay, honey?" Wendy asked, matching Pete's false look of concern.

"Miles away," Tim said. "Sorry."

"Would you like to order for us?" Pete said, obviously hoping to embarrass him, Tim surmised. He didn't know about his clandestine passion for France, did he? He assumed a Brummie with a comprehensive school education wouldn't know French from German. No match for his superior grammar school education that mummy and daddy paid for, funded by a Conservative government that loved to make people like the Averys richer.

"You can order for us if you like," Tim said, sounding petty and immature. He hated it when that happened.

Avery didn't need a second invitation.

Cue a needlessly excessive bit of French conversation with the maître d'.

"You speak French very well, sir," the maître d' lied.

Well, my arse. Tim counted at least twelve mistakes in their brief exchange, and his dated accent and turn of phrase had about as much inflexion as Stephen Hawking reading a VCR manual.

"Very impressive," Wendy said, pouting a bit before considering Tim's presence again.

A bit more butchery of the French language from Pete and they were left alone to converse in English again but still engaged in dialogue which felt as contrived as a Berlitz role play.

Wendy scowled at Tim for the first time, showing her distaste at how difficult he was making even light conversation. Pete ploughed on amiably though, keeping up the pretence that they were three chums together. Good old Pete; can't say he's not a trier.

What followed could be politely termed as being an uncomfortable silence, but this was not so much an uncomfortable silence as one with teeth. Tim took a sip of his Coke when he realized that he was baring his.

And that's generally considered to be bad table manners.

Tim vowed to stick to drinking soft drinks, avoiding alcohol altogether. A drink would make his nerves less fraught, true, but it would also serve to dull his anger and blunt his reflexes. Wendy would try to veto it anyway; she deplored him drinking alcohol.

Tim looked up and smiled derisively at the concern etched on their faces. It was beautiful. Things were not going the way they had planned. Instead of their anticipated mockery of Tim, they were the ones being mocked.

Wendy had quit giving Tim dirty looks, probably because she knew that he couldn't give a rat's arse. Wendy tried to pick the conversation up a little. Being contemptuous towards Pete would only cast him under more suspicion. So Tim smiled and thought of a real bastard of a question to ask Pete, one someone like him would appreciate.

"So, Pete," Tim said. "Ever taken that someone special to Paris?"

Pete, being a trier, clung to this the way a shipwrecked survivor grasps driftwood.

"I've been so many times I've lost count," Pete said. "Always on business, I'm afraid."

"Is that what guys like you call it?" Tim smiled conspiratorially.

Tim wanted to say more but willed himself to keep the conversation cordial.

"Never been myself," Tim said, keeping the conversation going. "Always wanted to."

For some unknown reason, Wendy apologized. They both ignored her.

"Maybe we should go as a threesome sometime," Pete said.

Touché! So Pete could take the mickey as well.

"I'd like that," Tim said, grinding his teeth to chalk.

Wendy grinned at Tim like a Cheshire cat; she could take the piss as well. When the conversation was strained and bordering on antagonistic Tim seemed to have the upper hand, so he went all sulky again.

Tim spotted the guilt of their seedy little secret as Wendy and Pete smiled tightly at each other. Tim's face remained a mask of hatred, his eyes ablaze with scorn. A real Kodak moment, as they used to say. Knowing Wendy, she probably wanted a picture of this catastrophe. Right on cue, Wendy asked the waiter to do just that.

The waiter had the habit of counting one, two, three, as if this held any significance before taking the picture; he only excelled in prolonging the awkwardness.

The waiter took three photos - a waste of good film.

They tucked into their food. The arrival of the main course was welcomed by all three of them, not because they were especially hungry but because of the simple fact that when you're eating there's less talk.

Pete's phone belted out the Bond theme and both Wendy and Tim laughed, but for different reasons.

Avery probably fantasized he was Bond. What a loser. What could Wendy possibly see in this guy?

Pete excused himself to answer it, leaving the table and the restaurant, pretending it was to get improved reception on his mobile.

Wendy's soft, smiling eyes turned into those of an Old Testament prophet. "What on earth do you think you're playing at?"

Unbelievable. "What am I playing at?"

"Pete's a good friend as well as a colleague," she said.

Oh boy, this is where she confesses, then the confessions will predictably become recriminations. Tim could almost hear her say, "What do you expect when I have this to come home to?"

"It wouldn't kill you to be a little nicer to him, you know."

"Excuse me." Tim got up, scraping his chair as noisily as he could manage, savouring the sound, like fingernails on a chalkboard, striding across the restaurant and into the gents.

To Tim's surprise, he felt his eyes moisten with tears. He caught his expression in the mirror. It was one of agony.

When someone entered the room, he rushed into a cubicle and slammed the door.

She had admitted it, even gloated – Tim didn't expect that, the heartless bitch.

Fresh tears were about to blur his vision when out of the open toilet window Tim saw Avery chatting on his phone in the rain-washed alley.

No one else around.

Tim took an inventory of the situation. He looked up: CCTV cameras? One camera fifty yards away; its unhurried sweep did not cover the section Pete was standing in.

Tim reached inside his pocket, the flick knife in his hand before he realized. Fluorescent light reflected in a thousand different directions off its blade. Tim was temporarily mesmerized by the glittering steel and the power it possessed to shape his destiny.

Out in the alley, the torrential rain had ceased, the rain-slicked floor washed an unreal sodium orange. Tim looked at a caricature of himself in a puddle, just a big joke.

Avery had his back to Tim, chatting away. Perfect.

Tim winced at every footstep, which seemed about as unnoticeable as a clap of thunder. Adrenalin took over, and he found it hard to distinguish whether the thumps were his footsteps or the blood beating in his ears. Tim resisted the urge to run at him.

Five feet away.

Four.

Avery too wrapped up in his small talk salesman slang of "yeah mates", "tell me about it" and "yeah-yeah-yeah" to notice Tim's approach.

Two feet away. Tim felt his stomach lurch as if he were standing on a cliff edge.

In a way, he was.

The blade poised, his forearm tensed and ready to bury the flick knife in him, right up to the handle. Below his navel will do.

Maybe a few inches lower; that would be more appropriate.

No, concentrate.

Tim had to make it count. To make sure Pete died.

Tim wanted to send out a message to men like Pete Avery. Men who assumed they could invade your territory as and when they want and not feel the consequences.

If Pete failed to turn around, Tim would grab him from behind and slit his throat with one efficient left-to-right motion.

The police? Right now, they had barely crossed his mind. He wanted it over quickly. Besides, he had heard that they never come down too hard on blokes like him anyway.

It starts raining again, and the only thing Tim is concentrating on at this moment is trying not to get too much blood on his clothes: that sort of thing tended to be a dead giveaway.

Tim hoped the heavy rain would mess with forensics.

He was within touching distance when he heard the one word he didn't want to hear from Pete.

Avery being the nobber he is, the word is Italian.

"Ciao."

Pete turns.

"Tim?" His forehead furrowed.

Tim wimped out, concealing the blade behind his back.

"I…"

"Yes?" Pete looked confused.

"I just want to say sorry."

This was the best Tim could do under the circumstances. Tim hated apologizing at the best of times, and to a shit like Avery, it hurts like you can't imagine.

"For what?" Pete said.

"The way I've been acting tonight."

"Not necessary." He broke into a smile. "Come on, let's go back in and start afresh, hey?"

Avery felt the need to punctuate this truce by putting a friendly arm around Tim like they were two mates emerging from their local at closing time. When they walked in like this Wendy's face told Tim she was confused by these turn of events, but her smile was one of hope.

COURSE III: DESSERT

Pete and Wendy passed on dessert because the menu was crammed with treats with enough calories to put a spare tyre on Kate Moss. Tim ordered crêpes with chocolate sauce, determined to at least salvage something from the night.

There were no more arguments until the bill came.

Pete offered to pay, but Wendy agreed to split it. It was the price of Tim's food that proved the sticking point.

"Look, to be honest," Wendy said, addressing the waiter, her voice subconsciously posher when complaining, "the only reason we came in here was because of your special offer."

She gestured at Tim. "He may be big for his age, but he's only eleven, and the promotional offer clearly states that kids under twelve eat free when accompanied by an adult."

Tim didn't know where to look. She was always embarrassing him like that. Tim thought about storming off in protest.

COURSE IV: AFTER-DINNER TREAT

His fortunes changed for the better when they got to the pictures, as Tim got into an eighteen! Can you believe it? The latest Tarantino movie too, Tim couldn't wait to tell his friends about it.

As for Avery? Well, there would be other opportunities. Better opportunities.

Pete had promised a trip to the Bahamas in July, and good old Avery had vowed to take Tim out on a boat fishing.

There are hundreds of uninhabited islands out there, he said. Islands so small and secret that they don't even show up on most maps.

Perfect.

There would never be a better opportunity than that.

Chapter Fourteen

"So you killed your mother's boyfriend on that fishing trip?" Rachel said, rocking back on her heels and backing away two feet; out of striking range. "When you were eleven years old?"

"Actually," Tim said, as though it made a difference, "I was twelve at the time."

"How did you do it?"

"Does it matter?" Tim said softly. So softly that Tia only just heard him.

"It matters," Rachel replied.

"He hit his head, okay?" Tim said. "It was an accident, I swear, but I left him to drown as I pulled up the anchor. And that's the God's honest truth. I separated from my mother, after that, and the unhealthy hold she had over me went for good."

"I changed," Tim went on in a pleading voice. "I was an evil, messed-up kid, but that's not me any more. I got therapy, I took yoga and t'ai chi classes, I moved on. I've tried to make amends. To be a warm person who is kind and helps people. You said yourself that you committed your crime as a child. You must understand better than anyone that that is not who I am now."

Tia stopped to consider this herself, her face one of concentration in the shadows, listening to their argument. Tia thought about the Tim she had met and developed feelings for in the short time she'd known him in this house. Not romantic ones like Rachel had, but a solid friendship built on the way he listened carefully, his thoughtful, considerate disposition and his sweet, unselfish nature.

Tia thought about how much she too had changed since childhood.

"Look, you know me," Tim pleaded.

Rachel's face remained unmoved.

Tia shifted position, wincing as a floorboard creaked beneath her Nike trainers. When she looked up, Rachel had rounded the corner and spotted her eavesdropping. Tim followed a second later. Both had stony, unforgiving faces.

"And what have you got to say for yourself?" Rachel said to Tia. "Still protesting your innocence? Or do you want to join our little group and confess? You killed your hubby, that's what everyone's thinking."

When Tia didn't answer, Rachel said, "Trust me, it will be better if you do."

Tim ran a hand through his cropped blonde hair, his cold blue eyes on Tia. He was expecting a confession too.

"It'll be better for you," Rachel finished, repeating herself to drive her point home. "We'll form our own little alliance to rat out our devious little mole; the Divine Leader or whatever weirdo cult name he has given himself."

Tia shook her head. They were both killers then: Tim and Rachel. Carrying out their crimes when they were minors, but killers nevertheless. A different breed from herself.

Tia was furious. Furious because of the mistake they had made in putting her on an island with these people. Tia had felt like killing her husband David many times, but she hadn't done the deed. A jury had cleared her.

As Tia left, Rachel called out, "Sooner or later you're going to have to come clean with us. It's only a matter of time."

What Rachel shouted out next got Tia's heart rate up and her step subconsciously quickened.

"If not," Rachel shouted out, "in all likelihood, it'll be you who's next, with a sheet put over you. You may want to think about that, Little Miss Perfect."

Frightened by this, Tia didn't stop running until she was out in the woods.

It was getting late, and it was getting dark.

Being out here all alone wasn't the smartest move.

Tia headed back to the house. Forming an alliance was the only thing she could do. Rachel had been right about that part. She didn't have to be in league with these two though.

Tia doubled her pace as the house came into sight.

If she stayed out here on her own, the odds were that she probably would be next.

Chapter Fifteen

The flat, emotionless drone of the Divine Leader's voice startled Tia out of a daze as it summoned the housemates to the living room.

The plasma screen read:

```
I know when you're sleeping,
I know when you're awake,
I know when you've been bad or good …
```

"Cute," Alice said. "But it's not Christmas."

The onscreen wording disappeared in a flashy graphical disperse effect, replaced with:

```
YOUR PUNISHMENT FOR LEAVING THE COMPLEX, WHEN
SPECIFICALLY INSTRUCTED NOT TO, IS SITUATED ON THE
TABLE BEHIND YOU.
```

Tia's head swung around to spot a small, wrapped gift she'd previously overlooked. It sat in the middle of the coffee table.

Harvey, nearest to the table, got there first to pick it up. "There's a note attached."

"It says," Harvey read out loud, "For the person who put this through my heart with their naivety, love – it's a foreign name – Eva? Spelt E-V-A."

"Does that mean anything to anyone?" Alice said, looking around the room.

"That's me," Phil said. He didn't look his usual confident self.

He wasted no time in ripping through the shiny red wrapping paper, revealing a small black metallic box.

Phil opened the box.

He pulled out a small handgun and a single bullet.

Tia appreciated that Phil had handled such a firearm before as he immediately placed the bullet in the chamber and snapped off the safety with a sharp, sinister click.

He looked at the screen for further instructions.

The plasma screen read:

THE HOUSEMATE CHOSEN AT RANDOM HAS TO IDENTIFY WHICH OF THE LABELS ON THE BOARD APPLIES TO THEM. WITH A DETAILED CONFESSION / EXPLANATION AS TO WHY.

This instruction disappeared, replaced with a further one:

PHIL - THIS TASK COULDN'T BE SIMPLIER. FAILURE OF THE CHOSEN HOUSEMATE TO CONFESS THEIR PAST CRIME WILL RESULT IN YOU FIRING THE BULLET INTO THEIR HEAD.

IF YOU FAIL TO COMPLY WITH THESE INSTRUCTIONS THEN YOU WILL TAKE THE CHOSEN PERSON'S PLACE AS THE HOUSEMATE TO DIE.

The board of labels popped up on screen again, displayed for all to see. Each had a question mark after it, with two exceptions. DEALER had Dale's name and smiling picture next to it and the presenter, Helen Westling, was now pictured opposite the HIT AND RUN DRIVER label.

The three labels at the bottom were still a cypher, having TBA before the double question marks.

After a minute or so, another text entry came onscreen:

THE HOUSEMATE TO CONFESS WILL NOW BE CHOSEN AT RANDOM:

Seconds later, the board shot into life as all their names appeared onscreen. The computer cycled through a list of their names at high speed.

TIM

ALICE

HARVEY

TIA

HARVEY

RACHEL

JENNY

ALICE...

"I can't take much more of this," Alice said, biting her fingernails. Harvey turned his back, unable to look.

HARVEY

RACHEL

ALICE

TIM

JENNY

TIA

HARVEY

JENNY

TIA

To Tia's horror, she realized the board had stopped on her name.

She was close enough to see her terrified expression reflected in the plasma screen.

"Oh, my God!" Tia said.

Phil wasted no time in levelling the weapon at her head.

The fashion with which Phil raised the firearm, holding it out in front of himself as though it were an extension of his body, meant that Tia was in no doubt that:

A – Phil could fire it at any moment, and

B – he would not miss the target that was her head.

Tia slumped down on the sofa, and Phil instantly adjusted his aim.

"No one has to die," Rachel said. "If you confess, Phil will put the gun down. Right, Phil?"

Phil nodded, not taking his eyes off Tia.

"Just confess," Harvey urged. "Please."

Tia looked at the screen, her name placed below the graphic title of "Confession Time" and with a question mark next to it, the criminal labels appearing underneath.

Tia looked at the board, taking it all in. She considered each of the labels carefully before looking back at Phil.

Phil's stoic expression shielded any hint of emotion, his posture ramrod straight.

Looking around the room, Tia saw Phil's icy demeanour and complete lack of compassion mirrored in the others' expressions.

Their united message was clear: Tia, you have to confess.

The Divine Leader started a countdown onscreen which overlaid the guilt labels in huge digits.

The count started at thirty seconds.

When the onscreen counter was down to ten, the screen glowed red, and Rachel broke the silence. "For God's sake, Tia."

Tia looked at the six available sinner labels, including the three cryptic double question mark entries below the last of these labels. Was she supposed to guess if one of these hidden entries applied to her if the other crimes were unsuitable? Guess her own crime?

Finally, she spoke, her pleading voice like that of someone else, not her own. "I'm not on this board," she said.

The countdown went down to three.

Two.

One.

The board dramatically flashed a deeper red: "Time's up."

Tia clamped her eyes shut; all she could hear were cries for Phil to reconsider. The others demanding Phil put the gun down and take a second to think things through.

Tia only expected a bullet between her eyes.

Death.

A wall of blackness.

Nothingness.

It never came.

When she opened her eyes, Phil was pointing the gun at the others; going from one person to the next.

"One of you," he said, swallowing hard with the tension. "Put this on the table."

There were fresh cries for Phil to think again.

"Which one of you was it?" His voice was eerily calm and determined. "This gift didn't grow legs and walk its way over here. So, who put it there?"

Phil aimed the gun, before firing it.

*

Phil fired at the plasma screen behind them.

Tia's heart leapt six inches.

The plasma screen did not shatter; it wasn't even marked.

"Blank," Phil said. "The bullet was a blank. I knew it from the weight as soon as I picked it up."

He placed the gun on the coffee table.

Phil was shaking, his complexion a sickly shade of grey.

The *Divine Leader* emblem came back on to the screen; it was not the standard pink and blue version but a black eyelid, eyelash and eye imposed on a white background; like a darker, pirated version of the familiar logo.

Jenny had mentioned the Dark Web as a probable platform for viewers watching this show. Tia had read about the Dark Web in *Cosmopolitan*. You had to download the Tor browser, and type ".onion" to gain access to this underworld of the internet; an uncharted territory unlit by the sane, safe highways of the Google search engine. A real upstairs-downstairs dynamic for the psyche. In Dark Web forums people freely discussed subjects such as cannibalism and torture preferences in place of the Brexit or gender equality debates going on upstairs.

Threads casually started with, "Does anyone know a reliable ex-forces hitman in the Los Angeles area?" or "How many bullets does it take to kill a cheating whore, when all the major organs and arteries have been deliberately missed?"

"You're going to have to kill me then," Phil said, looking around the room, meeting their eyes. "However, mark my words. The one behind that little charade just now better know this. I don't scare easily, and I'm hard to kill. So, look out!"

Phil marched out of the living room, striding up the stairs two at a time.

Seeing Phil lose his cool was perhaps the most unsettling moment in the house for Tia. She'd only just recovered from the fact that she was still alive. Tia could see the others in the room were as unsettled as her at the sight of Phil losing it.

Up until now, he had been their leader.

With this new development, it seemed the Divine Leader had the upper hand.

But then again, had that not been the case from the outset? The remaining housemates were at a disadvantage; the Divine Leader seemed to know everything about them, but they still knew nothing about the Divine Leader.

Or maybe, as Phil suggested, one of them did know.

Tia looked up at a camera perched in the corner of the room. A camera which existed for no other reason than to record their suffering.

Chapter Sixteen

A tense atmosphere was developing at the dinner table.

The guys showed their unease by knocking back alcohol and the food Alice served up as if it were their last meal.

Jenny had come clean about the whisky and beer she'd stashed away when she'd entered the complex as the first housemate, but not that Dale – entering as the second guest in the house – had been her partner in crime in doing so.

The last three entries on what Harvey had dubbed "the guilt board" and Phil "the board of shame" were counting down. Scheduled to be revealed in a matter of minutes, it put them all on edge.

Who knew what heinous act was going to appear there?

The women, in contrast to the men, were not eating anything. Jenny and Rachel kept disappearing to give Alice a hand in the kitchen, which confused Tia.

Outside, a downpour continued, hard enough to make it sound like static from a tuned-out radio. Darkness added to the claustrophobic atmosphere of impending doom that was settling in.

Tia could feel it in the pit of her stomach, that sickening feeling something awful was about to happen to her and there was absolutely nothing she could do about it. A feeling she had experienced throughout her tumultuous marriage to David.

One of the men at this table, looking at her now, could be something worse than the criminal acts already displayed on the screen in the living room. That's what Tia could not get out of her mind.

In a matter of minutes, there were more dire revelations to come on that board.

It struck Tia as funny how being seated at a table made you feel civilized, and how a lifetime of conditioning made you sit docilely at the dinner table when you should be acting.

What could I do, though? Tia's conscience answered for her. *These people sat across the table could have been victims just like you.*

If that were the case, then they should be working together. A clear divide already drawn between the sexes from the subconscious seating arrangements made this out of the question.

But could she trust Alice, Rachel and Jenny any more than she could Tim and Phil purely because they were of the same gender?

Harvey was acting too strangely to trust. He had necked far too much alcohol and could hardly sit up straight.

Tim's eyes were red-rimmed as Alice obligingly brought him some more coffee to counteract the fatigue that inevitably came with the stress of their situation.

When Alice brought in a dessert of lemon cheesecake, she motioned to Tia with her hands as Jenny and Rachel made eye contact. Both Jenny and Rachel left at the same time, fleeing into the foyer between the living room and the dining area.

Phil, seated closest to Tia, hadn't said a word. The mere mention of the name Eva earlier had crumpled his fighting spirit; he hadn't been the same Phil since. His gaze remained fixed, staring at something on the table in reverie and his face ashen. Phil's awkward lack of engagement persuaded Tia to get up and leave the dinner table.

Something unsaid was happening here.

Alice motioned her again with a come-hither gesture as she caught Tia's eye.

Alice had something important to say.

The rain continued to slam down with an audible din, allowing them to talk without whispering.

"What's going on?" Tia said.

"You need to see the screen," Alice told her.

They rushed towards the plasma screen; it spoke for itself. It answered all of the questions regarding Alice and Rachel's notably anxious behaviour in the past few minutes.

Tia felt her skin crawl and an icy flute play down her spine again.

Two more entries had appeared in eerie, gaudy, highlighted text:

RAPIST?

TRAINED ASSASSIN?

"That's why we need to get out of here now," Jenny said with urgency.

That elusive final entry on the board, counting down with less than five minutes to run before it revealed itself, added to their sense of foreboding.

It had to be something worse than a rapist.

Tia helped Rachel fetch two of the sleeping bags, thoughtfully provided in case of a falling out and some housemates opting to sleep elsewhere and to pack them full of tinned food, fruit and packets of biscuits. Alice and Jenny gathered up all the knives from the kitchen to use as weapons.

Jenny clutched the pyramid rack of the sharpest knives. The fierce look in her eye told Tia that Jenny did not trust any of them.

Tia reminded herself not to let her guard down as far as Jenny was concerned.

Despite the three men still being seated at the dinner table, the four women rushed out of the house not only unchallenged but unnoticed.

But they were not quick enough to miss the last entry on the board.

It would perhaps have been better for them if they had.

It took her breath away.

Tia was not the only one panicking, watching Jenny stumble into the patio door in her haste to open it and rush into the night and away from this house.

The flashing text, the final entry, had two words for them. Possibly the most sickening words Tia could have imagined. Those words were:

SERIAL KILLER

Chapter Seventeen

Serial Killer. Those two words dominated her thoughts.

One of them had successfully killed more than once and got away with it, and there were already two dead bodies on this island.

The night wind remained bitter and unrelenting. The rain continued to lash down in continuous straight white lines of iciness as if drawn from the pages of one of the Frank Miller graphic novels that her boyfriend Richard obsessed over.

The four women squeezed their way past the eerie graveyard of plastic mannequins, grabbing four coats from the dummies as they went, but not lingering long enough to try them on.

There were cameras following them, refocusing as they moved.

Alice was out front with the torch as they left the compound. There was some relief from the rain and wind as they left the cliff face and entered the small woodland area where trees sheltered them on all sides.

The torchlight bobbed in front of them, resembling a ghost's floating face. Eventually, Alice found the equipment shed. Tia thought she spied an owl as they passed the last of the trees, but it was merely the silent, unhurried, apathetic sweep of yet another camera.

What else?

Another camera looked down on them outside the shed. Its sound mics recorded the whispered argument over who would enter the door first, and potentially have their head blown off by Peter with his revolver and twitchy, sleep-deprived disposition.

They continued to argue until Tia took the decision out of their hands and rushed into the room. She stopped in front of Peter, seated motionless at his control desk.

Tia figured that wearing a dark anorak would prevent Peter from spotting her approach, and her sudden burst into the room would have the element of surprise.

However, Peter could not see Tia for an entirely different reason.

Nor did Peter see the three other women who entered moments later,

his emotionless, bloodshot eyes contained discoloured almost grey pupils.

When Rachel shook him, his head slumped onto the desk of the control panel.

Peter was dead.

If there was any doubt about this, the DL initials scratched into the wall above his head confirmed it.

The mobile phone on his desk had gone, along with the gun.

Facing the reality of this outcome, breathing heavily in that small dark room, Tia recalculated their odds of survival.

Her fear, which she thought had peaked, went up another notch.

Looking around the room, Tia discovered that she was not the only one feeling this way.

Chapter Eighteen

In that small, dark shed, silently contemplating their fate without the gun, they were roused from their bleak reverie by a shrill of static followed by a disembodied female voice.

She had an Australian accent.

They glanced up at the plasma screen in the corner. A woman paused, smiling weakly at them before she started talking again.

Tia's first impression was that the glamorous lady onscreen looked a lot like an older version of Jenny. But it quickly became apparent that she had nothing to do with Jenny.

"My husband Gary was such a kind, gentle soul," the onscreen woman said. "He was a devoted single parent to his only daughter. Devoted to a daughter who betrayed his trust and ultimately killed him."

"Switch the fucking thing off!" Alice snapped.

They all turned around to look at her. Although Alice tried frantically to find the controls, she couldn't kill the woman's voice or onscreen image.

"In the end, he was poisoned. Alice – his daughter – had been drugging him for months. Gary was already sick, and so none of this could be proved by the coroner, of course; but I knew. She was messing with his medication, overdosing him by putting it in the food she cooked for him. Gary was so proud of his daughter's cooking skills that he never complained or missed a meal.

"I think Gary knew on some level; only he couldn't accept that the daughter he'd raised so lovingly was killing him for his money. I mean, could any of us really come to terms with that?

"Alice ended up with pretty much all of his inheritance money. From the little I received from his estate, I reinvested in a gym. It had always been my dream to make it in the fitness industry. I started small in Perth, building a decent reputation and a solid brand, then expanded to Sydney, and then all over Australia. Now it's a multi-million-dollar company. Ironically, Alice squandered all of that money, trying to become a celebrity chef while I succeeded."

"Oh, you fucking bitch!" Alice screamed, clawing at the screen. Eventually, Alice broke it away from the wall. As soon as she did, the Australian woman popped up on another monitor, as if by magic.

"With the money I now have, I'll match the prize money for my take on justice. I'm offering the equivalent of one hundred thousand of your UK Pounds in Bitcoin to kill Alice. I want her to feel hunted for money like my Gary must have felt at the end. For me, this is true justice. Not only that, but the Divine Leader has provided a little extra incentive. Whoever kills Alice will be spared at the end of the game."

Game? Tia thought. *A game? That's what it is to these people. She's talking like a hostess revealing the mystery prize on a game show.*

The Killing Games.

"That's right, and anyone who kills Alice's conqueror immediately forfeits winning the game. In simpler terms, Kill Alice, and you are guaranteed to be spared by our killer."

"You fucking bitch!" Alice screamed again, breaking another screen. The Australian woman's face immediately popped up on a smaller TV on the control panel, like a mole burrowing out of another hole.

"Temper, temper. I can see you, Alice," the voice answered. "And if you're looking for the gun, you're very cold, honey."

The list of crimes they had come to refer to as the "guilt board" now flashed up on the screen, before disappearing in favour of the sickening image of leeches writhing in constant motion, eating up the screen. A close-up focused on one of them being picked up and put on the skin of an arm. The camera closed in tighter as they saw the leech draw blood.

The guilt board reappeared, the question mark after LEECH now changed.

LEECH = ALICE

The updated caption at the bottom reading WINNER AND SURVIVOR read WINNERS AND SURVIVORS now.

Tia imagined the Aussie hostess saying "and that, folks, is what we call a game-changer!"

But Alice wasn't there to see the caption change as she had bolted, followed by Jenny and Rachel a few seconds later.

Tia froze, before shooting into life again, sprinting to catch up with the others.

They were heading for the church.

At this stage, knives in hand, they were prepared to kill anyone or anything that came in their path.

They were, after all, on an island of criminals and murderers.

PART SIX
THE GAMES

Chapter Nineteen

Jenny stayed up talking to Rachel for a time while Alice slept. Tia felt that her best option was to pretend to be asleep, listening in on their conversation, a few feet away from where they were sitting up in their sleeping bags.

For the first hour or so, Jenny and Rachel watched the church door with interest, clutching the knives in their hands firmly, Tia noticed. Tia had a tense feeling of dread in the pit of her stomach.

After an hour, when no one had turned up, the tension eased with Jenny and Rachel breaking the silence.

Rachel led the conversation with Jenny, leading up to talking about why she was here, and the nature of the crime she had committed.

Tia knew that Alice was sleeping from her faint snore. Tia pretended to have her eyes closed in slumber, as she continued to eavesdrop on Rachel's confession.

With their backs to her, Tia risked a peek before closing her eyes again.

"I think the bully label is for me," Rachel said.

Jenny said that she did not have to explain, but Tia could sense in her tone that she felt Rachel owed her an explanation, considering that she had confessed her crime and that it would be easier to continue their friendship if Rachel admitted her guilt.

"I was thirteen," Rachel said. "There was this boy in my class called Daniel Sturgeon. We were mean to him like *really* mean. We nicknamed his family the Addams Family because they dressed in old-fashioned clothes, and were all weirdos. I knew he liked me, but I was awful to him. We played a trick on him where we invited him to go to the movies and then didn't turn up. It was kids' stuff, but I regret being so horrible to him. But kids can be cruel. How were we to know that he would hang himself?" Rachel wiped a tear from her eye. "I mean, I wish more than anything that I could take it back, but I can't – and I wasn't the only one involved."

Jenny put a consoling hand on top of Rachel's and patted it.

"You know when they asked us what was the worst thing we'd ever done?" Rachel said, looking into Jenny's eyes. Jenny was still holding her hand.

"Sure," Jenny replied.

"I nearly confessed," Rachel said. "If I had, I'm sure I fucking wouldn't be here now. But I just stood there silently, and they moved on. I had no idea at that moment that my chance of salvation had passed. There are thousands of unprosecuted criminals out there who deserve this a hell of a lot more than me."

Rachel wiped away her tears. "God, why didn't I have the strength to say anything?"

Jenny smiled. "I didn't confess, not even close," she said. "When they asked me, what was the worst thing I had ever done, I mean."

"Didn't you say anything either?" Rachel said.

"No, I gave them an answer." Jenny's serious face broke out into a smirk.

"What did you say?" Rachel asked as she smiled too in anticipation.

"I answered parking in a disabled space," Jenny said.

"You parked in a disabled space?" Rachel said in disbelief. "No, you didn't say that?!"

They sniggered into their hands, hoping to muffle the sound while checking that they hadn't woken Alice or Tia.

Tia wanted to say that she'd come up with something far wittier but had to feign slumber to glean some more vital information, information that could save her life.

"No shit?" Rachel said.

"No shit," Jenny confirmed.

A few minutes later, Jenny was feeling sleepy again.

Rachel, on the other hand, had adrenalin pumping through her system like a double espresso from the unburdening of her conscience and was finding it difficult to sleep. So Rachel agreed to take the first watch in place of Jenny.

Since early childhood thunderstorms had always bothered Rachel, she'd confided in Tia a few nights ago. "God's wrath" was how Rachel's religious mother had described it to her. A tree branch tapped on the church window in the wind, rattling on the glass like skeleton fingers, putting Rachel on edge. Another clap of thunder made her start again.

Tia saw Rachel get up to ease her anxiety; checking if anyone was lurking in the shadows to distract her childlike fear.

Rachel seemed to be even more afraid of the thunderstorm than the possibility that a killer may be lurking in the darkness of the dilapidated church they'd made their refuge. Tia watched in surprise as Rachel stood up and walked to the far side of the church; an area so steeped in darkness that Tia could only hear her creaking footsteps.

And then nothing.

*

Tia couldn't sleep. She couldn't stop thinking about who the killer could be.

A list of suspects turning over in her mind; bullying her thoughts.

Rachel had said to Jenny that she would have liked to have talked to Tim some more. Tim, like Rachel, had only been a child when he'd committed his offence.

But Tim was the last person Tia wanted to see coming through those church doors.

Rachel had stated on numerous occasions that she still didn't suspect Tim of being the killer because of his "kind, reflective persona".

For Tia, however, there was such a thing as a duality of nature, and the fact that Tim had been a child when he killed for the first time was not a pardon; it was a red flag.

Tim had admitted he was a prodigious twelve years old at the time of his heinous crime. With that simple fact very much in the front of Tia's racing mind, it meant Tim had to be the serial killer.

Had to be.

When pressed for the details on how he killed his mother's boyfriend by Rachel, what he described was sketchy at best. His island story was a bit too familiar for comfort; an island too small to show up on Google Maps. Like this one, maybe?

Tim didn't look like a serial killer, with his boyband dimples and Instagram-perfect toned abs. His eyes were warm and kind. An image struck her then, a powerful one. A well-dressed Ted Bundy smiling in court and waving to his fans. Dubbed "the pin-up boy of serial killers," demonstrating that looks counted for nothing.

Harvey hadn't been truthful from the beginning either. Tia had found numerous gaps in his stories.

Little inconsistencies that gnawed away at her.

Harvey had a tall, wiry frame capable of immense strength. Powerful enough to drown Dale, to string up Helen Westling, and to wrestle the pistol out of Peter's grasp. Strong enough to kill her in this dark church with his bare hands.

You could argue all you wanted about gender equality, but only one sex could strangle the life out of the other with its bare hands or overpower you and slam your head against a hard surface until it split open.

These types of encounters were occurring the length and breadth of the country behind closed doors. As though a significant proportion of adult men hadn't progressed in any meaningful way since caveman times.

That dreaded "board of shame" flashed through her mind again.

All those crimes.

Tia's heartbeat quickened to the point that it was pounding with an uncomfortable pressure in her chest. It felt as if a hand squeezed her heart with the fearful realization of the extent of her vulnerability here.

Tia willed herself to think of something else, but what else could she think about tonight?

Our survival instincts are programmed to override everything else.

No, it was Tim. Not Harvey.

Tim was the cliché of a child who had murdered because of his mother fixation.

Serial killers emerged in childhood, their skills honed as they became older, and she had to remember that the clever boy who had got away with murder now possessed the strength of a fully-grown man.

Tim, without a doubt, was the most innocently charming personality in that house. And the most widely travelled. Tia knew that two common traits of psychopaths are that they must remain on the move and have charm, to avoid detection.

Tia found herself thinking about Tim as she fell asleep.

And with Tia fast asleep, and Rachel absent, there was nobody to watch over them in that church.

Chapter Twenty

Jenny discovered the grotesque spectacle of Alice's corpse, her scream acting as an impromptu wake-up call for both Tia and Rachel.

Tia's blood froze when she took in Alice's resting form.

Her unnatural complexion cast such a deathly pallor she needed to advance no further from where she lay to recognize Alice was dead.

Alice violently murdered a few feet away from where Tia had slept.

"Her shirt has a tear in it," Rachel said. "Probably the result of a struggle."

Rachel stopped mid-sentence, her post-mortem examination cut short when she doubled over and wretched until her throat must have been raw.

Tia got up to comfort her.

When Rachel could breathe again, she opened up all the shuttered windows and dragged back the heavy oak door at the entrance of the church.

It was day, but barely, the light shrouded by a bleak, grey mist.

In the eerie half-light, Tia forced herself to look at Alice again. It was not a pretty sight.

"How did she die?" Tia asked, her tone childlike.

"Strangled, by the looks of it," Jenny replied. Tia reflected that a traumatized Jenny sounded as though she was being subjected to the same fate at that moment.

"She was definitely murdered, then?" Tia said, breathing hard. "God, this can't be happening. I mean, what the fuck is this all about? It's like a nightmare that won't end."

Tia studied Jenny. She recognized that Jenny's voice had recovered and her will had hardened.

I'm not falling for your Little Miss Innocent act. That's what her cold stare told Tia.

"What do you think it's about?" Jenny said, backed up by Rachel standing by her side. "It's about time you levelled with us about what you did in the past."

Chapter Twenty-One

You stubbornly refuse to admit you're guilty of anything. We know different, we know better.

That's what their looks said. They wanted Tia to confess.

But there would be no wearing her down, no admittance, no sign of remorse.

Because I didn't kill anyone, Tia's mind screamed. *What do I have to do to get that point across to you?!*

Jenny, tired of trying to coax out her past crime, eventually dropped the matter as they decided to check out the island as a threesome. All three women clutched kitchen knives in their dominant hands as they left that dusty ruin of a church.

Stepping out into the misty day had a surreal, dreamlike quality about it. Her reality felt like watching a movie running at a sluggish framerate, like a reality that was buffering.

A figure appeared on the horizon as though it were a glitch in this hazy reality. The retreating figure reduced to an ink sketch in the thick fog.

The figure, little more than an outline, was discernible only for seconds before disappearing like an apparition almost as soon as it appeared, dissolving back into the blanket of mist.

As the three women moved forward in pursuit, they came across their presenter's body. It was lying roughly in the spot they'd left it yesterday afternoon after Tim and Phil had carried her out of the church, but with one crucial difference.

Helen Westling, already in a state of decay, resided in a deep grave. The presenter lay staring up at them sightlessly, dirt covering her face and body. This grave, deeper than six feet, maybe even seven or eight feet down, was too far for any of them to climb down to inspect the body.

Maybe that was the point, her body and soul now unreachable.

A serial killer's marker, is that what this was?

Her limbs placed with care into a starfish position. A position that is more commonly known as the everyman position, with her hands extended overhead and her legs spread to form an X out of her four limbs, providing another unnerving detail for her traumatized mind to wrestle.

They moved on, the three women approaching the house with caution, moving through the plastic graveyard of mannequins.

Anxious to be out of the fog, Tia led while Jenny hung back with Rachel.

Although they were a threesome, they were not a united threesome.

The next unsettling discovery came in the form of a blood trail. Thick crimson spots led from the dining room to the back garden, ending at the foot of the wall. It told a tale of how the injured party had crawled through one of the tunnels to escape their tormentor.

The grim story of the hunted pursued like a stray animal by the hunter.

With caution, they searched inside the house, one room at a time.

They found the house deserted.

Tia sat down on the living room sofa for a moment, to catch her breath. She felt faint, on the verge of another panic attack, jumping at the sound of an unfamiliar voice.

Jenny and Rachel were as startled as Tia by the plasma TV bursting into life behind them.

An attractive woman in her early thirties appeared on the screen. She took long pauses between each of her sentences, before speaking as quickly as she could manage to get her words out. The distressed woman approached the start of each sentence as if it were a speed bump, accelerating through it and pausing before tackling the next one. Several times she broke down in tears.

"Peter was so kind to me when I first joined the network on an apprenticeship. God, just saying his name brings back awful memories. He seemed like a dedicated, professional man and above all decent.

"The sort of man who goes under your radar for arousing suspicion as a sexual predator. His conversation was more self-assured and interesting than the other, younger immature men at the station, and he seemed to listen to me and treat me as his equal. He seldom talked about himself.

"Little did I know at the time, that he wanted to find out as much as possible about me and give as little as possible away about himself, and his sick network of friends. Friends who took it in turns to rape me while the others – whose faces I will never forget – watched in silence, grinning.

"Looking back now, even in the beginning, I see how he was weighing up his options, calculating if he could get away with what his seedy little mind had in store for me. Being a girl just out of school, making her way in the big city, eager to impress and make new friends, he saw me as fair game."

All three women found that they could not bear to listen to any more of what this woman was describing. Going on what this poor, brave woman was building up to, it was a blessing that this depraved animal called Peter was dead.

But they had to focus on the here and now to ensure that they did not fall prey to somebody worse than Peter.

Chapter Twenty-Two

The silvery light and the slate grey sea all around them represented a marked change in the weather from when they had first arrived on the island.

It seemed a gauge for their fortunes too, their spirits depressed and their nerves more fraught by the hour.

Tia led again as they paced along the line of rocks on the edge of the woods overlooking the sea, mindful not to get too close to the cliff's edge in case one of the other women shoved her. The fall would kill her.

Tia risked a glance along the beach, spotting a red dot bobbing up and down in the distant waves.

"What's that?" Tia called out. "Over there."

"I can't see anything," Jenny said, with suspicion in her voice.

Tia could read the distrust in their eyes, but another woman in their group made them stronger and more formidable as a unit if it came to a straight fight. The only reason why they had kept Tia in their little group, she felt.

Especially now that their little band of four had been cut to three so clinically during the night.

They need me, Tia thought. *I can use that to my advantage.*

"It's over there, see?" Tia's voice became urgent. "Can't you see? You must, to the left of that big rock over there?"

Rachel, hugging herself in the muggy cool mist enveloping them like a curse, called out in confirmation: "I see it too."

The bright red jacket made it stand out, or else Tia would have never have noticed it.

It looked like a body floating face down.

"Who is it?" Jenny asked, now seeing what Tia and Rachel had pointed out to her.

"We'd better go down and see," Tia said.

The unspoken truth was that there might only be only two guys left to their group of three women; the odds perhaps stacked in their favour. No one much cared who it was at this point. Everyone's survival and self-preservation instincts were making their thought processes veer into sociopathic territory.

The easiest path down to the beach was to their right, a meandering trail leading down to a cluster of jutting rocks and a stretch of fine sandy beach.

Tia was the last to make the descent this time, lagging behind the others. She looked back, thinking about making a break for it while the other women made their descent. These two didn't trust her. Maybe she'd be better off going solo.

But the thought of being on her own on this horrific island, fending for herself, was too scary.

Jenny and Rachel were well into their descent before Tia even started down the steep decline.

This spot on the island was quiet with no birds calling out and only a light breeze rustling the trees, and the sound of their voices carried up to Tia.

"Come on, will you?" Rachel called out to Tia. "What the hell are you waiting for?"

Rachel looked worried as she stopped looking at Tia and glanced back towards the sea and then at Jenny.

"God, I think it's Tim."

"We'll soon see," was all Jenny could say in reply.

Tia, hugging herself, stopped her descent for a moment before she made her way down to the other two women waiting on the beach.

"Jesus, my nan moves faster than you," Jenny complained, eager to find out the identity of the body. "Come on."

Jenny seemed irritated at how casually Tia was taking this. That's what Tia read in her tone. That she thought Tia was somehow oblivious to the lurking danger when it was the exact opposite: Tia was terrified.

Tia shot into life; she too had to know who the identity of the body.

As she got nearer, Tia noticed that the body had its legs caught on a small rock. The lifeless limbs floated in fizzing, oxygenated seawater.

Tangled seaweed clutched the rock like tentacles, its bunched thickness caught up in the body's limbs, preventing it from either drifting ashore or floating out to sea.

Even though the water only came up to Tia's knees, it was freezing as she waded in; sending shockwaves up her entire body and stealing her breath.

Tia approached the corpse with trepidation, as though the body were poised to turn over and spring into life having tricked her.

Tia was comforted by the fact that Rachel and Jenny were right beside her.

Together they rolled the body over onto its back.

The face staring back at them didn't belong to Tim as Rachel had dreaded.

Or Phil.

Or Harvey.

Chapter Twenty-Three

The symmetrical face that they turned over in the surf, dressed in Tim's red North Face anorak, was not human.

A mannequin stared back at them.

Jenny was the first to spot the message etched into the plastic torso underneath the half-unzipped jacket. It read:

LOOK UP

DL

On the clifftop, a figure stalked them, the broad-shouldered outline of a man that could have been Tim, Phil or Harvey at this distance.

Or, equally, none of them.

They were too far away to make out any discernible features.

All three women moved out of the surf and onto the beach, the air whistling around them. It took Tia a second to realize that they were under fire.

A bullet grazed past Jenny's leg but did not hit her, as she cried out in shock.

Tia instinctively dropped to the floor, her bare hands meeting the gritty, firm-packed sand. She urged the others to get down too.

Out of the corner of her eye, Tia saw Jenny turn back towards the shore. Diving into the shallow water and submerging herself for cover.

To Tia's surprise, Rachel, in stark contrast, ran towards the cliff waving.

Rachel continued to wave her hands in surrender as if she were signalling a would-be rescuer.

"Rachel, no!" Tia shouted.

A second and third bullet flew past Tia, cutting through the air between her and a yelling Rachel.

The last bullet was close enough for Tia to feel it ripping its way past her. Near enough for Tia to feel the change in the air, like a high-speed metallic mosquito homing in on her exposed flesh, only it impacted in a puff of disturbed sand a couple of feet behind her.

Tia froze.

Rachel, uncaring that bullets were flying past her, carried on signalling the gunman. What Rachel shouted out made Tia gasp in horror.

"Stop firing, you hear me!" Rachel yelled. "I'm out of the game. I killed Alice, so you can't touch me."

No sooner had Rachel confessed, a fourth bullet sounded across the bay.

All Tia could see was a red mist, a spray finer than the fog around them. It formed around Rachel's head.

How Rachel dropped to the floor with a thud told Tia that her fellow housemate was dead.

Tia did not waste any time in following Jenny into the cover provided by the water. Only Jenny had disappeared, and Tia wasn't going to wait around to look for her.

Once the water reached waist height, Tia kicked off her shoes and swam to her left and behind a collection of rocks jutting out from the cliff. When she heard another gunshot roar out, Tia dived underwater.

She swam underwater for about thirty feet before coming up for air. Tia immediately ducked back under the water and swam for another thirty feet.

Underwater, Tia's face tingled.

She experienced a strange sense of tranquillity as she slowly propelled herself forward in an underwater breaststroke.

I'm still alive! Tia's numbed head declared.

But for how long?

Once past the rocks, a smaller bay revealed itself, the rocky shoreline in place of a sandy beach. But Tia dared not swim ashore in case the shooter was lurking overhead, waiting for her to emerge out of the sea.

Tia couldn't help but look up at the cliffs.

What she saw startled her.

Three dark figures, followed by a fourth and fifth figure seconds later, walked along the cliff's edge, stalking her.

The one nearest to her held a shotgun by their side.

She thought she heard them call out her name in unison, their shouting voices hoarse with concern, but couldn't be sure with the water in her ears. Bobbing up and down in the waves, her view of the cliff kept tilting. This far from the shore, Tia could barely keep her head above water in the choppy sea.

Alarmingly, a current was sweeping her further out to sea as she drifted around the cliff face, sighting another bay. When she had a chance to look up again, there was no one on the cliff.

Was that because they couldn't climb up to that part of the rock face, or was it because they weren't there in the first place?

Her eyes and ears playing tricks on her?

An occurrence throughout her childhood and well into early adulthood. Schizophrenia ran in her family. On her mother's side – her stepfather, who'd raised her (if you could call it that), had been keen to point out that undeniable fact at every opportunity. Tia had crazy genes.

And you could do what you liked to crazy children without out any fear of people believing their accusations.

When Tia looked up again, the looming cliff was so high, its rock face so steep in its natural construction that anyone who might be lurking up there would be out of sight altogether.

Tia kept swimming around the island in the freezing water, fighting the current. When she passed a trident-shaped rock at the end of the bay, she saw a small cave in the distance.

She could hardly breathe, icy knives digging into her numbed body and engulfing her head and lungs. Tia's face tingled as if frostbitten, tenderized by a hundred sharp needles.

She feared dying of respiratory failure.

Her jaw chattered as she anxiously looked up at the cliffs for the shooter.

Tia remained determined she would get the better of him.

If I make it to that cave, I'll survive.

Tia kept swimming, that's all she could do, fighting the choppy waves that made her bob up and down on the surface every few seconds.

Although Tia knew she was making progress with her strokes, the cave didn't seem to be getting any closer, and she guessed it was maybe half a mile away.

Perhaps it would be better to die in the sea than to be butchered by that psychopath and have 'DL' carved into her flesh, like a fucking trophy kill in his sick game.

Tia felt angry, and this much-needed adrenalin kick made her swim faster. Her strokes grew more assured and efficient. She aggressively cut a path through the water. The waves suddenly seemed smaller, the sea less choppy, and that cave a lot closer.

Tia kept swimming.

Swimming for her life.

Chapter Twenty-Four

Tia swam under an opening in the sheer rock face and into an enclosed lagoon.

The water was warmer in the cave as she swam around a rock formation resembling a dragon.

I've made it, she thought, raising herself out of the water with stiff arms and climbing onto the dragon-shaped rockface.

Exhausted, she lay down for several minutes.

After an hour or two, and almost dry, Tia no longer sat hugging her knees for extra warmth. During that time, her mind had wandered. She knew that she was still in shock, replaying the earlier events in her mind, attempting to put some mental distance between her and the horror that had unfolded on the beach.

Not just the beach, her whole experience on this godforsaken island.

The first thing Tia had done after catching her breath was to check out the walls of this cave, as every other part of this island had cameras installed so that sick voyeurs could watch them die one by one on pay-per-view.

Tia lay down to rest but could not shut her eyes in sleep. She was still shivering, not from the cold now but from her traumatized thoughts. Thoughts she could not escape.

When she felt physically strong enough, a barefoot Tia, dressed in damp jeans and a thin sweater, finally left the cave.

Thankfully, there was a shaft of rock face providing a dry route out for her.

*

She must have spent the entire day in that cave as she could see a sparkling night sky above. The dimensions of this rock shaft were snug enough for Tia to be able to press her back against one side, dig her bare feet into the other and inch her way up the shaft, all fifteen feet of it.

Her heart spasmed when she lost her footing, but she held on and was able to progress.

She was surprised to find that the top of the shaft had smooth brick walls; circular brickwork in fact, as she emerged out of a well.

The well situated at the rear of the dilapidated church, cast in silvery light by an eerie full moon scarred by clouds as black as chimney smoke.

Tia crept around the side of the church. She had ventured no more than a few yards before she encountered another corpse.

Alice had been dragged out of the church, rearranged in the same fashion as Helen Westling's dead body.

The limbs made a neat X, buried in a deep grave, this one well over eight feet.

Tia experienced a sense of dread that her fate was out of her control.

She realized that her knife was back on that beach, lying in the sand somewhere.

Tia gritted her teeth and moved on.

She had advanced no more than a few yards further before she found another grave. Tia knelt and peered over the edge of what was more of a burial pit.

This time it was the corpse of a man staring up at her, also spreadeagled on the floor, dressed up in a smart black suit, his limbs spread out in the same X shape. His corpse untampered with, except for the DL carved into his milky white torso, an inch below where his toned, hairless chest ended with his shirt torn open.

His pale face devoid of colour except for his bright but lifeless eyes.

It took a moment for Tia to appreciate that this was another mannequin and not a person.

The words SERIAL KILLER seared into her traumatized mind.

Tia focused on the fact that there were three more male opponents to contend with on this island, each of them bigger and stronger than her.

Movement in the woods startled her.

Had she fallen for the second trap of the day, having already been fooled by the floating mannequin earlier?

Tia feared she'd be left staring at this decoy body as the killer pounced. Her last act born out of naivety and stupidity.

The sound turned out to be nothing but the mechanical creak of a camera adjusting its focus to zoom in on her.

A startled Tia scampered towards the house, climbing up on the raised platform resembling a fashion catwalk providing access to the front entrance. She made it as far as the front gate of the *Divine Leader* house before she encountered footsteps and heavy breathing.

Chapter Twenty-Five

Tia had to think on her feet.

The heavy breathing sounded like it belonged to a man.

A silhouetted outline taller and broader than herself confirmed that fact.

Moonlight caught a metallic object at his side.

A gleaming pistol.

Peter's pistol: The one that had gone missing?

Had to be.

The figure's face was indecipherable in the dim light as he approached her.

Tia improvised, darting into the mannequin crowd to her right; the one move available to her.

He held a loaded gun.

Tia, weaponless, could only hide.

Time stood still as the figure swelled in her vision, edging nearer.

Had he sensed her presence in the shadows?

The tall, athletic figure strode with purpose.

It wasn't until he was right in front of her that Tia could see the freak was wearing a mask.

He came close enough for Tia to recognize a pentagram at the centre of the masked man's forehead.

The mask itself was certainly not the type you'd wear to a masquerade ball. It was not that elegantly made, more like something you'd buy from a corner shop for a Halloween costume party.

Eyes stared with intent out of that mask, eyes that didn't look panicked.

Quite the opposite.

This bastard looked focused.

He looked like he was enjoying himself.

All dressed up, a firearm in his hand, he was ready to have a ball; searching for victims to be terrorized for his amusement.

The heavy breathing under the mask Tia recognized to be from excitement rather than laboured dread or panicked exertion. Maybe the sick bastard even had a hard-on.

Tia found herself unable to breathe. She wanted more than anything to scream and let her fear out but held it together.

She wouldn't give him the satisfaction of being the damsel in distress.

Once again, that feeling in the pit of Tia's stomach crippled her will.

She felt nauseous.

The same feeling of disempowering panic she had before auditions.

This masked madman was going to kill her and deface her body as though she were a worthless piece of meat.

In the darkness, though only a few feet away, he seemed unable to pick her out from the sea of plastic around her.

"What have you got to say for yourself?" the masked figure said.

Tia froze, revulsion taking over her entire body.

"Well?"

Tia stood in silence. It took her a second or two to realize he was addressing the crowd of mannequins and not her personally.

It was his stupid, childish sense of humour.

Perhaps he did possess the mind of a child.

If Tia could have laughed without giving away her position, she would have. Inwardly she did laugh. He hadn't seen her.

He moved on, looking to her right.

All Tia could do was remain statuesque. Stay still for as long as she possibly could.

When he finally jogged on past the Divine Leader house and towards the cliff's edge, Tia breathed again.

Tia grabbed an overcoat and found a pair of trainers her size before shimmying out from the cover of the mannequins.

She headed for the house.

A thought came over her as she entered the house through the open front door.

I'm not going to let that psycho kill me.

Not without a fight.

Chapter Twenty-Six

With no one in it, the empty house seemed enormous as she moved through the living area towards the kitchen.

Every sound she made seemed heightened.

Inside the kitchen, there were no knives; nothing available that she could use as a weapon.

He could come back at any moment.

Think, Tia, think!

She had to hide somewhere.

But where?

She rushed into the girls' bedroom to consider a gap behind the walls; a gully built for a camera on a runner and a built-in space for a person filming them behind one-way glass. Having not spent any time in that bedroom, the killer wouldn't have known about it.

Frustratingly, it proved too tight to fit in.

Tia found she couldn't rip the panelling off either to squeeze in, no matter how hard she struggled.

The urge to leave the creepy house proved too much. The cameras felt like peering eyes. At least outside she would be covered by darkness.

Outdoors provided space in which to run, and Tia had always been a strong runner.

But she could only run so far on this island, of course, before she became trapped. The other option was to retreat into that cold sea.

That same cruel sea that had nearly killed her this morning.

Tia rushed back out of the house. She had probably been inside the house for less than five minutes. She forced herself to move more slowly than she wished to. Tia knew that nothing attracted the naked eye more than rapid motion.

Using common sense, she also tried to keep low to the ground, squatting down behind trees and shrubbery where possible.

The masked loony's wayward bullets when firing at them from the clifftop proved he wasn't that good a shot. With any luck, he was running low on ammo.

At a distance, she could make him miss until he ran out of bullets.

Tia didn't want to test that theory out, though.

Anger started to rise in Tia as she sat down behind a pine tree in the darkness, its sweet, natural scent filling her nostrils.

Why had she been put on an island with the likes of these people?

This cult was about justice, about producing a higher standard of justice than what society had provided.

She had committed no crimes in her twenty-nine years, and yet here she was with a mass murderer, a rapist and a whole host of sociopaths.

Here, fighting like an animal for her life.

How was that even fair?

Where was the justice in that?

Tia found herself more determined than ever that she would triumph in this situation. If she didn't make it off this island (and she was beginning to accept that she might never leave) then at the very least, Tia would avoid becoming another trophy kill for this sicko.

Tia found she could think with clarity as she started to formulate a strategy in her mind.

Tia stared up at the night sky; a jewellery box of sparkling diamond stars on a black velvet cushion. Those beautiful sparkling stars looked on apathetically from outer space at this murderous spectacle. They would still be shining as brightly millions of years from now.

Tia hugged herself in the darkness.

The fleece coat she'd acquired from the mannequin stopped her shivering.

Would it be better to attack now, covered by darkness?

Climb up on the roof, and drop a rock on him perhaps?

Such things only happened in books and movies.

In reality, that kind of precision was an unlikely manoeuvre.

She had to come up with something better than that.

Tia's life depended on coming up with something better than that.

Chapter Twenty-Seven

It didn't make sense.

It was Peter Tia had seen running through the woods.

Peter had anointed one of the bodies before striding off through the woods like some wild nocturnal animal who'd been disturbed; she had nevertheless had a good enough look at his features to identify him.

And yet she'd seen the corpse of Peter in that control room, splayed out over the monitors.

Were her eyes playing tricks on her?

She was distraught, after all, and it was feasible that she had mistaken him for someone else.

Tia, hearing the crackle of a branch, crouched down under the natural cover provided by the foliage.

Jenny's face seemed supernaturally illuminated in the moonlight as she crept through a clearing. Jenny looked more beautiful than ever, with fierce determination etched on her doll-like, unwrinkled features. She froze when she spotted Tia crawling out from the long grass to greet her.

She visibly shook at the movement.

"Stay back!" Jenny said, waving a hand at her. "I mean it."

There was fear in Jenny's voice.

The poor thing looked scared shitless, and for the first time, Tia felt genuine empathy for Jenny.

Although she had suspected Jenny, solely because of her lying about her involvement with Dale, Tia stopped fearing her; the terror on her face was no act.

She was suspicious of Peter now, sure that he'd faked his death like that judge in the Agatha Christie story.

"We have to stick together," Tia said. "Please, Jenny."

An almost out-of-breath Jenny seemed to see reason, agreeing with a nod before looking around anxiously.

Jenny motioned Tia to follow her towards the equipment shed.

They'd barely crept behind the back of the wooden shed, and out of sight, when they spotted Phil perched there, panting heavily, his head slumped against the wall of the shed.

He immediately got to his feet, ready to do battle. How he carried himself – his left elbow clutched closely into his side as if propped up on an invisible crutch, his right arm cupping his midriff as if holding his guts in – told her that he was injured and in no condition to fight.

Phil still moved with purpose, determined to give it his all.

Tia called out to him with a whisper. "Relax, it's only us."

Jenny shot her a scolding look, but Tia could see in Jenny's eyes that she didn't fear Phil either, especially in his current condition.

Phil was a soldier, not a psychopath.

Tia's intuition, working overtime in the isolation of that cove, had long since concluded that Phil must be in the armed forces. If she saw Phil again, she'd sworn to make him an ally.

Her intuition had been off before, but they had all misjudged Rachel's character.

Tia knew their chances of surviving were better if they trusted Phil. He was the one with combat experience.

Now was the time to start making smarter decisions.

Again, the naked expression on Jenny's face told Tia she felt the same way.

"Where to now?" Tia asked.

"There's a cove down here," Phil said, pointing beyond the silhouetted trees rustling in the wind. "I came out of hiding to grab some food from the house."

Phil handed them tin cans he'd stuffed under his jumper, the reason why he'd been clutching his side, alerting Tia to the fact that, although undoubtedly injured, he wasn't as badly hurt as she'd thought.

"We'll be safe there?" Tia asked.

"I think so," Phil said, grimacing with discomfort and looking around.

Phil pulled two more cans of tinned soup he had tucked under his arm next to his wounded side.

"Here, take these, will you? We'll need them to keep our strength up."

Tia hadn't thought about food. She hadn't eaten anything since this time yesterday.

*

Scrambling down the rocky hillside, and climbing gingerly over a steep rock face, it took the three of them several minutes to reach the sheltered warmth of the cove.

Phil performed a quick three-hundred-and-sixty-degree scan, to ensure that no one had seen them enter the cove. He was moving with greater freedom, his range of motion notably increasing as he wasted no time in lighting a fire.

He had a solitary sleeping bag stashed in his little hideaway.

"Who attacked you?" Jenny asked Phil.

He looked up for a second, confused. "Somebody jumped me in the woods. I walked straight into their trap. I fought them off, barely."

"But who was it?" Jenny persisted.

"It was pitch black," Phil said. "It was a man, but I couldn't say who for sure." Phil shook his head as if to clear it of the memory. "I lost some blood from a knife wound in my side which thankfully didn't penetrate my ribcage; my only thought was to get out of there. I was in survival mode, scrambling on my hands and knees."

"Did he have a mask on?" Tia said.

"Didn't get a good enough look at his face to tell," Phil replied.

"Could it have been Harvey?" Jenny asked.

"Harvey or Tim," Phil said. "I honestly don't know. Whoever it was, they must have expertly tracked me through those woods. It happened so fast. Had it not been for my combat training, I would be long gone."

*

A troubled Tia's face worked in different directions, a neat wave of silky-smooth ripples forming on her forehead like a calm, shallow surf. The tension in the air was palpable.

They want me to confess, that's what they're expecting.

Phil as well as Jenny.

They want to know which of the labels on that board applies to me.

Tia could see it in their set faces. I must tell them.

Tia saw that what she said next caught them both by surprise. It was not the juicy confession they were expecting. It was yet another example of her unusual, slippery nature. That's what Jenny was thinking. Her face wouldn't lie. She still couldn't trust Tia.

They couldn't perceive that she was innocent; the anomaly in this game and the control subject in this experiment.

Tia had no idea why her innocence was such an incomprehensible concept for them.

"I saw a ghost earlier on," Tia said, shifting in her seated position. "Like I saw one when I was a child."

"A ghost?" Jenny said, sounding annoyed. "What are you talking about?"

Tia, staring zombie-like into space as if something interesting was projected on the wall of rock behind them, remained oblivious to Jenny's negative tone.

"We lived in an eighteenth-century barn house. A haunted house, at least that was the rumour," Tia said. "She used to come to me in the dark. And during the day sometimes. Nobody else could see her; she was my special friend."

"Like an imaginary childhood friend?" Jenny said. "That's what you mean by a ghost."

"No." Tia felt frustrated. "I mean an actual ghost; a living spirit. She was smart, funny, independent, unafraid and aggressive; everything I'm not. She said that she'd lived there long before there were cars and streetlights outside. When the town was just fields."

Tia pressed on, ignoring the puzzled facial expressions they were giving her.

"My stepfather tutored me at home," Tia said. "I wasn't allowed at school, you see. My mother would have disagreed, but she left and never came back, so it was just him and me. Until this ghost. I know how it sounds, but it's the truth."

Tia chuckled to herself. "He used to write things on a chalk blackboard when I performed poorly academically; labels for me. Like cry baby, slowcoach, thick, loser and pea brain, to name a few. They were silly but spiteful things to shock and shame me into working harder. But one day she wrote a few things about him. Things he didn't like: Jesus juicer was a silly one but made us both laugh out loud. He put me in the closet for hours for that one."

"Did you kill him?" Phil asked, his voice a whisper.

"What?" Tia said. "Of course I didn't kill him, he's my dad. He's still alive today."

Phil looked at her with confusion; this was not the confession he was expecting.

Tia was disappointed with Phil. He'd been taken in by Jenny. Fooled by Jenny's looks even though Tia knew she was lying through her back teeth.

Jenny seemed to lie for fun. Sociopaths don't lie when they need to they lie for the thrill of it. They lie to manipulate others. Like doting Phil, wanting so desperately to believe Jenny because the way her jeans-clad ass looked when she bent over. The men in her life had always been such a disappointment to Tia and Phil was proving no exception.

Jenny had killed her husband, but not in the fantastic fashion she had described. Sociopaths always need to be the victim too.

It was an invitation to yet another of Jenny's games of misdirection, that's all.

Tia decided in the firelight that it had to be Jenny who was part of the cult, teaming up with one of the others.

There was evidence.

For one thing, Jenny kept looking up and to the right, the opposite direction to where stored memories based in reality come from in our neuro filing cabinets. The top right of the brain is where we create using our imagination. On occasion, Jenny looked to the left, as the best lies often have an element of truth to them. Jenny was hiding something.

Phil, with all of his military training, must have spotted this too.

Jenny used the fact that Tia had no confession to give, because she was innocent, to keep Tia under suspicion. She kept using that tactic over and over again to poison everyone against her. Except her lies were starting to show in this cove.

"So, we *still* don't know why *you're* here," Jenny said, as if on cue. "On this island."

"I saw a ghost again earlier," Tia said, changing the subject from her childhood and back to the supernatural.

"That's what I was building up to - I saw a ghost for the second time in my life."

Phil was taken aback by this "You what?"

"I saw Peter," Tia replied.

"The Russian guy?" Phil said, looking concerned. *The rapist*, he'd almost said, but didn't want to alarm himself or the others by voicing those words aloud Tia saw.

Tia nodded as Jenny looked at them both. "No, Peter's dead. I saw his body with my own eyes."

Tia became angry for the first time, raising her voice. "I saw him with *my* own eyes too. He was doing something to one of the bodies. Standing over it and reconfiguring their limbs as though they were a piece of art in an exhibit, anointing them with something."

Phil got up from his slumped seated position. "Hang on a minute. It makes logical sense. Think about it for a moment. Peter was the one who was orchestrating all of this from the start in that control room. Remember the message too?"

"What message?" Jenny said with scepticism.

"The message that said there was make-up available," Phil said. "Should the need arise to fake his death, remember? The message he cut short so that we couldn't hear the rest?"

To Tia's surprise, Jenny's face lit up with the idea. "I didn't look at his body for long," Jenny said, "but there was a lot of blood. Maybe too much of it. Maybe that sort of thing can be faked."

"Of course it can," Phil said, "with the right materials. I mean, one Halloween a make-up artist made me up to look like a zombie. My wounds were so convincing that I looked like the living dead. I think that Peter is in on it and that Tim is the Divine Leader of this whacko justice cult. The two of them are behind all of this, for sure."

To Tia's horror, Phil got up to leave the cove. He winced in pain as he got to his feet, but moved with fluidity from the renewed vigour the theory appeared to have given his system.

"Where're you going?" Jenny looked puzzled and then afraid.

"Well," Phil said, clutching his injured side. "That control room isn't far from the cliff above us. It will take me two minutes to get up there to prove our theory one way or the other. If Tia's right and I believe she is, we will at least know who our killer is. I'll be right back."

*

Tia moved to the other side of the almost spent fire, clenching her fists tightly.

I don't trust her.

Phil had stated that he'd only be gone a few minutes. Ten minutes at the absolute most she expected.

It had been much longer than that.

"Why do you hate me?" Tia squinted as she looked over the naked flames. These were the first words spoken since Phil had left. Tia conversed with Jenny so that she could get an idea of Jenny's position in the darkness rather than to get an answer to her question.

"I don't hate you," Jenny replied. "It's just that I can't relax around you until you confess your crime. I mean, for all I know you could be any one of those things on that board."

Maybe even the serial killer was the unspoken sentiment.

If Tia could shift the suspicion onto Phil, she might get Jenny to focus her attention elsewhere.

"Have you noticed Phil hasn't explained in any kind of detail how he got his injuries," Tia said in response.

Jenny did not reply. An uncomfortable silence ensued, the shadow of Jenny's knife moving in the flickering firelight, stretching out far enough to almost be touching Tia.

It's not Phil I'm worried about, though, Tia's mind whispered. *It's you.*

The fire eventually died, casting them into complete darkness.

There seemed to be a brief snigger of laughter coming from Jenny. Like a childish shriek of pleasure.

She's crazy, Tia thought, considering leaving the cove. But, boxed in, she would have to pass Jenny in the darkness to do so.

At the same time, it seemed as though another person had stepped into the dark confines of the cove; that ghostly presence lurking in the shadows Tia had described.

It was the same feeling Tia had when she was being watched in the shower a couple of days ago.

No more laughter came, only silence.

Tia could hear her laboured breathing.

And the beating of blood in her ears.

Footsteps?

Jenny on the move?

Someone creeping up behind her while she was distracted by Jenny?

Tia wanted to move but found herself paralysed.

If she moved, her assailant would know her position, so she remained still, holding her breath.

Tia could hear the heavy breathing of someone getting louder.

A bright light made her eyes swell with pain as Tia cried out.

*

An apologetic Phil shone the torch under his chin to show it was him. Phil looked like he had seen a ghost himself, his face devoid of colour, eyebrows knitted together in a combination of exertion and fear.

He held a Dell laptop, gripping it in his hand with his gym glove. The glove he'd worn since she'd first met him - the glove which hid his mechanical hand.

The laptop he'd recovered from the equipment shed, booted up to reveal a screen split into eight segments displaying real-time camera footage of the house; four cameras covering inside the house, four more sweeping over the surrounding grounds.

Phil tried to raise a smile but couldn't quite manage it. In place of a smile, a grimace formed on his lips.

"Peter?" Jenny asked the question on Tia's lips.

"Oh right," Phil said, still panting from exhaustion. "He's dead, slumped over the control panel. Just as you described, Jen."

Great, I've lost Phil's trust, Tia thought. The gamble had backfired.

Phil shone the light to the other side of the cove where Tia was sitting: "Whoever you saw, it wasn't Peter," he said, bending over to catch his breath again.

*

Tia, her body shaking from the chill in the air down here, lay awake in her sleeping bag, looking up at a rock formation where the cove curved around, giving way to smoother stone. Tia found the sound of trickling water sluicing over the rock face soothing. She was situated a good ten metres from where Phil and Jenny were talking. Phil was still trying to relight the extinguished fire.

Tia changed her mind and decided that she felt safest when close to Phil (even if that meant being closer to Jenny too).

When Phil finally lit a fire, wincing with a pain in his shoulder as he did so, he reverted his attention to the laptop screen. Jenny and Tia sat up, hugging their knees and rocking back and forth to keep warm as the fire started to grow into long licks of flame.

A few minutes later they could absorb the warmth of the fire, their silhouettes like primaeval cave drawings.

"So, if Tim's the serial killer," Phil said, with conviction in his voice, "Jenny's the celebrity killer, and I'm the soldier-stroke-trained-assassin, just who are you then?"

When Tia didn't answer, Phil followed up with, "There's a price – for staying here with us, you know."

Jenny subconsciously nodded, backing him up. "You need to tell us."

"You need to *own* it." Phil looked unflinchingly into Tia's eyes. "Trust me when I say that it's the only way you'll find peace."

Tia nodded but didn't answer.

"I guess I'll go first then," Phil said, shaking his head in disappointment. "But by the time I've finished my story, you'd better come clean with us, or Jenny and I are off, you hear?"

"You'll be alone," Jenny said. "Fending for yourself."

Again, Tia nodded her acquiescence but didn't speak. She was keen to hear Phil's confession.

Phil started his story, a story which stretched back years. A tale about a past love named Eva from another age, another country, another war; a time when a wall separated East Berlin from the West; when West Germany was cut off from East Germany by the infamous Iron Curtain. East Germany – or the GDR as Phil referred to it – committed to a life of control and observation, not unlike this island.

Chapter Twenty-Eight

Phil's Story: The Wall of Shame

I

Phil put two sticks of chewing gum in his mouth and pulled his hood down.

His trigger finger slipped into the guard of his .308 Winchester rifle.

It was showtime.

The target was a Ukrainian diplomat, a known arms dealer and would-be dictator. A figure stepped out of a blacked-out limo. Agent Andy Reuss, hunched down next to Phil, looking through infra-red binoculars confirmed that the man stepping out from the limo was not the target.

This man, attired in a glove-tight suit, possessed a bowling ball-sized shaved head and no neck: the bodyguard.

Phil sucked in a breath and eased the pressure on his trigger finger. Under the hood, he was sweating. He told himself it didn't matter, as long as his trigger finger remained bone dry.

The target emerged, an egg-shaped head with a tuft of thinning blonde hair and rimless spectacles. Phil realigned the crosshairs of his rifle sight, focusing on a red-wine tie and a white shirt. This tie soon to be accompanied with a matching wine-coloured shirt, Phil thought.

He mentally recalled the photos he had seen of this man.

He'd seen him seated next to Gorbachev, standing on a steelworks factory floor wearing a hard hat, kissing his wife and daughter. He compared them to what he was seeing.

It was a match – this was his man.

"Target confirmed," Reuss said.

Phil squeezed about three pounds per square inch on a trigger that required five, but no more.

"Target confirmed… why aren't you firing? Phil?"

Everything moved in slow motion; he was hallucinating. Between the crosshairs of his rifle sight, the man's face transformed into Eva's. Her arm moved in flickering notches up to an unruly lock of her dirty blonde hair, which she stroked back with a single elegant sweep of her hand.

This wasn't happening, couldn't be.

It wasn't Eva; he must fire.

He willed himself to fire.

"Fire, Phil," Reuss's laboured voice breathed. "For God's sake, Phil, fire!"

His training took over; he fired.

"Get down, then," Andy said. "They'll be looking for where the shots came from."

Phil didn't listen this time, but he lowered his rifle sight. The figure sprawled on the kerb was Eva, her sightless eyes staring heavenward, a thin thread of blood trickling out of her mouth.

He woke up in a tropical sweat, screaming.

Phil looked at the green phosphorescent digits of the motel alarm clock. They told him that he had been sleeping for forty-five minutes; likely to be all the sleep he'd get tonight.

His body revolted against him in allegiance with his treacherous mind and prevented him from drifting into the oblivion he needed to soothe his sanity.

He kicked the balled-up sheet off the bed in frustration, the first flecks of molten gold making the crepe-thin motel curtains transparent.

The fact that he couldn't afford to rest crouching behind his every thought prevented sleep.

He switched on the shaving mirror in the motel bathroom to reveal wide, hunted eyes staring back at him. The harsh white light revealed the gauntness around the eyes and cheekbones. He looked twenty years older than his twenty-eight years; not necessarily a bad thing considering his predicament. He had three days' growth of beard that was itchy as hell and a nondescript baseball cap took care of his head. It would do but was not a disguise he could feel comfortable with for longer than a few days.

It was time to get out of Berlin, a divided city politically that had given him no answers and little cover. He would take a taxi to the S-Bahn, then who knew where. He could speak seven languages well, three passably. France was a possibility or Italy. Phil wanted to see some of the glorious Amalfi Coast again before they caught up with him. He had planned to go there with Eva. Just rent a car, take turns driving and … he stopped himself; that sort of thinking wasn't going to do him any good.

A spider's web formed on the bathroom mirror where he'd punched it in frustration. The dull pain in his knuckle and the thin trickle of blood in the grimy basin did little to satisfy his destructive urges.

He towelled the blood off, showered, and left.

II

At six a.m. hardly anyone rode the subway, and Phil had a carriage to himself. He sat halfway up the carriage and side-on, a precaution so that he would get a good look at anyone entering from either direction long before they approached him. In the next carriage, a man speaking to himself in clipped, colourful German you wouldn't find in any Berlitz guide peered out of the train window; he had caught the wrong train.

Phil read the scrawled graffiti on the back of the seat in front of him. A declaration of love: Sven and Anna forever 4/4/88. An attestation to Bayern Munich as the best team on God's earth and a four-line satirical poem about the state of inner-city transport that Phil thought wasn't half bad. The usual deplorable racial slurs and right-wing sentiments about blacks, Jews and Muslims; like a stain society couldn't hide.

A whoosh of air announced the arrival of two severe-looking individuals entering Phil's carriage. Both were attired in black overcoats and held briefcases. Both wore expensive gold watches which Phil thought was a faux pas – he couldn't conceive that even in this age when materialism was gospel, anyone would wear that sort of jewellery on an inner-city train.

Agents pretending to be German businessmen perhaps? KGB? They gave Phil the once-over, and he was on his feet and scrambling into the next carriage before they had reached halfway down the aisle.

To Phil's surprise, they didn't follow, and he was resigned to the fact that these were businessmen after all. Stockbrokers, or men of that ilk, holding a high-pressure job similar to himself, Phil surmised. Their clinical mannerisms were redolent of cold-hearted assassins.

In the age of cut-throat capitalism defined as the Eighties, where a million pounds could be gained or lost in a morning's trading, they no doubt took their professions as seriously as his own.

After that scare, Phil boarded a coach to Stuttgart.

He slept on the coach, the motion of travelling helping him to drift off. Phil had a bitter taste of acidic saliva in his mouth when he awoke with a start.

The coach stopped at two service stations on the way, and so didn't arrive in Stuttgart until late evening. He had only one concern, a burgundy Volvo following the bus at a discreet distance for the best part of an hour since they'd left the service station. At Stuttgart railway station he nestled between waves of tourists, watching the two men get out of their vehicle. They looked suspiciously like the two "businessmen" on the train, and Phil began to wish that he had not dismissed them so readily and had taken a better look at them.

Mingling with a coachload of Dutch tourists, Phil darted for the exit. He jumped into the first taxi he came across.

They, whoever they were, didn't follow. At the airport, Phil reserved a seat on the next available flight to Nice, with Lufthansa at eleven-fifteen a.m. the following morning, paying with a substantial wad of his thinning cash.

He checked into a nearby hotel that was little more than a hostel. The room possessed that cloying, earthy smell of damp that settled on poor people; the sheets looked unwashed, the en suite little bigger than a telephone box, but at ten Marks a night it was cheap enough – and close enough to the airport – to suit his needs.

It wasn't like Phil was going to be able to relax tonight, even if he'd been staying at the Hilton.

With no complimentary glass, Phil took a long swig from the litre bottle of bourbon he'd bought across the street. He sank onto the bed, gasping and taking another swig.

The warmth of the liquor spread in his stomach and deadened his frayed nerves. The effect lasted until he glanced out of the window to see if the room at least had a view.

It didn't.

In the seedy backstreet below, to his horror, he spotted the two men from the train again.

Phil decided to leave via the wrought-iron fire escape as soon as the opportunity presented itself. But the opportunity never came, as they didn't dash into the hotel as expected, but stayed there, covering his escape route.

Which could only mean one thing; there was another of them on the way up to him. The man at the front desk would have given them his room number by now and pocketed some Marks for doing so. They, whoever they were, would be walking along the second-floor corridor, seconds away.

It was too late to make a run for it; opening the door would get him a slug in the face for his troubles.

Phil turned off the lights, went into the en-suite bathroom and ran the shower as a distraction. He hunched down by his bed, waiting to spring on whoever came into the room. If two men emerged then he would be dead, of course, but this type of work was often carried out by loners who trusted no one to back them up – he should know as he was one of them.

Odds-on a single assassin, whether a KGB agent or someone from his own Agency. It was a small circle he worked in; only a few men and women had the stomach to kill again and again (and who would have thought he would have fallen for one of them?).

Phil watched the spear of light under his door. It was split in half by the silhouette of someone lurking outside.

With no chain on the door, it would fly open any second now.

III

Phil, because of the strict security of customs getting into West Germany, had no gun. The Agency and the KGB would always get somebody to send you your "package" once you were over there. Now, having deserted both, he had no one to get hold of a piece for him. Phil had a hunting knife; that was it.

A quick grab, and a left-to-right slash across his assailant's throat, ought to be sufficient though.

Phil tucked the knife into his side, crouching low to avoid giving his position away to his assailant when he entered.

The faintest of scratching noises and the door opened with a click; the receptionist must have given the man a pass key. A size twelve boot showed, then a familiar figure almost as big as the doorframe: it was going to be Andy Reuss then, his pal from the Agency, chosen to administer the death blow. He had a garrote in his hands.

Nice.

Keep your friends close but your enemies closer, the joke they'd shared.

Not so funny now.

Reuss was the worst opponent Phil could have picked to engage in hand-to-hand combat. Six-five and the physique of a front-row rugby player, he had a natural aptitude for this type of work. Phil had taken the same combat courses as Reuss at the Agency, had been in the same class of seventy-five in fact; Reuss had finished first in those combat classes. Phil fifth.

The running shower decoy worked, buying Phil a split second, but Reuss, despite his size, was too quick for him.

Phil executed the grab-and-slash manoeuvre he'd mentally rehearsed for the past few seconds, but Reuss read him.

He bent back Phil's wrist at a right angle and jerked it back up.

Phil howled in pain as he did it again.

The knife flew out of Phil's hand and across the room, clattering against a windowpane.

Reuss, behind him now, slipped the garrote over Phil's head and pulled its ends with strong hands that made a noise like a zip-line descent.

Phil's left hand automatically went up to protect his throat. He managed to wedge it between his neck and the razor-sharp wire; an instinct which saved him from certain death.

The pain in his hand, however, was excruciating and he wondered how long he could bear it before he passed out. The wire was pulled as tight as a finely tuned piano.

It sliced through Phil's skin and muscle and severed the bone at his wrist as if it were brittle charcoal. His left hand was left flapping limply, joined to his forearm by a single uncut tendon.

An arc of blood jetted from the wound, spraying the wall and carpet.

Black spots filled Phil's vision, the half-dozen dots became a galaxy of swelling planets, but he somehow remained conscious.

Reuss, in the meantime, lifted him off the floor to administer the *coup de grâce*, and in doing so afforded Phil a chance to butt the back of his head into Reuss's nose.

Reuss had a delicate nose, broken and reset many times; his weak spot. The cartilage in his nose broke like chalk and tears filled the big man's vision. He loosened his grip on the garrote wire. It was the split second Phil needed, pulling his hand free. The motion caused his hand to sever and thump onto the uncarpeted floor.

Phil barely suppressed a scream.

His instinctive training taking over, Phil picked up the knife and with a measured thrust buried it in Andy Reuss's trachea. Reuss, still blinded by his tears, didn't even see the blow coming. Shortly after administering this death blow, Phil slumped to the floor himself, the loss of blood he'd suffered causing him to pass out.

IV

Phil came to in a hospital bed. He had a room to himself.

A room to himself except for the blank-faced man sat in the corner guarding him. The guard got out of his chair and alerted the nurse that Phil was awake.

Phil took a quick inventory of his surroundings. The room was devoid of any distinguishing signs indicating what part of the country this was. Out of the window, Phil couldn't make out a landmark or particular style of masonry.

There was no written chart at the end of the bed to give him a date either.

The guard spoke flawlessly enunciated English. "Settle down. You are amongst friends."

Phil noted with distaste the bandaged stump at the end of his left forearm, wincing as he tried to raise himself.

The man ordered him to relax again. He explained to Phil that he was in Berlin and that Phil had caused a lot of trouble going AWOL but was in safe hands now.

"Berlin?" Phil was astonished.

Only when Sandford came in did Phil believe the guard.

Commander Charles Sandford dismissed the guard, sitting down next to Phil.

"How are you feeling?" Sandford asked.

"Confused," Phil said.

Sandford nodded.

Phil tried to speak some more, but his mouth was dry, so Sandford ordered the nurse to fetch him a glass of water.

His throat lubricated and his thirst satisfied, Phil spoke again. "Reuss?"

"We know; double agent for the KGB." Sandford shook his head. "Who would have guessed, eh? Old Andy."

"Anyway, that's history." The Commander smiled. "Thanks to you."

Phil couldn't believe the part about Reuss being a double agent, but at least the Agency weren't after him.

"How long have I –" Phil rubbed his forehead.

"Been out of it?" Sandford said. "Two days. You lost a lot of blood and needed a transfusion. I expect you're wondering why I'm here and not Alec. There's no easy way to say this. Alec's dead, along with two other of our top agents and the Commander-in-Chief."

"The Commander-in-Chief's dead?" Phil was incredulous. "How?"

"That's what we would very much like to find out. It looks like we have a new agent in the game, something of a super-agent. We believe this same man killed all four top-ranking officers."

"Why do you think that?"

"Our killer leaves a unique calling card." Sandford grimaced as he reached into his pocket. He removed a small, green plastic figure: a toy soldier holding a bayonet rifle. "I'm not kidding; this is how our mystery agent marks his kills."

Charlie Sandford produced another toy soldier, also green but this one had a parachute.

"One of his kills was an ex-air force pilot," Sandford said. "Cute, hey?"

To Phil, the figures looked cheaply manufactured, as if they'd come out of a Christmas cracker.

"We think it's a reference to Agatha Christie and the ten little soldier boys," Sandford said. "They're manufactured in China." He cleared his throat. "As regards the more important details, Alec was in his Embassy office at the time. His toy soldier was a general; it's undergoing forensic analysis as we speak."

"His office? How did that happen?"

"Again, we don't know yet," Sandford said. "But this assassin ghosted past security. And you know how tight security is at headquarters. The chief security officer for the secret service is on it, Special Branch too. So far, we have nothing. No one's talking. No name, not even a sighting. We think this guy must have had inside help because the CCTV cameras at headquarters failed to capture anything. It's a worrying time, I can tell you."

"Charlie, I need you to answer something for me."

"About Eva?"

Phil was stunned. Sandford smiled. "They don't call us intelligence for nothing, you know."

But Phil wasn't smiling. "Eva was murdered by someone in the Agency."

"It won't do any good –"

"I need to know."

"Okay, okay. Eva was deemed a threat and eliminated."

"By whom?"

"Don't know. And that's the honest truth. Not that I could tell you if I did, Phil."

"I thought they didn't call you intelligence for nothing." Phil studied Sandford's face, looking for any tell-tale signs that he was lying; there weren't any. "A name, Charlie."

"They don't tell me that kind of stuff." Sandford spread his arms wide. "Look, all I know is that someone in the Agency took a dislike to her, suspected her of leading you into a trap –"

"That's bullshit and you know it," Phil said.

"Whether it is or it isn't, it's really beside the point," Sandford said. "The point is I don't know who ordered Eva's execution, I don't know who carried it out, and it isn't our business to know, okay? That sorted, what I do know is that we have a real threat on our hands and a dangerous

Soviet agent who needs to be retired before he does any more damage. Not that he hasn't done plenty already."

"Why should I care now?"

"Get a hold of yourself." Sandford had lost his patience. "You signed up for Queen and country, remember? Not to carry out some vendetta for someone who never loved you. She used you. It's what women in our line of business do. So I'm telling you – no, ordering you – to cease with this personal crusade on behalf of Eva right now; do I make myself clear?" Sandford didn't wait for Phil to answer. "Besides, there's another reason why you should care. A good one too."

"Yeah," Phil said. "And what would that be?"

"This assassin," Sandford said. "Whoever he or she may be, appears to be working methodically from the top down. The next agent on the list is Harry, then you."

Sandford, seeing that Phil wasn't in the mood for a further chat, turned to go. There was no real mission directive to go through because intelligence had yet to compile anything on his opposite number (which Sandford seemed more than a trifle embarrassed about).

When Sandford left, Phil found his thoughts wouldn't get past Eva. It was the Agency then. Somehow, some part of him, knew it to be the truth. Might it have been Reuss? It was a possibility, but there were plenty of other suitable candidates. It wouldn't do him any good to dwell on it though; Sandford had been right about that at least.

Better to let it go; he would never find out, no matter how hard he pushed. It was not his business to know such things.

Phil instead found himself forming a mental picture of this phantom Soviet agent – which didn't help his dreams when they came.

V

Phil had been on the run from the Russians and the Agency, his survival instinct keen for weeks on end. He had to approach everything in the here and now, unable to see beyond the next minute, the next second. In that state of mind, no past and no future existed, only the present.

He'd been afraid to shut his eyes at night. Now that instinct was back again. His situation wasn't quite as desperate as it had been; he no longer had the Agency attempting to eliminate him for being a rogue agent as well as the Soviets. He also had Harry to watch his back. It had been a week since Sandford had informed him of this deadly Soviet assassin, and since then there had been no more casualties. That détente period, however, had done nothing for the Agency's nerves. Phil currently resided in Harry's Berlin flat with the lights dimmed.

The flat overlooked parkland and the Berlin Wall separating them from the East.

Phil's uneasy feeling about this had lasted all week. Harry was the next target on the hypothetical list, but it was by no means a sure thing. The tension had become unbearable at times, and Harry had more than once intimated that he was more than a little scared by this unknown hitman. Harry joked that if the assassin turned out to be the Grim Reaper, it wouldn't surprise him.

It was unprecedented that an agent should have been so active without even a scrap of information on him emerging from some remote resource. No past endeavour or minor indiscretion had come to light.

Phil looked out of the window. The wispy, low-lying mist shrouded the street the cobblestones like the tops of skulls. He shuddered at the thought.

"Christ, the way things are going," Harry said, with a grin that looked painted on his face, as they changed shifts window watching. "Even Maggie's not safe at number ten."

Five minutes elapsed before Harry spoke again. "Hang on. Yes, there's our boy. It's your turn to collect the pizza."

Phil got up, his knees creaking. Out of the window, he saw the delivery boy get off his scooter. "Just don't scare the boy off this time, Captain Hook." Harry was making another attempt at humour regarding Phil's prosthetic hand, which he still hadn't fully got used to, and was beginning to wonder if he ever would.

"Keep your eyes peeled. And Phil…"

"Yeah?"

"Don't hang around," Harry said. "I don't mind telling you that this guy, whoever he is, gives me the willies. This guy is in and out. He'll gun you down in the street and be gone. We still don't even know what he looks like, remember."

Phil heard a clunk as Harry put the chain on. The old lady in the apartment across the hall from Harry's smiled at Phil as she passed him in the hallway, and Phil nodded to her. Thinking he was unobserved, he waved at the grille of the surveillance camera as he passed by. The old lady, still fumbling in her purse for her key, gave him a funny look as if she doubted his sanity. Phil looked back and smiled.

The pizza boy, his acne-scarred face not unlike the food he was delivering, thanked Phil for the generous tip and sped away on his moped with a sound like a plummeting bumblebee. Phil checked the street. The mist had thinned, and he could make out parked cars on both sides. The same ones that had been there for the last hour or so. An unseasonably cold summer night felt like an omen, the air chill enough to plume his breath.

Phil inspected the pizza toppings as he rode the elevator. No anchovies on his. Good. Extra garlic for Harry.

Harry's appetite never ceased to amaze him. He'd snacked on toast and croissants at five o'clock as well as a hefty lunch. Phil wondered how the man stayed so slender. Frayed nerves making him overeat, he thought. It had the opposite effect on Phil; he doubted he would even finish half of his pizza.

The elevator door chimed. Phil got out, gave the corridor a quick once-over. But the apartment door remained locked; Harry wasn't answering.

Phil dropped the pizzas, drew his pistol and put his shoulder to Harry's door. It didn't budge.

"Harry?"

With all of his body weight behind a kick, the door flew open. He covered the corners of the room with his semi-automatic handgun.

He found Harry slumped against the tiles in the bathroom.

It was Eva all over again.

Momentarily, the two images merged; he saw Eva with the hole in her head and not Harry.

Something caught his eye. Next to Harry's corpse, in a pool of blood, was a toy soldier. The same model, size and shape as the ones Sandford had shown him, except this toy soldier wore jungle camouflage, referencing Harry being in Africa before his reassignment to Berlin.

Phil ran into the street. It was empty apart from a young couple getting into a sports car across the road. He couldn't believe what had happened. He double-checked the apartment; empty. Harry's killer was long gone.

How had he missed him coming out of the building?

Phil checked the roof. No one there either – it defied belief. He'd been outside no more than ninety seconds, two minutes at the most.

VI

Phil went over the apartment again. What was he not seeing? A slight draught from the bathroom window drew his attention. Too small for even a dwarf to squeeze through. He checked the windows of the apartment; all locked. The ledge outside was an impossibility, being too thin to take a foot and too precarious for even the most skilled acrobat to attempt.

It was like one of those Ellery Queen locked room mysteries. How on earth had it been done? Reverting to his original thoughts about a dwarf, Phil checked the air vent. Its screws were loose, but inside he saw that that the channel narrowed to letterbox dimensions; no one had come through there.

He smashed the bathroom mirror. There was no false back to it; no one had got in from the apartment next door.

Phil spotted a note on Harry's dressing table; unsigned and on the back of a business card for a Berlin dry cleaner's; a toy camouflage armoured RV acting as a paperweight. The handwritten message said:

I know how to avenge Eva.

Phil pocketed the note before any of the investigating agents could notice it.

The one thing left to do was to check the surveillance camera. Phil went over every angle at the slowest speed setting. Harry, opening the door, looking around, deciding no one was there, shutting it. Himself arriving on the scene with the two pizzas finding the door locked.

A shot to the head and Harry had fallen to the bathroom floor of his apartment.

Baffling.

He sorted the formalities out with the police, returned to headquarters. It was a quarter to one now, and the frustration and fear had passed. Phil found himself in awe of this agent. This agent was a bloody magician.

The realization that he was next on the proposed hit list didn't escape him. Phil, back in his West Berlin flat and in his favourite armchair, sipped vodka as he played a copy of the tape headquarters had run off for him on his VCR.

Sections of the tape were missing, he was sure; the significant parts. There was no sign of him waving to the camera minutes before Harry's demise in the footage from the hallway outside the apartment. The clock in the background skipped two minutes in the middle of one of the sequences. The footage suspiciously jumped to him at the door, indicating a splice in the film. The shooter, when he arrived, could not be made out no matter how much he slowed the footage down. The CCTV camera capturing the footage was too distant and too grainy in quality.

Phil checked the footage over and over, even though his head throbbed, and he was red-eyed through lack of sleep.

He finally gave it up. Soon he would get his answers. Phil only hoped he would live long enough to act on them.

VII

After a string of soaring hot September days, a thunderstorm was looming. The overcast sky resembled a melting lid, caving in. The claustrophobic pressure of his situation – being hunted by a formidable agent – was getting to Phil more than ever. He had nearly shot a Russian student on the street, convinced he'd spotted his man at last. Knowing that attempting sleep would be a fruitless exercise, Phil sat up reading the files of possible suspects the Agency had sent him. The first dossier was on Mikhail Chevrolenko.

DESCRIPTION: Age: 32. Height: 6' 1". Athletic build, broad shoulders, a former gymnast. Blonde hair, usually shaved or closely cropped, aqua-blue eyes, a small crescent-shaped scar running from his right temple to the top of his jawline, thought to be caused by shrapnel, a fragment embedded in his skull. (NB: frequently wears headwear to conceal the scar on his temple.)

ORIGINS: Born and raised in a mining town a hundred miles north of Moscow. Degree in inorganic chemistry and mass spectrometry from Moscow University. Promising gymnast; comment by coach relates to his vigorous preparation and an unswerving will to win. Patriotic, but antisocial, something of a loner. He didn't compete in the Montreal games because of a torn rotator cuff. Turned over to the KGB, picked out as an excellent marksman and having the right temperament for such work. Hand-picked over several other hopefuls because of his specialist knowledge in explosives. His early career involved cross-examining defectors' families who sought to betray the Soviet Union. Section commander says (roughly translated) that he "carried out the work with gusto".

Thought to have been behind the NATO bombing in Strasbourg in 1980.

PASSPORTS: Various.

MOTIVATION: Saw his father executed by a drunken soldier at their dinner table when he was eight years old. His father, a miner, thought to have owed money having lost a bet of some kind to the soldier. Note his intolerance for ill-discipline amongst fellow officers (several brutal incidents are referred to on page eight, including hanging a soldier for not looking after his footwear). Thought to be mainly asexual; killing having replaced the need for satisfaction of his sexual drive.

COMMENTS: Chevrolenko is possibly the most dangerous Soviet agent in current circulation. His executions are preferably distant, either as a sniper or by explosives. Hand-to-hand combat skills exemplary; extremely strong and flexible. No known weaknesses, he lives like a monk. Trying to win his confidence seems an unlikely and risky strategy.

Phil finished his second shot of neat vodka, a craving he'd developed naturally enough from being a UK agent working in Russia. After a final detailed scan, he put the file away and brewed a pot of coffee.

He needed to stay sharp. If he carried on drinking and Chevrolenko came through the door, he would be powerless to stop him. Not that that was a likely outcome. Chevrolenko would more likely be lurking on the roof of the department store across the street, either to fix him with his rifle sight or to detonate a couple of pounds of plastic explosive. The chances, however, of this agent being Chevrolenko were slim, considering the man's invariable preference for keeping his distance.

This guy had come right inside Harry's apartment room.

Phil looked through a couple more files, four men and one woman named Olga Stravensky. Stravensky's photograph showed a woman in her late twenties who would have been achingly beautiful if not for the cold immobility of her dark brown eyes. Stravensky, he read, preferred to get up close, bedding her prey before emasculating them, and on one occasion causing a Czech commanding officer to choke to death on his severed manhood.

He put down the last of the files. No, it seemed unlikely any of these agents were going to turn up on his doorstep. Besides, he knew the others' methods well enough. Stravensky and Chevrolenko were the only two he hadn't been in the same room with at one point or another in his work as a double agent.

This hidden agent was someone new to the game, he was sure of it, and not one of these candidates; an agent with all of their strengths combined and none of their weaknesses. That was how it appeared. Right now, this agent was a magician. And since magic is about misdirection, Phil promised himself he wouldn't let himself be sidetracked from the facts – he knew the answer was on that tape somewhere.

The person who'd edited it knew the truth.

Phil continued hunting for clues, focusing on the facts.

Like all magic, once the answer revealed itself, you question how you could have come to any other conclusion. So what had he missed, where was the misdirection?

Hang on, had he got his first breakthrough? The shadow on the wall, thrown by a lamp, but no person on the tape. How? He rewound the tape, pausing moments before the sequence where Harry, understandably edgy, opened the door to look into the corridor. Why? There couldn't have been a knock at the door because the corridor surveillance camera showed it to be empty.

Someone came from behind, shooting Harry in the forehead as he turned.

Harry had let them into his apartment.

Harry must have known the person and thought them to be friendly.

"Why did you do that then, Harry?" Phil said to himself as he gulped down the dregs of his coffee, which was now cold. "Why didn't you react?"

He rubbed his temples.

Come on, what am I not seeing?

He told himself there was maybe a book in this, once he retired if he could spot what a whole team of investigators were unable to see. He turned it over in his mind some more as he went into the kitchen to put a fresh pot on the coffee maker. What was it Sherlock Holmes had said? "When you have eliminated the impossible, whatever remains, however improbable, must be the truth."

Something like that. It didn't help Phil in any meaningful way, though. He had eliminated all the impossibilities, and there was *nothing* left.

The only other answer was that this agent had some sort of supernatural power.

He laughed at this. A coldly rational man by nature, he was not easily given to lending credence to matters of the occult.

But why not? Some people believed unswervingly in such phenomena. Yes, but people also believed in the Loch Ness monster, mistook Venus for a flying saucer and swore Elvis was alive and well and living on Mars. He dismissed such fanciful thoughts and went back to the task at hand. He sipped his coffee – which he took black and sugarless – and rewound the tape.

The figure moved too rapidly to be captured clearly on camera.

His head lowered in notches, as he slumped further down into his armchair until he was asleep.

Phil was walking in Special Branch headquarters. There was no one at the front desk; no one human, that was. Two uniformed mannequins were seated at the end of the long, narrow corridor, behind the signing-in desk. Their plastic flesh glistened under the fluorescent lighting. Was this some kind of joke? He knew the men on the desk at this time of day as Martin and Stan. His blood congealed when he got closer. The dummies' facial features didn't have the flawless symmetry and reflection of a department store mannequin but shared the houndlike face of Stan and the snub-nosed, flinty features of Martin. Martin's flaming acne even showed in places, but paler – as if wrapped in cling film. Phil touched the face with his fingers, bracing himself for the eyes to dart open as he did so. They didn't. The "skin" felt unyielding, like a doll. What the hell was going on?

Phil walked past the desk and into the adjoining corridor that led to the headquarters canteen. There were two men, paused in mid-stride.

They were blocking his path, so Phil had to push them over to get past; they fell as rigidly as surfboards as he did so. In the canteen, a whole exhibit of waxwork dummies was in evidence. The chef behind the counter dripped tomato puree from his serving spoon. The man nearest to Phil was in the process of putting a fork in his mouth; the food must have slipped over the moulded tongue, slid down the plastic oesophagus and into the set bowels.

Phil saw a lightning-fast flash of black in his peripheral vision. A darting figure had gone out of the exit leading to the L-shaped building where the Agency's head office was situated. Phil ran in pursuit. The dark figure exited the corridor as Phil entered it, the assassin clad in long, billowing black robes. He was heading for the Commander-in-Chief's office. Phil broke into a sharp sprint, exploding through the double doors; surprised his assailant had left them unlocked until he'd finished his work.

He was too late. The Commander-in-Chief had a black hole where his right eye should have been. There was no blood. The flaps of his broken skin were like jagged seaweed around the gaping wound.

Phil took in the assassin for the first time. Inside the hood of his black robe, there was no head, no face, only a black oval – reminding Phil of a kendo faceguard. With no lips to form words, the black oval face spoke directly into Phil's mind. It said, in a dark and silky voice, "Next time it will be you."

Phil reached for his gun; the weapon was in his hand for a second before he realized he possessed no left hand and it clattered to the floor. The black figure swelled in his vision, enveloping him.

Phil awoke, clawing at the air and crying out. It was some time before he got back to sleep.

VIII

Phil's thoughts dwelled on Eva. Waiting for the assassin was sadistic torture alright, but this brooding over Eva had a bittersweet intensity of torment all its own.

Phil had as good as killed her himself with his naivety. As if he had put the gun to her head and pulled the trigger. Phil should have listened to Eva and her protestations; her belief that the Agency would not trust her. Why hadn't he been smarter?

Because he thought he was fighting for the good guys is why, and the good guys don't kill without reason.

He laughed at his naive belief that the Agency would set it up so that Eva and himself could disappear. He thought about the times when he had become so involved in his role as a Soviet agent that Phil had forgotten his other self and wondered if he might slip into it indefinitely. It required no real conscious effort on his part, more a surrendering, a drifting; a sort of beautiful euthanasia of his will. Beautiful was the operative word because at times it seemed so enticing to become somebody else – to wipe the slate clean and begin anew.

The more he thought about it, the more he recognized he had done it before, many times. Everyone did; it was part of the make-up of life. Meeting Eva made him realize this; the closed-off loner he was before loving her became a faded memory. Yes, love was beautiful euthanasia. Being remade, a new person.

But Eva couldn't be remade anew unless she existed in one of the countless parallel universes.

Maybe this killer was from a parallel universe, and kept switching from one to another to remain undetected; that's what his dreams were telling him.

Maybe he had something there, or perhaps he should lay off lacing his coffees so generously with whisky. Either way, it was melting the tension away. Right now, the needy, drill-instructor survival voice had been dormant these past few days, blessedly tuning out; maybe this was a cut-out mechanism of the brain to ensure his sanity remained intact. Who knew how the mind worked, with all its meandering corridors and undiscovered subterranean streams of thought?

A knock at his door murdered his musing with a single blow.

IX

Another knock on his door followed. Phil recalled the phantom knocker on the tape, immediately preceding Harry's demise.

"Wait a moment please… coming," Phil said in a strained voice.

Phil picked up the walkie-talkie, muffled its broadcasting screech-whine with a pillow, and spoke in a low, urgent voice. "There's somebody at the door. Over."

Sandford, on the other end, replied. "Copy. I'll send somebody around to pick them up. Treat them as hostile and don't answer the door. Repeat, treat as hostile."

"Sure," Phil answered, putting the walkie-talkie down. "Over and out."

Phil went into the bedroom, staying down and away from the window. The apartment building was crawling with friendly agents, eleven in all. Nine in the building, two outside; they slept in the apartments next door, above and below.

Another knock.

"Phil, it's okay. It's me, Agent Clarke."

A long second passed. The scratch noise of a walkie-talkie jumping into life as Sandford announced that it was okay; it was a friendly agent at the door.

Phil let Agent Clarke in.

Sandford told Phil he would feel better if there was another agent in the room with him. Phil wasn't going to argue with him, and so Clarke stayed.

An hour passed without incident. Phil noted his dummy self at the window as he passed the bedroom en route to urinate in the en-suite bathroom. He guessed that the dummy had been the trigger for his nightmare earlier. The bedroom lighting dimmed by a specialist with all the skilled precision of three-point lighting on a movie set. The bedside lamp showed enough of the outline of the dummy for it to look convincingly real. With the bedroom door open, it provided an extra distraction should the Soviet agent make it as far as his apartment.

The Agency was nothing if not thorough, and Phil didn't mind that they veered towards overcautiousness considering the formidable quarry he was facing.

Phil was still in the bathroom when he heard the first shots. Two low, flat thuds – unmistakably a nine-millimetre fitted with a silencer. Phil groped for his gun, before realizing that he had left it on the living-room sofa.

He had to get out of the bathroom before his quarry located him, so he ducked into the darkness of his bedroom, staying low to the floor. The room's dimensions were sketched lightly by a dim bedside lamp and moonlight.

A flash of light as he felt the whoosh of a bullet fly past his right ear, the second shot just nicking it.

The sound of the door crashing against its hinges followed and bright lights made Phil's eyes swell. Three agents filled his apartment in a heartbeat, followed by three more moments later. Had one of the agents fired shots? The smell of cordite was still in the air, but no assassin.

Phil took from this that he was in a state of shock. He must have lost track of time.

No one could move fast enough to evade multiple agents blocking all exits.

He found another card placed on the bedside table. On this occasion, a different Berlin dry cleaner's; a meeting date and time written on the back. The card held down by a tiny green toy soldier: a private talking into a walkie-talkie.

Phil eventually went to sleep in yet another run-down motel on the outskirts of Berlin. Only with the aid of vodka was he able to close his eyes.

X

Phil found the doors of the Berlin dry cleaners open at 8:30 p.m., but empty inside.

He did a double-take, unsure he was in the right place. He had the correct date and time.

Phil had told no one he was coming here, of course.

After a few moments, an old lady entered. She had iron-grey hair pulled into a tight bun. Phil recognized her straight off as the old lady from the apartment next to Harry. She was the last person he'd suspected of killing Harry, based on a stereotype of being harmless and incapable of an assassination.

So it was a different person each time. That was the trick.

Multiple assassins.

Each of them made to kill to escape punishment or blackmail from an unseen, persecuting organization.

And like all tricks, once revealed Phil questioned how he hadn't seen it earlier.

An over-reaching organization – undetected by the KGB or the Agency – with someone wiping the security tapes, covering tracks, recruiting people at every level of their organization; an inside job.

The woman seemed unperturbed that he'd recognized her.

"What did Harry do?" Phil asked, but received no answer.

The old lady ignored all of his questions, as she handed Phil a piece of paper. This time it was a brochure for holiday cabins set in sunny, secluded Bavarian woodland. Inside the glossy brochure were directions.

Phil grabbed her arm as she attempted to pass him and exit the dry cleaners. When he dropped the holiday leaflet, she picked it up, thrusting it back to into his hand, looking around nervously. Phil could tell she was afraid, and that she thought somebody on the street was watching them.

"Here," she said. "Take it. What they wanted of me is done, you understand? I don't have any more answers for you; they made me do it. I held no grudge. I never met this Harry before, you understand? Please leave me alone."

She left before he could think of a response, leaving Phil looking dumbly at the brochure in his hands.

XI

To get to the cabin, Phil had to make his way on foot through secluded woodland. The woods were a battle of coppery browns this time of year with trees close enough together to block out most of the light.

Phil slipped over as he passed an ancient oak tree whose thick roots resembled arms reaching out of the mud, clawing their way to the surface.

Five minutes of walking proved more of a crawl, the branches clawing at Phil as if making him prove himself worthy of entering, and then he was out onto the tapered path the map so vividly described.

Gazing across a landscape that had once been wild, it struck Phil how people could overlook its natural presence. Ragged weeds and nettles comprising a jungle of overgrowth were all the uninitiated saw.

He understood its power at that moment; could feel its pull drawing him in like a magnet.

Almost dusk now, the fading sunlight offered little warmth as the chill of the night asserted itself, and the abandoned woodland landscape started to take on the aura it merely warned you of during the day.

The only signs of civilization out here were when Phil trod on soggy newspapers and comic books or stepped over Coke cans and crisp packets. Sidestepping puddles on rusted sheets of corrugated iron to get to a path which crossed a small stream, Phil sensed he was nearing the cabin.

He spotted a rat staring back at him, holding his gaze for a full three seconds with eyes as slick as olives, before darting out of sight.

Other eyes were on him; he sensed it.

Such intensity of primal feeling transcended this derelict woodland, as the forest floor snapped and crackled into life like a firecracker under his feet, as he strode over it.

Impatient to see the cabin, Phil gazed skywards at tissues of black and grey clouds.

With minutes of daylight left, he didn't want to lose his way out here after dark.

He didn't feel like an assassin, a secret agent; he hadn't felt this powerless since childhood.

Phil sucked in a breath and concentrated, as a thousand thoughts tried to gatecrash their irrational way into his mind, foremost of all a growing sense of foreboding.

He stumbled across a pair of red panties on the ground as he approached another path.

Phil imagined a young couple out here all alone. He imagined them kissing passionately and not being able to resist making love before they'd reached their cabin; screwing while at one with nature.

When he came to the bottom of a steeply rising hill, he turned right, where the map directed him over even harsher terrain.

The woodland area remained bone-hard where rain had not penetrated, softened only by a thin carpet of pine needles.

Phil stopped to catch his breath, looking up at the sky.

The dying sun emerged behind a cloud, pillars of sunlight standing out in the wood.

Eager to get out of here, Phil slalomed up the tapering path. Starting on another incline, he checked his wristwatch; it was getting late now and he'd still not reached this damned cabin.

Up a steep grassy bank, a series of S-bends outlined by weather-worn orange tape tested his resolve. It felt like fiery hot pokers were embedded in his calves as he pressed on, his stride lengthening to cover the uneven ground more efficiently.

Out of the woodland, the chill in the air hit him, the wind had picked up, but he pressed on, expecting to find his answers in that cabin and not another tantalizing clue.

Phil left the thick woods via a barren, boggy field resembling the Somme, feeling the dreaded sticky pudding pull underfoot that can take it out of your legs if you're not in shape; his mud-caked trainers feeling like moon boots for the first few yards until the mud worked its way loose.

I've gone off the bloody path to the cabin, Phil thought with genuine dread. It would be easy to get lost out here in the fading light.

He spied a small lake down to his right that was more of a boating pond, its gloomy depths mirrored by the murky sky.

At the end of the pond, a cabin awaited, standing by itself like an evil sentinel challenging Phil with its faceless thousand-yard stare.

Who would come out here? This place wasn't romantic. *It's downright creepy.*

The obligatory cabin in the woods you find in horror movies, alive with menace and rebuke for innocent passers-by.

And hapless secret agents without a gun …

Phil approached the cabin with caution.

"Open up, it's me," he whispered.

Phil realized how dumb this sounded, but he was tired and on edge.

He knocked and waited, receiving no answer he forced the door open with a powerful kick of his right boot.

Phil fumbled for a light in the unlit cabin. He knew he wasn't alone, sensing eyes on him.

He located a switch, illuminating part of the cabin; spotting, with a jolt to his heart, a fair-haired woman in a floral summer dress slumped in a wicker chair. The second thing that struck him was nausea from the putrid smell assailing his nostrils. He put a handkerchief over his mouth and coughed into it.

Phil didn't even bother to check for a pulse, the reek of decay overpowering him.

The blonde woman's eyes remained motionless, her unflinching gaze fixated as if a movie were playing on the floor; a mesmeric but unexciting one.

Her arms were flung wide in a beggar's pose with a belt strap cinched around a bicep causing a sickly pale yellow pigmentation on the skin with a roadmap of purple veins. A syringe stuck out of the rigid flesh.

The proportions of the veiny bicep made Phil appreciate that this was not a woman after all.

He tilted the victim's head as carefully as he could, the dirty blonde wig slipping a half-inch, enough to reveal closely cropped hair underneath.

The light but skilfully applied lipstick and eyeliner did little to disguise that this was the face of a secret agent he knew.

Phil knew him because he'd worked closely with Eva.

Although far from an expert, Phil guessed that this man had been dead for at least a week.

Phil didn't need the note on the table and the sprawled photographs to know that this was Eva's killer. The dress he was wearing, the necklace, rings and the blonde wig were all Eva's. A symbolic message that this was her killer.

Phil sat down at the table.

On the table were ten soldiers, nine of them broken in half.

Next to the toy soldiers, three photos were upside down, which Phil turned over one at a time. They were black and white shots of a meeting between this man and another person he recognized.

Charlie Sandford.

Old Charlie then. The one who had ordered the hit on his Eva.

Mister "they don't call me intelligence for nothing".

Phil went outside and lit a cigarette with a shaky hand. Almost dark now, but there was enough light left for him to make out a figure at the other side of the water, in the bushes, calmly watching him.

Studying him. Making sure he'd got their message.

Phil thought about pursuing, but the man retreated into the bushes.

Phil reread the note, pocketed the photos implicating Charlie Sandford along with a toy tank, and left.

He'd noticed initials carved on the man's thigh.

The same initials on the signed note but in full; the name translated roughly to Divine Leader.

Phil later discovered this was a cult specializing in providing justice where society cannot.

Believed to have been started in Germany, and behind the execution of the high-ranking Nazi war criminals living in exile in Brazil and Argentina after fleeing Germany at the end of the Second World War.

A small, but obsessively loyal following, residing in every country worldwide.

A week later, Phil killed Charlie Sandford in his apartment. He'd bought the gun on the black market. Without a silencer, Phil improvised by muffling the shots with a pillow. He placed the cheap toy tank, a toy that looked as if it had come out of a Christmas cracker, next to his body to keep their little mystery going; and to divert suspicion away from himself.

The organization never caught up with Phil to ask him for a favour in return. Phil left Germany and the army shortly afterwards, and that was the last he'd thought about it.

Until Dale's body, and this cursed island.

Chapter Twenty-Nine

Phil finished telling his story looking at Tia. It told Tia that he was more interested in her opinion of him than what Jenny thought. Tia felt this to be encouraging.

"So, what's on your mind?" Phil said.

Tia shook her head as if to clear it. She couldn't think of any questions to ask.

Jenny asked a few questions about Eva, but Phil couldn't talk for long before it became difficult to continue.

"So?" Jenny looked at Tia.

"What?" Tia replied.

"Your story," Jenny said. "If you don't tell us what you did, Phil and I are off in the morning, and you can fend for yourself. Right, Phil?"

Tia got up exasperated, which surprised Phil as much as it did Jenny, she saw.

"How many more times!" Tia roared. "I haven't fucking done anything to merit being here."

The savage look on Jenny's face said *You're not going to get off that easily.*

"Leave her," Phil said, much to Jenny's annoyance.

"Leave her? She's the one who can leave, right fucking now!" Jenny shouted, pointing at Tia. "She could slit our throats in the night."

The ferocity scared her so much so that Tia deemed it necessary to move to the end of the cove, putting distance between herself and Jenny as she nestled down into her sleeping bag.

"We'll give you until morning to think about your priorities, sweetheart," Phil said, loud enough to carry.

*

Hiding in the bushes with a blanket draped over her shoulders, Tia hugged her knees and stared at the ground.

They're both against me now, so I'll stay hidden.

A coin-sized moon meant that Tia could see along the meandering, luminous stretch of beach.

The sand resembled cremated ashes on this sacrificial island of death. Several trees stirred in the strong breeze and black skeletal fingers clawed at the night sky with silhouetted cliffs as extended bony hands.

A Gypsy-looking girl with thick mascara around her fiercely determined eyes emerged on the beach; a primaeval creature in an animalistic night world of black and white never shades of grey, perfectly suited to this evil backdrop.

Tia, hiding in the bushes, rose to her feet to take a closer look, and to her horror, she saw the assassin dressed in a skin-tight black jumpsuit running straight for her.

Maybe she's not human; her eyesight like that of a lioness picking out my eyes blinking from hundreds of yards away.

The whole thing reminded Tia of the part in the Bible where Jesus was alone in the desert tested and taunted by Satan.

Tia had said to her stepfather once, with childlike innocence, "If Jesus was all alone out there in the desert then maybe Satan was a part of Jesus, and that's why they crucified him."

She had been thinking that if Satan's marker was an upside-down crucifix, then it was still Jesus nailed to it, but upside down. That made perfect sense to her.

Her stepfather slapped her in the face. Hard enough for her to feel the blow down into her socks.

Tia hadn't mentioned Jesus or Satan again.

Why had that memory come back to her now? Because she needed someone to save her?

Knives in both hands, the female assassin advanced, an edge of menace in her fixed gaze; the mysterious eyes of a Gypsy.

A fresh sea breeze brushed against her fringe and clothes as Tia dropped her blanket in preparation for running away. She felt that she shouldn't turn her back on this woman, that to do so would make her angrier – and twice as fast.

Outrunning her was not an option.

Tia stayed still, the woman moving closer, close enough for Tia to see the freckles on her face as she whispered into the bushes: "You were right not to tell them any more about me when they pressed for more details."

Tia found she still couldn't move.

"Trust your instincts and come out."

A gravitational pull tugged Tia forward as she emerged from the bushes and onto the beach.

"You were right not to trust them. Where there's a rat, there's always going to be nine more waiting in the shadows. Remember that time the rats came into our bedroom, what Dad said?"

"My dad?"

"*Our* dad."

"You're talking about Phil's story?" Tia said.

She bared her perfect white teeth in a hiss. "No! I'm talking about the people on this island; all of them! They're the rats in our bedroom, don't you see? You can see one, but there's always nine more watching in the darkness."

"You're saying I shouldn't trust Phil and Jenny?"

"I'm saying you should trust *me* to take care of it. Why else are you out here alone, breaking away from the others?"

Tia nodded to herself, but she still didn't understand, and to ask more questions would only piss this cryptic psychopath off further.

Tia had one question left. "How did you get on this island?"

"What you should be asking," the assassin said, "is how *you* are going to get off it, and I'm the answer."

As the assassin came closer, Tia noticed that her freckles were not freckles at all but a fine mist of blood covering her warrior expression.

"Can I trust you?" Tia asked.

The Gypsy warrior nodded, pleased with Tia for the first time as Tia looked down at the knives by her side that dripped fresh blood onto the moonlit sand; another sacrifice imminent. "Maybe that someone you've been desperately wanting to save you from this nightmare is already here," she whispered. "Closer than you think."

*

Tia awoke with a start.

That's the most vivid nightmare I've ever had.

The sensory detail so powerful, so visceral, it felt more like real life than waking up here.

Tia felt a strong hand tug at her shoulder. She could feel the cold metallic zip of the sleeping bag bite into her back as she turned over.

What's the matter? Tia wanted to say, but Phil pressed a finger to her lips to silence her.

"Let's go," he whispered.

It took a disorientated Tia a moment to register that Jenny wasn't leaving with them. That wasn't in Phil's plan.

When they left the cove, the whispering of the ocean became silent replaced by a rustling breeze of trees stirring in the woods. Phil spoke again. "I believe you. About Jenny. About her and Dale. All of it."

"You do?" Tia replied, her voice childlike. Relief, appreciation and desire rushed through Tia's mind all at once in a dizzy cocktail of pleasure released into her bloodstream after hours of pent-up dread and hopelessness.

The release felt something like falling in love. Phil's trust on this deadly island was that important to her.

"I don't trust her any more," Phil said.

Tia couldn't help but smile.

Finally, he believes me.

She trusted Phil. Tia couldn't have said why, but she knew he wasn't the one behind this.

Perhaps it was because he, like herself, wasn't good at hiding emotions.

"Thank you" was all Tia could think to say as they looked for a suitable hiding place in the moonlight.

"Not much further," Phil said, picking up on her unease. "I promise."

It was difficult to make out the cliff's edge in the darkness, the only light to guide them restricted to the moon and stars watching on like eyes imbued with a supernatural glow.

Tia could make out the beach a few feet below, her forehead creased in confusion, "look at the beach," Tia said.

"What about it?" Phil's eyes scanned the shoreline, looking puzzled.

"Rachel's body's gone."

Phil considered this for a moment. He shook his head. "No, that's the beach around that corner. Not this one."

"Are you sure?"

"Positive," Phil said. "I came across her body earlier. Now come on, before someone sees us."

Tia was scared as Phil was leading her into darkness.

A small cave announced itself near the shoreline, so that's where he was taking her. Can I trust him?

If she had this wrong, she would never leave that cave.

But Tia had to trust somebody. Phil was military trained, and unlike the others, he'd committed his crime in the line of duty. And hadn't she guessed Phil was in the army herself, days ago, when they were doing the washing-up?

She could see only one sleeping bag when they reached the cave.

Phil didn't take long to light a fire, providing her with a sliver of warmth and orange light.

Tia had already relaxed when Phil surprised her with a bottle of Scotch whisky.

She surprised herself again when she snuggled up next to Phil to take a sip of it.

"When we get off this godforsaken island," Phil said, "we can go anywhere in the world. So, where do you want to visit first?"

Tia smiled. "Like I said before, Paris."

"Ah, yes," Phil rolled his eyes. "The walking cliché goes for the city of love. The city everyone gets so misty-eyed and romantic about - except for me. Like I said before, I despise the place. It will be more bearable with you by my side, though."

"Will it now?" Tia smiled that little bit wider. "Well retrieved."

"Thank you," Phil said, his smile broadening.

"So where are we going, Philip?" Tia said, faking a solemn, displeased look at his lack of planning.

"Philip? God, no. My father called me Philip, and I hated the bastard."

"Really?"

"Like you wouldn't believe." Phil caressed Tia's belly button, circling it with his forefinger before picking at the bow on the waistband of Tia's panties. "Anyway, I was thinking Spain," he said. "In the morning we'll take a hire boat, sail it to a secret beach and skinny dip. In the afternoon, we'll sip Guinness at a beach bar owned by a cute old Irish couple who've owned it since the Eighties or Nineties, who made a success of it against all the odds."

Tia smiled. "Paddy and Sian."

Phil grinned. "Paddy and Sian."

"And in the evenings?" Tia said, gasping a little as Phil's sensuous fingers traced the line of her hip bone.

"And in the evenings, we'll..." Phil paused a second for thought, inspiration coming a few moments later. "In the evenings, we'll eat at a tapas bar and sample local wines and beers. Light ones so that you don't get too fat," he smiled, as Tia playfully punched him in the arm.

"And then?" Tia said.

"And then. Well, we'll wake up the next morning and do it all over again."

The warmth of Phil's muscular arms felt comforting.

The cave's entrance showcased the beauty of the moonlit beach. It didn't seem real, as though it were a portal to an imaginary world: a magical doorway to an enticing otherworldly paradise, like something out of a fantasy tale by C.S. Lewis or J.K. Rowling.

The crescent of white sand, shaped like the languid smile on her lips, stretched out of sight but Tia knew from memory that it went on for no more than a hundred yards or so.

The ocean continued to whisper.

Which ocean, though? The Atlantic?

That's what Phil believed. Earlier, he'd commented about the disorientating helicopter journey and how this island could be in the Irish Sea, the Celtic Sea or the English Channel, which wasn't exactly narrowing it down. She knew what he meant though; she'd felt woozy when she'd been blindfolded and thrust into the helicopter. They could easily have slipped her something in her drink, as she couldn't recall how long she'd been in the air.

They both agreed that it was too warm to be one of the islands in the Hebrides.

The moon became scarred by a cloud before disappearing behind it.

The effect of engulfing darkness was world-altering for her mood; closing the imaginary portal to her fantastic universe.

The fear came back, the dread crouching behind it.

Tia didn't know what time it was, but her body clock told her it was still the middle of the night, leaving maybe five or six hours of this darkness left to survive until daybreak.

Tia tried to focus her mind on something else, but darkness dictates your mood, bullies it into submission.

Like the Divine Leader.

Like this island.

Like this killer.

"You want to tell me about what happened that day?" Phil said.

Tia felt for the first time that she did. She wanted to get it off her chest, and she knew Phil wasn't the judgmental type.

Chapter Thirty

Tia's Story

One year earlier

Sunday 29 October

Tia had married a shit.

It was official.

Today she hated her obnoxious husband and wanted to kill him.

If not kill him, then to hurt him badly.

To make him suffer as she was suffering.

Maybe take his son away from him.

Just for a little while.

To make him feel something.

Tia knew that made her sound like an awful person, but no one knew what it was like to be in this relationship.

David had been a complete and utter shit all morning; there was no other word for it.

In truth, Tia was having more and more of these unbearable days with David, and a happy, incident-free day felt like an aberration, something like a bank holiday, a birthday or Christmas.

He walked on ahead, ignoring her.

In the pit of her stomach, she felt a growing tension and a fear she was going to be sick.

Her head started to ache.

More than ever, Tia wanted a drink to calm her anxiety, something light and soothing. A tall glass of rosé or a delicious Chardonnay would do nicely. Some blessed relief to take the edge off, to help her drift away from this cruel man she still loved like a fool and pathetically wanted to keep.

He'd lived up to none of his promises that he'd take this Sunday to be exclusively a family day as Debra had dictated in their last marriage guidance session. He'd been on his phone all morning to agents, none of them hers, fretting about his business which meant more to him than herself and Alex.

Tia put her sunglasses on, despite there being no sun, so that she didn't give David the satisfaction of seeing how much he'd upset her with his comments on how she looked.

Huge bags hung under her eyes like a caricature; she hadn't bothered with make-up, and putting her hair up in a ponytail didn't suit her. She looked like she was, quote, "tired all the time", fucking unquote. Which, for a model, is not a good look.

Daring to age, and nearing thirty was not a good look.

David suggested she'd hid her eyes because she was using again. *God, do I look that awful?!*

Tia ended up fumbling in her Gucci handbag and emptying the contents to prove to her asshole of a husband that she had no pills on her.

Not one.

He walked on again, not even looking at the contents of her purse.

When no apology was forthcoming, and Tia couldn't take any more of his unnecessary put-downs, she walked on ahead, and he had the nerve to shout out the accusation *she* was the one being childish.

Her.

Tia wanted this to be a family day and made an effort to make peace with David.

For a while, it worked.

The weather turned as they found themselves heading for cover under a marquee.

She cuddled up to him.

Briefly, very briefly, they were the happy couple again to the other people taking shelter with them.

An older couple and a tall girl dressed in a leather jacket and black jeans stood next to them.

David hated making a scene in front of an audience.

1.26 p.m.

Alex and Tia spotted the lion emerging from behind a bush. Alex smiled as the lion yawned; a gorgeous photo.

Alex looked so cute, smiling and surprised at the same time.

She showed it to David, but he waved her off with a hand. He was on his mobile again, in his self-absorbed world. The slightest of grins made Tia suspect he was conducting some business of a different nature.

Arranging his "busy schedule", my ass.

Arranging his busy schedule …

With that slut.

Tia scolded herself when she overheard him talking about the Murray account. She knew this to be a legitimate business deal with a BBC TV mini-series in production; she'd already been through all the emails on his laptop, having cracked his password last week.

His password turned out to be an amalgamation of his favourite football team and his company, and it had stung her more than it should that she no longer featured in it. Tia knew that at one time he had her as his password. The pet name he had for her.

Tia felt needy today.

She wanted to feel desired; was that such a crime?

To want to feel loved by your husband?

It suffocated him. He'd told Debra as much several times. Enough times for Tia to get the message.

It wasn't what he wanted.

And when Debra asked him what he wanted?

To be left alone sometimes.

That's what he said.

It's all he bloody well said.

She forgot all about her husband momentarily, looking down at her son. She was worried about Alex, his face redder than usual as he sneezed.

Her fretting about Alex having a cold and asking David's opinion on this was wrong.

Today she couldn't do anything right.

Today, she felt ugly, old beyond her years. Just three years ago she was a successful model and YouTube influencer for gym wear and lingerie, and David had promised that his secret Channel Four producer multi-millionaire contact would provide her with her big break. Now she felt fat and bloated, her opportunity missed. Tia felt as unsexy in this baggy black high street raincoat and polo neck ensemble as she could ever remember.

Tia felt as low as she could remember; a useless wife and a hopeless mother.

Tia noted she was attired all in black, from head to toe, as if attending a funeral.

It certainly felt that way.

As soon as they sat down in the café and ordered drinks, David moved away from her so he could make another business call over the noise Alex and she were making. She spotted that he'd not even bothered wearing his wedding ring today. His excuse that he was lifting weights earlier and he'd taken it off to avoid damaging it and had left the ring in his gym bag.

Tia was disgusted with him, her icy gaze told him as much.

When David informed her (spoken as though addressing a spoiled child) that he needed to drive to his office to go over a contract, Tia couldn't hold it in any longer.

He used the familiar micro-aggression that she didn't know what it was like to have a deadline since she wasn't working any more. Tia made a note of this to inform Debra in their next session.

I'm not working because you, as my useless fucking publicity agent, can't find me any work and are too chicken-shit to ask for help from your big-shot producer friend. Either that or you're too chicken-shit to tell me that your big-shot producer friend is a mere acquaintance who won't help. Or chicken-shit option number three: I'm not a marketable enough prospect to promote which you can't say that to my face.

When Tia looked up, he'd made his way out of the café, striding towards a girl dressed in black.

She was pretty and very much his type; younger than her too.

She'd followed David here, that was it; They'd had an affair.

When David walked straight past the girl as if she wasn't there, Tia dismissed the idea.

Tia yelled at him to come back if he valued his marriage. Melodramatic, she knew, but by this point, she was furious with him. She continued shouting over the babble of children milling about in the café.

Tia chased after David in the rain.

David didn't walk so much as march. Out of breath and a headache looming, Tia gave up trying to catch him.

She was far too upset to rush back to Alex right away.

Tia tried to ring her sister and then Debra to tell them what a heartless wanker she'd married and about how he'd mistreated her today.

1:39 p.m.

Tia felt too angry to cry.

She rang her counsellor Debra, and then her sister, only reaching voicemail for both of them.

Tia's anger left her the moment she looked down at the pushchair.

A half-eaten Halloween toffee apple in the pushchair the only trace of Alex.

Tia frantically scanned the zoo café.

She addressed the nearest adult she could see, a grandmother.

"You must have seen my son?" Tia said. "He was right here, strapped into his pushchair."

Children played energetically around Tia, making her feel as if she'd stepped on to a carousel. She looked down at the children milling about, key witnesses without care or comprehension of what had taken place under their noses.

"No! What do you mean, no?" Tia shouted. "He was right here. Somebody must have unstrapped him."

"I'm sorry, I didn't see anybody unstrap him," the elderly lady said, apologizing and indicating that she had her hands full with her grandchildren.

Dread hit Tia brutally in the pit of her stomach.

"Are you alright, dear?" the concerned grandmother asked.

"No, I'm not alright. How could I be?"

She used anger to cope with the impending panic attack.

"How could I possibly be alright?" Tia screamed hysterically; too alarmed to cry.

"I'm sorry," the grandmother said, leaning across Tia. "But that pushchair belongs to me."

Calling her son's name over and over again, Tia made a circling route around the zoo café. On exiting the café, she jogged over a grass verge leading to a boating pond where ducks were pecking at breadcrumbs and getting in her way.

Oh my God, maybe he's fallen into the water!

She shouted, "Alex! Alex!"

As soon as she stopped running, she started to shake.

Tia couldn't see him anywhere in the murky water; the water shallow enough here to see the bottom. Further out it got quite deep, however.

She ran back along the path, approaching a young couple, whose faces grew alarmed as Tia spoke, their expressions turning vacant and uncomprehending. Tia gave up appealing to them, suspecting they were foreign tourists.

"Alex!" Tia screamed again as she broke into a run.

She passed another couple, expecting them to drop what they were doing and help her, annoyed at their puzzled looks. "My son is gone!" she shouted, showing them the screensaver picture of Alex on her phone.

This time the couple sprang into life and helped Tia search. Tia was too overwhelmed with anxiety to convey her gratitude. Someone had acknowledged her and was helping her look for her baby.

Minutes passed as more people joined the search, including the zoo staff and security guards. Minutes dragged by with each uncomfortable heartbeat thumping and indicating that time was getting away from her.

Tia fell over more than once on the slippery grass and flung herself back up again. She composed herself long enough to stop and think about what she was doing.

Breathless, she wandered back to the café table and sat down next to an empty pushchair. She rang David over and over again to check that Alex was not with him, leaving messages on his voicemail imploring him to come back to the zoo right away.

Her phone vibrated in her hand.

Incoming call.

Debra.

"Debbie?"

"Listen," said Debra's distorted voice on speakerphone. "David has told me that you've been following him all day."

"You don't understand –"

"Alex is missing, is he?" Debra said. "But no one has seen him with you."

Tia looked at the phone as if it were an alien object. "How could you possibly know that?" *How could she know that when it had only just happened?*

"You must leave the zoo," Debra said. "And come and see me now; I'm free until four. And Tia –"

"Yes?"

"Please take your medication."

The phone slipped out of Tia's grasp.

The café faded, with black spots filling her vision; ink blots expanding in size until they obliterated her peripheral vision, and she felt her legs go weak. Her vision disappeared like a TV monitor thrown down an elevator shaft as she fainted.

3:51 p.m.

When Tia came round, she saw David's concerned face. David! Had it all been a dream then?

His face told her it wasn't a dream.

She hadn't eaten more than a slice of toast today, washed down with black coffee.

"Look at me, Tia," David said. "This is important."

"Alex is missing," Tia interrupted.

"There is no Alex," David told her, unable to keep the disgust off his face. "This isn't the first time this has happened. We decided that we wanted to pursue our careers, so we terminated the pregnancy. That was when we were together. I don't want you following me around any more, do you understand?"

Tia nodded, but her attention was on the woman dressed in all black. Lurking behind them; watching.

David thrust his hand forward, holding two pills. "I found these in your bag; you need to take them."

The woman in black seemed to object. Her mascara thick, like warpaint, around hooded eyes brimming with menace. She resembled a disgruntled Gypsy; an unsettling mystique hung around this woman.

Tia wanted to shout out, "Why are you hanging around us?" but found she was too afraid to meet the woman's fierce gaze, remaining submissive to her aura of supernatural bestiality.

"What are you looking at?" David sat down next to her on the grass, a tear in his eye. "Is it Alex? As a little boy?" Tia could see he knew it was hopeless. She wanted to cry and hug him.

He does care for me.

She could see it so plainly it hurt them both.

Tia glimpsed the man she had married; the man she wanted.

David attempted to become authoritative again, but his voice faded away in the helplessness of the situation.

Why couldn't he have shown me this caring side when I told him I was pregnant? Or when he talked me into having an abortion on an overcast Saturday afternoon in a packed Kensington pub with drunk men shouting abuse at a match on a television screen?

Tia felt trapped by the thought, as she had never been trapped before in her life. She felt penned in like the imprisoned zoo animals around her, crashing against their cages.

The Gypsy girl approached David at speed, like a witch about to cast a spell.

Tia's voice was too hoarse and weak to warn him as she produced a knife. A knife that sliced across his exposed throat.

David looked stunned. He looked hurt at first and then angry. Controlling, abusive David emerged as he lashed out at *her.*

Tia took a step back as he weakened, fury overtaking the shock on his face.

The girl stepped in again, slipping between them, slashing him in the midriff twice and in the shoulder and torso in lightning-fast blows as he failed to protect himself.

It all happened so fast there was no time to react.

David's blood splashed the grass like experimental art.

Blood covered his tailored white shirt as well as his suit jacket and trousers. Always smart in public, dressed formally, as if he knew this day would be his last.

Tia couldn't watch as the Gypsy girl ran away, leaving the corpse of David on the slate-grey circular sundial patio, the stone matching the colour and tone of the bleak sky. The widening pool of blood leaking out of his body like rain clouds moving in a facsimile of the heavens above them.

Tia caught her reflection in that pool of blood, not recognizing her face. David grabbed her arm when Tia crouched down, before his grip relaxed in death; his splayed body's limbs outstretched in an unnatural everyman pose on the stone patio, a pose showing how he had fought death right until the last moment.

Tia pursued this savage Gypsy woman attired all in black like the angel of death. Around the winding path, she spotted her tossing the knife into the murky boating pond before sprinting out of sight.

Tia rounded another bend in the park trail, but there was no one on it; she had vanished.

Never to be seen again, not even by witnesses at the trial.

Not until she appeared ghostlike on this cursed island that seemed to be tailor-made for her.

Chapter Thirty-One

Phil put his human hand on top of hers. Tia could tell that he was relieved. But he also looked confused by a story which raised as many questions as it provided logical answers.

"God, if you're innocent," Phil said, "then there's a killer on the loose around London; a real femme fatale. Couldn't the police find the murder weapon? The knife, I mean? Surely it would have had her DNA on it." An inner cloud passed over Phil's expression. "No, it would have been wiped clean by the water, I suppose."

"You probably won't believe me –"

"I do believe you," Phil said.

"What I was going to say," Tia said. "Is that the police never found it, but that's the first time I've recalled seeing her throwing the knife into the water, just now. Right by that copse with the small oak tree, it was. How could I forget such a detail? I blanked it out completely; my memory was a meaningless haze at the trial."

"Due to the trauma?"

"Yes," Tia said. "I guess so."

"What else do you remember? It could be important in clearing your name. I know that you were found not guilty in court, but still…"

"You can say it, you know."

"Someone else thinks otherwise," Phil said. "Or you wouldn't be here, and you should put them straight."

"I don't recall anything else," Tia said, her gaze distant. She shook her head as she looked away from Phil. "No, nothing else."

When she glanced back at Phil, she caught a look of hopelessness passing over his features.

Phil didn't have any more questions, much to Tia's relief.

He took a slug of whisky before passing her the bottle.

"Down the hatch," Phil smiled. "That's it."

"We need to forget the past," he added. "And get some rest."

Tia rested her head on his shoulder.

"Try and think of something nice" were his last words, before sleep smothered her.

*

What seemed like moments later, Tia was awake, roused by a scream so full of pain and fear it iced her blood.

The scream sounded female. It had to be Jenny.

Phil stirred from his sleep, sat up and said, "Sounded to me like it came from the woods."

He grabbed his trainers, crouching to lace them up.

"Don't go," Tia pleaded.

"I'll be careful," Phil replied, attempting a smile of reassurance. Tia looked down for a moment, thinking of something to say that would make Phil stay. To prevent him from investigating; a rationale to keep them both safe.

By the time she had looked up, let alone spoken, he'd gone.

And the quietness of the night was all she could hear.

Until the screams started up again.

*

The screams had stopped, but the last anguished cries replayed in her head, convincing Tia that they may have come from a tortured man.

Tia couldn't get it out of her head, for some reason she thought about the day of her husband's attack in the park.

Tia emptied her mind until whispering ocean waves blended into the whisper of tree branches swaying in the breeze. Those two noises were almost inseparable to her ears, a phenomenon of nature. As if this world were not real but an artificially simulated environment; one noise copied from the other in this virtual reality.

Tia trod with care to reduce the crackling noise of her steps. She kept as low as she could manage to avoid being seen by anybody, or by the numerous cameras fixed on trees. Her only previous reference for this type of creeping movement was paintballing as a child, but it proved a legitimate survival instinct.

Someone out there had a real gun, of course, filled with bullets and not paint capsules.

Tia sensed movement to her left, dropping to her knees behind a rock large enough to use as cover.

It took Tia a moment to realize the movement was coming from the sky and not the ground.

Another patrolling drone.

A handy device to check people's whereabouts on this island so that they could be located, stalked and killed.

Leaning her body weight on the rock, Tia felt a strange sponginess in the palms of her hand, and not the cold hard rock face biting into her skin she'd expected.

She thought at first that this must be moss covering the rock, but a quick inspection proved that not to be the case. This rock had a uniform surface; made entirely out of what felt like plastic.

Closer inspection revealed a thin gap, and a metal detail Tia recognized as a brass hinge.

A brass hinge on a fake rock?

Tia stood up and lifted: half of the rock face rose with ease; it weighed practically nothing.

It proved to be not a rock at all, but a hatch covering a concealed opening in the ground.

Gritting her teeth, Tia climbed into it and descended into darkness.

*

The hatch swung shut above her in the breeze as she lowered herself down the ladder lining the shaft.

It was warmer down here, her hands breaking into a sweat. At first, Tia thought that this was why the rungs of the ladder were so hard to grip, but it appeared that it was slippery from some oily substance. Taking care with the slick metal rungs, Tia made her descent with careful deliberation until the ladder ended about four or five feet short of the bottom of the shaft.

Tia dangled feet-first before dropping to the floor so as not to injure her ankle. She was conscious of the fact that she might be required to make a run for it again at any moment should the killer show up.

After a few strides, Tia found herself in a small room, a soundless chamber in which Tia could hear nothing but her laboured breathing.

An air raid shelter built for a wealthy family fearing nuclear war, perhaps?

In this silent bunker, a long concrete-grey corridor stretched out to her right, and another one opened close behind her, opposite the ladder.

After a moment's debate, Tia decided to head for the corridor behind her.

Lights stabbed at her eyes, her sight slowly adjusting having been in darkness for so long.

Her vision cleared to reveal only an empty corridor. It was one of those motion-detection devices of the energy-saving variety, triggered by her movement and not by a person; the same way the lights were programmed to operate in the Divine Leader house.

It took several seconds for her vision to fully return, but significantly longer for that feeling of dread and foreboding to leave her gut before she started moving down the corridor.

To do so felt like stepping into the mouth of a monster.

Hearing footsteps, she ducked inside the first room she came across.

Bright lights were once again activated as she entered the room.

Tia almost cried out at the spectacle in front of her.

Harvey stared into her eyes, his face cold and unmoving.

Chapter Thirty-Two

It was Harvey, and yet it wasn't.

His face possessed a glassy, plastic sheen under the harsh white glow of the overhead lighting.

In softer light, it could have been Harvey.

The likeness was eerie; his chiselled features carved with greater detail than most of the celebrity waxworks Tia had seen in her visit to Madame Tussauds last summer.

Two more figures of starkly varying heights lurked behind Harvey with sheets draped over their heads like a cheap cliché of a ghost.

Tia felt she'd entered horror-movie territory, studying the figure's arms carefully for fear they would spring to life and grab her.

When Tia's nerves had settled enough for her hands to be sufficiently still, she pulled the sheets off the waxwork figures' heads.

They both represented people on this island. Resembling Jenny and Tim, they were equally as lifelike as Harvey's mannequin.

Another awful vision from a movie struck Tia.

House of Wax. A movie where real bodies were sculpted into lifelike wax statues and preserved for a demented voyeur with a twisted take on art.

What had she stumbled upon here: the serial killer's sick trophy room?

If this were true, it meant Phil and herself were the only ones left to fight the Divine Leader, as there were no wax figures of them down here.

Tia peeked out of the room to check that the corridor outside was clear. Fear prompted the hairs on the back of her neck to prickle with gooseflesh.

I've got to get out of here, her mind screamed. *And fast - before this psycho turns me into one of these statues.*

Thinking she'd head back where she'd come from, Tia found her way into a control room entirely by accident.

Large, TV-studio-sized cameras hovered overhead, elevated on a mezzanine level pushed up against the thick glass.

Tia stared into the empty kitchen area of the Divine Leader House through a one-way mirror. More cameras were pointed at other areas of the house, raised high to capture the bathroom and shower areas discretely.

I'm directly under the Divine Leader house itself, Tia thought. And I still can't find my way out of here.

She had to find Phil.

She scanned the six TV screens in front of her, focusing on the three monitors where there was movement.

The other housemates; still alive!

Harvey.

Jenny.

Phil!

Thank God!

Phil's on-screen expression looked pained, matching her reflection. She wanted to call out to him more than anything.

He looked trapped, unsure of his surroundings.

Tia felt frustrated that she didn't recognize the backdrop of Phil's on-screen location.

Where are you, Phil?

As Tia pondered where his location on this island might be, a shadow hit the floor behind Phil. Unaware, he didn't react to it. Someone was creeping up behind him.

Chapter Thirty-Three

"Oh-no!" Tia watched television screen number two, biting her lip. "No-no-no. Look out!"

On Monitor two, the stalking figure popped up in the bottom right-hand corner, on Phil's blindside. Jenny had disappeared from monitor screen three altogether.

"Look out, Phil!" she shouted, each word ripping Tia's throat raw.

The long blonde hair of a woman now appeared on the same screen as Phil, distracted, and with his back turned, he was still unaware of her presence.

Tia could see it was Jenny and she was holding a knife.

Watch out for her!

To Tia's relief, Phil turned around to spot Jenny at the vital moment. He didn't seem at all alarmed by her.

Tia couldn't believe her eyes, as they sat down, grinning at each other.

Maybe he's trying to get information out of her, Tia thought. *Phil was using his military intelligence to lure Jenny into a position of trust to gain the upper hand.*

Yes, that had to be it.

Unable to hear their conversation, Tia could only go by their body language. They seemed to be pretty amicable, but again they would be if Phil was trying to trick Jenny into giving him the information he needed.

Tia took her eyes away from the monitors for a moment, looking around the room, recognizing the mini-maze of glass cabinets, filled to the brim with glowing lights and spaghetti junctions of cables; a rack of servers.

A tap dripped somewhere in the room, but Tia couldn't locate it.

She was sweating due to the heat of the room. The whirling noise of a fan emanated from the servers, lowering the temperature of the expensive hardware but doing nothing to cool her down.

The faintest sound of voices came from screen five, like somebody whispering in her ear.

Harvey and a woman off-screen were talking. She recognized the female voice, but couldn't quite put a name to it. It was tantalizing with the sound quality too scratchy to make out the identity of this woman.

Tia focused instead on what Harvey was saying.

She noticed Harvey's gore-soaked trainers as he bent down to pick at them, theatrically looking at the spots of blood on his hands like a broken Lady Macbeth. "No, I'm not willing to play along," Harvey said. "Who knows what that psycho bitch will do to us."

Tia stood up. *It's a woman then. For God's sake. Who, Harvey? Who's the killer behind all of this? Who's the Divine Leader?*

"There's a reason I was physically sick in the sink when I first saw that board," Harvey said. "I wasn't acting then. One of those labels belongs to me. I didn't see it in the script they sent me. They've set me up, I know it; set me up for their sick pleasure."

Script? Tia said to herself. *What was he talking about - a script?*

"What did you do?" The still unidentified woman off-screen moved closer. Tia could make out her shadow almost touching the seated Harvey, who was scooping up sand in the palm of his hand and dropping it as if measuring time as he spoke.

"One of those labels on that board was their little wildcard," Harvey said. "All part of their fun and games, I'm sure. A subplot to the main feature. The whole point of this fucked-up show is to take you to breaking point."

Harvey shouted in an outburst of frustrated rage. "Well, guess what? I've reached it."

What did you do, Harvey? Tia said to herself.

The onscreen Harvey answered right away as if he'd heard her: "I used to stalk a woman online, okay? It was a rush for me. Then I started following her in real life until, one day, she committed suicide. Hell is other people."

Expecting a full confession, Tia was disappointed when none came.

So Harvey's the stalker. The voyeur and stalker on the board of shame.

Harvey wasn't a threat then.

Tia still wanted to know who the elusive "psycho bitch" he kept referring to was.

In the background, behind Harvey, a never-ending pattern of waves broke and reformed, like fresh sins discovered and dismissed in this wretched, spoiled world where only nature could be said to be pure and free.

"You need to get ready for the new direction we've been given," the woman said, but Harvey ignored her.

When it was evident that nothing more was going to be said, Tia turned her attention back to screen two. Phil and Jenny immersed in their conversation.

If only I could hear what they were saying.

Tia spotted a navy-blue metallic box with "audio" written on it. Its interface had six buttons. Six buttons for six screens?

That made sense.

She pressed button two.

After a screech of static, Tia could hear his faint voice over the noise of the fan, but she could barely make out what they were discussing, catching the odd word or fragment of conversation here and there.

She turned a dial on the box to her right up to maximum, but she still couldn't make out their words. The dial didn't alter the volume as she'd hoped.

Tia had an idea; maybe the volume was voice-activated.

"Control room," Tia said.

No answer.

Tia smiled to herself. "Divine Leader," she said.

"Yes, Peter?" the Divine Leader's voice answered.

Tia almost fell off her chair at the sound of the flat, inhuman voice greeting her.

"Divine Leader," Tia instructed, wiping sweat from her brow. "Turn up the volume on Monitor Two."

It was an improvement. Tia could make out some of the words they were saying over the fan noise.

"Louder," Tia said. "Louder still."

With the volume set at almost one hundred, Tia could make out every word. It was even a bit too loud for her liking. "Divine Leader," she said. "Set the volume to eighty-eight."

Eighty-eight proved the perfect volume.

The more she listened, the more Tia began to wish she hadn't found that audio volume command.

Chapter Thirty-Four

Despite feeling sickened by each word spoken, Tia found she was unable to tear herself away from the TV monitor.

"I hear we have the same agent," Phil said. "Ryan Thompson."

Jenny rolled her eyeballs. "We did."

"He dropped you?" Phil said, sounding surprised.

Jenny nodded. "Guy's a prick."

"I won't argue that one. That's cold, though," Phil said, unable to suppress a grin. "Seriously though, he's not worth it."

"Well, I got this gig without him."

"You go, girl!" Phil smiled when Jenny shot him a disgruntled look. "Look, I'm not knocking you; I'm happy for you."

Jenny changed the subject, "Anyway, you were showing me what to do on this laptop."

"Right, it's simple," Phil said. "If she starts talking, you hit the record button. Any confession or detail around the death of her husband is like gold dust to these people. Anyway, the app is always running; minimized in the taskbar. As I say, hit the red record button whenever Tia speaks, and we're good to go."

"Isn't like every part of this island covered by audio and a camera of some description?" Jenny fiddled with a pea-sized camera on her jacket button as if to underline the point.

"Don't even start," Phil said, exhaling with frustration. "There's only a million quid riding on her confession; do you seriously want to leave that to chance?"

"Understood," Jenny replied with a noticeable change of attitude. "So, that's all I have to do with it?"

"That's it," Phil said. "Here's the thing, though: don't give away that you're recording, subtly glance at the screen now and then to make out you're checking the CCTV cameras for our killer. The cameras run on a loop as a glorified screensaver."

"I am an actress, you know," Jenny said, looking insulted.

"I know," Phil answered with a smile. "You're the second-best actor here."

Jenny rolled her eyes.

"Lucky for you," Jenny said. "Tia isn't the sharpest tool in the shed. She didn't work out you're not old enough to have been an experienced agent in Berlin in 1989."

"I'll take that as a compliment," Phil said with a smile.

"The guy originally set to play Phil pulled out at the last minute," Jenny said, "when he landed a speaking part in a Martin Scorsese epic, I heard. Worked out okay for you, though."

"Yeah, I heard that too; we'll have to find out who his agent is."

"I tell you who can't act," Jenny said. "That fucking halfwit playing Dale."

"Yeah, well," Phil said, "there's a reason he got knocked off first. I could see his ribcage going up and down when he was supposed to be dead. That's why I wrote the DL on his back so that I could roll him over. I moved Dale out of Tia's sight quick-smart too, and got Peter to swap Dale with one of his waxwork dummies at the first opportunity."

Jenny nodded. "I tell you who's a tool too, that guy playing Harvey. He can't even work out if he's playing gay or straight. She picked up on that right away. To be brutally honest the only other professional authentic performance, aside from the two of us, was from Helen Westling, and that's because she's a presenter in real life."

Jenny looked down at Phil's metal hand.

"You're wondering how I got this?" Phil smiled.

"I wasn't." Tia could see that Jenny was lying.

Again.

"It's okay," Phil said. "Everybody does. It was in a car accident when I was a kid. Boring, hey?"

"I don't know about you, but I'm still pinching myself over the advance I got for this," Jenny said, changing the subject.

"Not too bad is it, and I guess you haven't got Ryan Thompson leeching his percentage off your pay packet to feed his coke habit now."

"Nope," Jenny said, smiling up at the camera almost as if she knew Tia was watching and going out of her mind in the process. "The bonus they're dangling in front of us is pretty nice too. Anyway, let's get back into character before she comes back."

"Fat chance of that," Phil said. "She's about half a mile away in that cave opening. Even if she isn't sleeping, she'll be too afraid to wander out on her own."

"Do you really believe this programme will be a success," Jenny said, looking serious. "Even with Tia's confession?"

"Funny you should say that." Phil turned the laptop to face Jenny and maximized the messenger window. "Our generous benefactor gave us some encouraging news an hour ago. They've recovered the knife from the boating pond. They were able to locate it based on what she described to me."

"So now they have the murder weapon." Jenny seemed to perk up at the news.

"Now they have the murder weapon," Phil said. "Which sounds like it may be enough to reopen the case. And we get our fat bonus, after all, despite some of the most horrendous overacting and low-budget special effects ruining the suspension of disbelief."

"It's only Tia who has to believe it, though," Jenny pointed out. "And she looks scared out of her mind."

"Yeah," Phil said. "Trust me, at the moment she'll do anything I say. And I need that money."

"Don't we all," Jenny said.

Alongside her panic, which was growing with each sentence they uttered, Tia felt like she was going to throw up, her guts doing acrobatic flips and cartwheels.

To Tia's continued amazement, the actors playing Alice and Dale ran in, panting for breath as they came on screen.

Her presence on this island had been a mystery to solve. Tia had been unable to find a label on the board of shame to describe herself, and she hadn't been able to relax since.

Time and again, her thoughts had dwelled on her reason for being here. *Was she the control subject? Or the odd one out? The non-criminal amongst a cast of stranded offenders chosen purely for experimental purposes? Or had she been doomed due to a dumb administrative error?*

The motive, now revealed, was the worst conceivable outcome for Tia; one she couldn't have foreseen.

A wave of dread overcame her senses, so strong it caused dizziness to rush through Tia's body and mind.

Any movement felt sluggish, as though she were underwater. Tia sank into her chair.

The screens in front of her wavered and started to roll on their sides.

It wasn't as if they were strangers acting weirdly again; the truth was much crueller than that.

It was as though Tia had attended a masquerade ball where they had all suddenly unmasked; revealing grotesque, monstrous faces underneath the one's they'd been presenting thus far to her.

Tia couldn't help but draw parallels with Rosemary Woodhouse saying, "There are plots against people, though, aren't there?"

This elaborate deception being just such a plot.

And, like Rosemary in *Rosemary's Baby*, no one was on her side.

Tia felt her anxiety soar to new levels.

They're actors, all of them.

Even Phil.

And they're all against me.

Chapter Thirty-Five

Tia couldn't help but continue watching.

Watching this horror TV show unfold onscreen as Dale and Alice came into shot on monitor two to join Phil and Jenny.

Somewhere in the room that infernal tap kept on dripping. A distracted Tia had to locate it. It was an OCD thing, driving her further into madness.

"What the hell are you doing?" Phil said. "For fuck's sake, you're supposed to be dead. You're going to ruin the whole thing."

"Shut up!" Alice said. "Just shut up and listen for once. The game's over, you hear. Tim's dead."

"Of course he's fucking dead," Phil said. "It's in the script."

"No," Dale said, raising his voice. "She means for real."

Jenny looked at Phil with disgust. "They're having us on."

"Look at our fucking faces, you stupid bitch!" Dale screamed. "Do we look like we're playing a prank; he's dead, okay?"

"Are you sure?" Jenny said.

"Am I sure?" Dale mocked. "Gee, I don't know. His throat has been slit; he has more than a dozen stab wounds. I'm no doctor, but you can't get much more dead than that, can you?"

"Fuck," said Phil.

"I'm calling my agent," Alice said. "I'm supposed to be in *Emmerdale* next month. This show was only supposed to be a stepping stone for me. I don't care about the money any more."

"Seriously?" Dale said. "That's all you can think of right now?"

"She's gone all Ellen Ripley on us," Dale said, starting to calm down a notch after his outburst. His laughter still sounded mentally unsound. "That's what's happened. There's a good reason why she hasn't confessed."

"And why's that?" Phil asked, crossing his arms.

"Only because she doesn't believe she's done anything wrong," Dale said. "Psycho killers generally don't feel remorse or the need to confess their crimes. Kind of a spanner in the works of the 'genius' who concocted this little island adventure script, wouldn't you say? Great for TV, great for your career they said. Do a social service in the process. Get a killer to confess her sins, they said."

My God, they think I killed Tim.

David too, that's what they're saying.

"Look, calm down." Phil was typing on his laptop. "I've alerted whoever is monitoring this by messenger. Whoever picks this up will send someone for us. We've just got to stick together and stay alive for the next hour or two before they get here. Safety in numbers. Piece of cake."

"Good," Jenny said to herself more than the others. "That's good."

"She probably killed Tim while he was defenceless, or playing dead," Phil said. "She can't be that dangerous. There's all of us and only one of her. Let's go get the others."

Phil stuttered, his next sentence cut off by something happening off-camera.

"What is it?" Alice said to Phil.

Distracted herself, Tia wasn't watching any more. She had located the dripping tap noise.

A liquid flowed off the back of her chair, dripping like soup onto the damp floor around her.

Tia felt cold all of a sudden, hugging herself.

It was freezing in here, not tropically hot.

It wasn't sweat coming from her forehead either.

A thick, viscous puddle had collected at her feet.

Tia realized why she was so wet.

From head to toe, she was dripping, covered in warm blood.

PART SEVEN

BEHIND THE SCENES

The Actors' Testimonies

Dale (Michael Garrott) – Drug Dealer

Q. Now, Mr Garrott, what the court would like to know with regards to your testimony around your participation in this so-called justice reality television experiment, is why you decided to take part in it in the first place? Especially as you seem so critical of it now.

A. I read the script and the part of Dale leapt off the page, as though it had been written just for me. At least, that's what I thought at the time. The character intrigued me, I have to say. I'm a singer as well as an actor by trade, you see. And of course, there was the fat pay cheque; with a handsome non-disclosure pay-off that I had to look at twice to believe my eyes.

Q. Five hundred thousand pounds for the episode, as well as three-hundred-and-fifty thousand for a non-disclosure agreement, is that correct?

A. Come again? I was offered two hundred K and another two hundred for keeping my mouth shut. You've got to be kidding me. Who was offered that?

[Some laughter from the gallery]

Q. Settle down now. If you could focus on my questions, please? The court would like to know about the part where you faked your death.

A. That part was easy. Nothing to it, really. Alice – the actress playing Alice, I should say – she put something in Tia's cocoa to make her drowsy that morning, so that she wasn't at her sharpest, like. The others made sure they crowded her out, just enough so that Tia saw a glimpse of me being fished out of the pool and turned over, but no more than that. When she went back into the house to look at the board of shame with the others, the special effects guy told me to get up and he placed a dummy replica of me on the ground and put a sheet over the dummy for good measure. The dummy even smelt bad, like it was rotting, so she wouldn't uncover it, I guess.

Q. I see, and where did you go after that?

A. He led me to a hatch.

Q. A hatch?

A. A hidden opening in the ground. I remember saying to him he had to be effing kidding, I wasn't going to spend the rest of my time on the island in a friggin' bomb shelter. He laughed, and I saw what he meant pretty much right away. The hatch was an entrance to a massive, lavishly equipped underground bunker beneath the cliff face. There was even a natural water feature running through it. That became my new home. They had video games, plenty of food and drink – being the first to die, I got first pick of everything – and I could watch the show unfold on the big screen. I had a ball; it was better than being in the house, with that psycho waving knives at people, I can tell you that much. That gets old real fast. The only downside was that I couldn't get my guitar and that oddball Russian, Vlad. He considered himself a method actor and didn't want to converse with me out of character if you can believe it? He even turned up to the island a week early to get into character, right down to pretending that he had no recollection before arriving here.

Q. So you're confident that Tia had no clue what was going on? That you had covered your tracks sufficiently well?

A. Of course; there was only her against all of us. Everyone played their part in convincing her it was real. Social proof it's called, isn't it?

Q. It is indeed. And you have no moral reservations about tricking someone in this fashion?

A. She was young and fit, wasn't she? She wasn't going to keel over, that's how I looked at it. And seeing what that psycho was going to do to one of the other participants I can say that I will sleep soundly tonight, thank you very much. So no, not at all.

Q. I see that you don't, Mr Garrott. Thank you, you can step down now.

Helen Westling (played by herself) – Hit-and-run driver

Q. Can you state your name for the record, please?

A. Helen Amy Westling.

Q. And you're a daytime television presenter by profession, is that right?

A. That is correct. I've presented shows for the BBC and Sky. *An Eye for a Bargain, The Entrepreneur, Women's Football Round Up* and the *Divine Leader* show, to name a few. I've been a Radio DJ for the past three and a half years. Or I was up until the end of last year.

Q. And it was because you presented last year's Divine Leader show that you were approached for this project?

A. Yes, they wanted me for the authenticity angle. To suspend the disbelief, to create the illusion of it being a mainstream show. That was what I was led to believe by my agent. I have a new one now, for the record.

Q. You say mainstream show, as opposed to what, Ms Westling?

A. As opposed to, I don't know, snuff TV, a freak show, whatever cult status the online showings of the killing have turned it into.

Q. As you so clearly disapprove of how the murders have been sensationalized, what attracted you to the show in the first place? Was it the idea of administering justice through reality TV?

A. Nothing so altruistic. I have two mortgages, your honour.

Q. I see. So, your agent set this up and you happily went along with it not knowing what the outline of the show was?

A. I don't know if anyone knew exactly what the outline of the show was, as you put it. There was plenty of room for improv. Some knew more than others, put it that way.

Q. You're suggesting that you were kept in the dark about the exact intentions of the show other than it was a reality TV justice experiment. Would that be accurate, Ms Westling?

A. And if that isn't the fucking understatement of the year.

Q. Don't use profanity in my courtroom. Go on, please.

A. Yes, it is accurate.

Q. After you knew about the killing of... let me see my notes... Mr Henderson.

A. Who?

Q. Christian Henderson. The actor playing Tim? Surely if you didn't know that from being on set you must have seen it on the news afterwards.

A. I've been in rehab for the past month.

Q. For alcohol addiction, is that right?

A. Yep.

Q. The same alcohol addiction that led you to have your accident last year. The one that lost you your job on national radio and the *Divine Leader* show itself, is that correct?

A. Two out of two; you're on a roll, Your Honour.

[a snigger of sarcastic laughter from Helen Westling, met with laughter from the gallery]

Q. I'm glad I amuse you. However, I would like to remind you of the serious nature of this line of questioning.

A. Noted. Please continue.

[faint sniggering again from Helen Westling that the committee judge ignored]

Q. I'm reading here that your accident injured a young couple. Was this played to the full in the show?

A. There was an implanted video suggesting that the couple had died, instead of just having whiplash – which the jury is still out on, by the way; when you're hit at ten-miles an hour – anyway, it was on the screens when Tia was queuing for her audition. Fake news. God, I sound like Trump, but that's what it was. They spliced real-life footage of me being arrested, the courtroom with two people killed in their car. I have to admit they did a professional job on it in that it looked like a real news bulletin. All the other actors in the house were shown this video beforehand and briefed on the scenario to enhance its authenticity. Good enough?

Q. Yes, thank you, Ms Westling. That goes a long way toward explaining the premeditated nature of this show. Wouldn't you agree?

[Helen Westling shrugs]

Q. So?

A. So what?

Q. The show was premeditated to cause distress for Tia, wouldn't you agree?

A. Look, at no point has anyone suggested otherwise. They tried to beat a confession out of her psychologically. The show was to pull no punches. You really like to grandstand, don't you?

Q. This is how things are done in such proceedings, Ms Westling. We have to consider each part of the case so no detail is overlooked. You were saying.

A. I was finished actually.

Q. Well, thank you for your testimony.

A. No, thank you, sir. That was so worth the three-hour trip from rehab.

Alice (Caroline Pennant) – Leech

Q. And you played the part of Alice, is that correct?

A. It is.

Q. And what is your recollection of the events which ensued in the early hours of 25th September?

A. I want to state for the record that I don't blame Tia for what happened?

Q. And why is that, exactly?

A. She was pushed too far. I said so at the time. Do you think they would have ever treated her like that if she were a man? Think of all the men who have killed their wives in the past year. And they picked a woman for this radical role-playing study. This psychoanalysis based, patriarchy-researched-and-funded bullshit that tortured her mind until she went crazy. Did you know they had her entire internet search history on hand? Nothing was left to chance, and I mean nothing. Even at the end when we were supposed to appear as the undead at night pleading for her to confess her murder so that she didn't go to hell like us. We were supposed to come out of the sea at night holding hands and chanting. This was from a nightmare she'd described to a friend on WhatsApp. Did you know that they even –

Q. Thank you, miss… we get the picture. Now, what can you tell us about the drugs you gave her?

A. I was supposed to put a dosage in her food. To reduce the odds of her reacting violently to the events that were to unfold. But the drugs only seemed to make her worse; giving her paranoia and raising her anxiety, and I felt bad for giving her them.

Q. Why did you do it then?

A. My kids. I'm a single mother with two children. A part-time waitress struggling to hang on to my shifts. This was too much money for me to turn down. I figured it was legit considering the budget and scale of the programme. And when I heard Helen Westling was involved –

Q. I see. At what point did you start to have concerns about the way things were being run?

A. To be honest, when I saw how many non-disclosure contracts I had to sign. But I went ahead with it anyway because I needed the cash so badly. On the island, I told them that they should have pulled the plug when Tia nearly died. But I was shouted down by the others.

Q. How did she nearly die?

A. She swam way out to sea. We all watched from the clifftop. For a moment I thought she had reached breaking point and was going to swim for the horizon. After a while, it became clear that she was headed for the shoreline behind the cove and a strong current started taking her out to sea. Tom was poised to dive in. He's a strong swimmer. I thought at the time that it was to save Tia, but I later realized that Tom was only protecting his precious cash cow from drowning before she confessed.

Tom was the one who pushed the group to keep going. I could see the pound signs in his eyes.

Q. Tom?

A. Oh yes, the actor who played Phil? Why, aren't we doing real names?

Q. Okay, thank you. Who were you fighting to have the programme stopped? The experiment called off, as it were.

A. Everybody. Nobody else seemed to care about what we were doing any more. The justice element angle was no longer there. If it was ever there in the first place. Everyone became obsessed with the show, the money, the potential fame it could bring, to the point that no one seemed to stop and think of the consequences.

Phil (Tom Stafford) – Assassin

Q. You played the part of Phil, is that correct?

A. Correct.

Q. What I'm unclear of here, is why exactly did you agree to be on the show? You're not an actor like the others. What I'm reading here is that you're a soldier by profession.

A. That's not entirely correct. I'm also a theatre actor. I never wanted to be famous like the others, if that is what you're getting at? Money and the promise of more of it. Cash for participating and the promise of more of it for a successful completion was too much for me to turn down. Military service doesn't pay too well, I'm afraid.

Q. Indeed, I sympathize with your situation. You served in Syria and Afghanistan, I'm reading here.

A. Yes sir, two tours.

Q. Would you like to expand on that?

A. Not really, no. [The committee impresses upon Mr Stafford that a fuller explanation of his military record is required.] I was a communications expert, put it that way. I started in this role at the tender age of twenty-two. I continued this role into the Gulf War and later in Syria and Afghanistan. I can't divulge any more than that.

Q. And this is what you do now?

A. I work in Learning and Development these days, non-operational. And I moonlight as a West End actor.

Q. I see, and your military skills led you to be the one who radioed for help. How did you do that?

A. I tried to hack their system. When I failed, I reassembled the radio that had been smashed to bits outside the church. I managed to find someone on a nearby frequency.

Q. Why didn't you do this earlier?

A. You make it sound easy. I was surprised and relieved that it worked as well as it did. It took me a whole day to do it. We'd all still be stranded on that island if I hadn't.

Q. You've been described as being 'money-driven' in your actions on the island. Would that be an accurate description?

A. Seriously? We're all money-driven. The others could have stopped at any time, but they didn't, did they?

Jenny (Jenny Sadakis) – Celebrity killer

Q. You played the part of Jenny, is that correct?

A. Yes, that's right. I played Jenny, the same as my name in real life. Whether the producers thought that being from Essex and a woman, and more inexperienced as an actress, I would lapse and forget my stage name, I don't know. I had a particularly grisly backstory I had to memorize. About a husband I'd killed based on a fake news story advertised to Tia's Bing news feed. It was supposed to bond us closer together and induce her confession.

Q. Why would that grisly backstory, as you put it, bring you closer together?

A. She was abused by her ex-husband, or so she claims.

Q. You've mentioned several times that you thought that this experiment, as you put it in your own words, should have been stopped. Why didn't you stop it yourself?

A. Don't think I didn't try. After the incident where Tia came out of the shower brandishing a kitchen knife à la Norman Bates, I said to Mike at the time –

Q. He played the part of Dale?

A. Yes, I said to Mike, what's the use of having a million pounds if you're not around to spend it?

Q. By a million pounds you're referring to the danger money you were offered as insurance in case of injury?

A. I am. I was offered a hundred thousand for the confession; again my scuzzy agent – and me being a young woman, of course – swindled me out of the other nine hundred thousand offered to some of the others. There were other bonuses on offer. Anyway, I had serious concerns about health and safety measures being overlooked throughout the show. I was the first to say that Tim – Christian – shouldn't be wandering around the island on his own in that dumb mask. Peter – Vlad, I mean – was supposed to be with him at all times. At no point was anyone supposed to be left alone with Tia without at least one other present. That quickly went out of the window. The worst breach was when that son-of-a-bitch Tom – playing Phil – left me in that dark cove with her. I'm still suffering from PTSD now, and I'm having to take Prozac daily.

Q. Do you have a written copy of the health and safety procedure, or an agreement to ensure the safety of the actors while on set with Tia?

A. Barry, the producer guy, sat us all in a room and did a kind of boot camp session that lasted all morning. The others will tell you. A fat lot of good it did though. Especially when you consider someone died.

Q. Indeed, I couldn't put it better myself, Miss Sadakis. Have you anything more to add?

A. I haven't. My lawyers have instructed me to not give any more details, as I'm going to sue the pants off my former agent and the production company that put me on an island with a deranged killer.

Rachel Whitehouse (Dawn Kennedy) - Bully

Q. Why is your testimony so vague compared to the others?

A. After I was shot, or rather pretending to be shot, I thought I must have hit my head on a rock in the sand, or something, as my head started throbbing. Later I realized it was the onset of a migraine. I felt exhausted and a bit hazy. I slept for hours in a dark room before I was awoken and told that Christian had died, Tia was on the loose and I was to join the others for my safety.

Q. I see. Did you feel the loss of Christian more because of your closeness during your time in the house?

A. Look, I'm a professional, and I did my job. I shared a kiss with him, but that was all. I know it's hard for binary men such as yourself to understand but I'm bi and I have a girlfriend who I'm very much in love with. So no, I didn't develop feelings for Christian or his character, Tim. It was all part of the act and now it's done I'd rather know less about what went on while I was out of it if you don't mind.

Q. One more question. Do you have any remorse, or feel that you could have done things differently?

A. That's two questions, and it's an emphatic no to both of those. As I said, I'm a professional actress who did the job she was paid to do. No more, no less.

Harvey (Tony Ward) – Voyeur and Stalker

Q. Can you state what part you had to play in this reality TV show?

A. That's not an easy question for me to answer.

Q. And why is that exactly?

A. I was supposed to be the stalker, that was what was written in the script.

Q. And what did that entail?

A. I was given access to her personal information including Tia's very private emails that I was meant to disclose to her to give me credibility in this role. They even provided me with her Gmail password to log in and do some research before I came onto the show. I was to say that I'd seen her Instagram photos and quickly became obsessed with her. This wasn't the first time I'd become infatuated with a beautiful woman. I longed to see her naked and watch her shower. I rented one of the high-rise apartments across the street so I could keep a close watch on her. I was then to disclose that I'd followed her that day in the park and watched in horror as she stabbed her husband to death. But I didn't tell a soul because of my reverence for her.

Q. You say you were "supposed" to be the stalker?

A. That's why I feel so guilty. I contacted the *Divine Leader* production team by messenger while I was on the island. They agreed that I could swap roles with Christian if my state of mind wasn't up to it. Chris was eager to take the limelight and have an opportunity of grabbing the extra cash her confession would net him. I was nervous about what might happen when confronting her, with good reason considering what went down. It should have been me that died, not him.

Q. I see. I understand now why you said your part in this TV show was not an easy question to answer. There's one final aspect which is troubling us.

A. I used to stalk an ex-girlfriend, that's why I thought they chose the role of a stalker for me. In the original script, they gave me it was just voyeur. I became paranoid when I saw the stalker label appear. My state of mind was such that I felt unable to confront Tia. Chris comforted me, as did some of the others.

Q. That's not what I'm getting at. I'm talking about the other roles on the board. Something we still need to clear up. So, before you traded roles, you were supposed to be the stalker and Tim the serial killer?

A. Correct. The serial killer role was just a glorified walking role. To stride up and down the island in that silly mask with a weapon in hand to scare the wits out of Tia.

Q. I'm confused. Were you also the voyeur, as you say that you longed to watch her naked in the shower?

A. From what I gather the voyeur entry wasn't scary enough on its own, or the equal of the other criminal acts on the board. So, they added the stalker bit to it to give it more weight. The script, remember, was designed to destroy her on every emotional and psychological level. At least, that was how it was supposed to go.

Q. Do you have a copy of this alleged script?

A. I do, it's a PDF in my Dropbox. I can send it over to you. It will verify everything I've told you.

Q. Thank you, Mr Ward, there will be no further questions. I'll add one further thing for the record. Forgiveness is for everyone. You need to forgive yourself for your chequered past and for not confronting Tia in the role you were given. It sounds like Christian didn't need much persuading, and ultimately your decision not to divulge this information to Tia was the correct one. It saved your life. There are several counselling services we can put you in touch with if you so desire. You can step down now.

Peter (Vlad Karloff) The Rapist and Games Administrator

Q. Hello, Vladimir

A. Vlad.

Q. Right, Vlad. I believe you have something for us?

A. I do [hands over six pages of printed documents]

Q. What are these…emails?

A. I managed to get them off the server. They are from the missing producer Heinrich and demonstrate his involvement with the director and writer of the show.

They fill in some of the gaps in terms of the evolution of the show at the production level.

Q. Well, we better thoroughly examine them then.

17 Jan 23:07

From: magsthewriter@gmail.com

To: heinrichschrader@cupidsislandltd.com

Heinrich,

I've found a lawyer who agrees that multiple personality disorder is a very questionable mental condition for a legal defence outside of the United States. It's rare for sufferers to be violent or aggressive. He's got to do some more research before agreeing, but he seemed confident in our Skype session that a strong case could be put together on these grounds.

Mags

2 April 18:39

From: magsthewriter@gmail.com

To: heinrichschrader@cupidsislandltd.com

I can't believe this has happened.

I feel sick.

Not in my worst nightmares did I foresee her walking away scot-free.

Not guilty! How is she not guilty of killing our baby boy?

What sort of justice system would arrive at that conclusion?

I saw your face at the verdict. I felt so much love and sorrow for you at the same time.

Please come over. Neither of us should be alone tonight.

Mags

8 April 06:01

From: heinrichschrader@cupidsislandltd.com

To: barrysaunders@cupidsislandltd.com

Barry,

I'm suspending the Cupid's Island autumn show. I'm keeping the house and the set, but with some alterations. I need your design team to work long hours over the next few days.

I've wired one million pounds to your account as a show of our friendship as well as professional partnership. Money means much less to me than this project.

This is more than business for me, it's personal.

Heinrich

30 July 08:24

From: barrysaunders@cupidsislandltd.com

To: heinrichschrader@cupidsislandltd.com

Heinrich,

My main concern is how certain we can be to entice this Tia? What if she doesn't want to be on the show? We will email her and set up advertisements on her laptop at every opportunity? We have her IP address. Our report shows that she watches a lot of YouTube focusing on fashion and acting, which is ideal to set up a private video ad recommended exclusively for her account, stating that the Divine Leader show is looking for new housemates. I will set up the audition in our sister company's old premises as this will be close enough for her to attend the audition without any travel expenses. If she is at all interested then she will go for it.

Barry

31 July 05:16

From: heinrichschrader@cupidsislandltd.com

To: barrysaunders@cupidsislandltd.com

Barry,

Margaret says that she's fame-mad. She will do anything to be on television. She's already applied for reality TV shows in the past. I know it will work.

Please keep me posted on any new developments regardless of the hour.

Heinrich

22 August 14:27

From: barrysaunders@cupidsislandltd.com

To: heinrichschrader@cupidsislandltd.com

Heinrich,

I have splendid news - she showed for the audition!

I made up the fourth-panel member myself, and I guarantee that she bought it.

She didn't speak to anyone there, I'm told, so she didn't know the others were auditioning for Cupid's Island. The whole thing went flawlessly.

We will leave it a week before we send out her acceptance letter and travel details.

Barry

Margaret Susan (Mags) Fairbanks – Writer

Q. You wrote a script for the actors to follow. Is that correct?

A. I wrote a teleplay for a TV show with characters optimised to Tia's warped sense of reality.

Q. And would you say that you feel guilty creating this piece of work considering its outcome?

A. The world has seen who or rather what she is. That's all that matters to me. I consider that to be a success.

Q. But you are sorry that someone has lost their life over this project?

A. Of course, it haunts me. I'm not the sociopath here. She would have killed again in the outside world, left to her own devices, so maybe I've saved lives.

Q. Please answer the questions I ask you.

A. I thought I was.

Q. I understand that getting revenge for your son's murder was your motive for creating this teleplay for reality justice TV, as you put it. But can you expand on this, please?

[No answer]

EPILOGUE

PRE-PRODUCTION COSTS

Six months earlier...

Mags was supposed to attend a charity coffee morning with her friends after yoga.

That had been the plan.

Then a relaxing Champneys Spa appointment mid-afternoon to relieve the stress.

In between, Mags was going to watch that new RomCom she'd recorded on her Sky Plus box.

And early evening, she was going to round off the perfect day by finally getting around to doing some writing.

In the end, Mags never did any of those things.

Mags couldn't get enjoyment from any those routine things any more; the things she used to love.

All the colour had gone out of her world; all her warm, positive feelings were memories.

Mags headed to the scene of the senseless crime; the zoo where her son had been murdered, finding she couldn't stay away.

Having received an advance, Mags felt guilty she was shunning her writing time in favour of this obsession. She had developed storyboards for a brand-new reality TV show focusing on cheaters; the first two episodes concentrating on a rogue-trader ripping off the elderly and an ex-professional footballer serial love rat with multiple aliases on Tinder.

And her novel hadn't been touched in weeks either - based on the true story Mags had learned about from a holiday tour guide. A woman found guilty of rigging stage equipment to kill her abusive husband, the most famous magician in Paris in the 1890s. Mags switched up the setting to an almost present-day London, but her editor disliked the gore and the domestic violence running throughout her first chapter, and Mags had to rewrite it.

She had been looking forward to it, but like everything else, it had faded into the background of her depression and her morbid desire to revisit the scene of her son's murder.

Despite a media frenzy to find the murder weapon, a murder weapon that had to be in that zoo parkland area somewhere, not one line of enquiry had proved fruitful.

Mags checked the portal which updates the victim's family of any progress in the investigation. There was nothing on there. When she phoned to query this, they told her that it wasn't an IT error. The case had been closed on the system due to the outcome of the trial. And that was that.

The unsaid sentiment: accept it and move on with your life.

If only it were that easy. If only.

Mags sat down in the zoo café drinking a double espresso and chewing on a croissant.

Was this such a surprise? After the trial, and the gut-punch of that ridiculous "not guilty" verdict, Mags knew she was going to have to do her own digging here.

She looked around the café.

Noisy kids came and went as they had on that fateful Sunday afternoon. Margaret sat at the nearest available table, less than ten yards from where her son, a certified coffee addict, had drunk his last cappuccino.

She straightened in her seat. The killer had watched David. She didn't want to refer to her by name, couldn't, other than the necessary detachment of "the killer".

Anyway, she – the killer – had left via the same exit; the exit Mags was facing.

It had been raining, so her approach had been masked by an umbrella. Putting her umbrella up made her anonymous. She hadn't taken it down until the last second; that's why no one had seen her.

Possibly.

David's mobile phone had been found on the outskirts of the zoo on a pathway through a small wooded area leading to an estate. A jogger had discovered his body.

A few parked cars were on the road where a low, wilting railing fence, much in need of repair, bordered the zoo.

The half-arsed police theory suggesting her car had been parked there, despite CCTV footage of that afternoon capturing almost all the number plates of passing vehicles and those parked on the street. Not a single ANPR hit on any of the cameras.

Officers had been over that footage time and time again, interviewing close to a hundred passers-by.

The footage cleaned up by Met cybercrime techies with state-of-the-art software – and still no leads.

So, what was she going to find?

Anything needed to get this damned investigation reopened - only it never quite happened.

Maybe because they were looking in the wrong place, it wouldn't be the first time.

That murdering bitch may have lied about everything else in her statement, but she had told the truth about one thing at least. The coffee here was lousy.

Margaret's stale croissant was equally as bad; smelling of old feet and tasting like cardboard.

Mags walked over to a railing fence where a father and his two sons were kicking a plastic football at a goal made up of two jackets laid down on the grass as goalposts. She had done that with David when he was little. The rear of the zoo café was still visible from this vantage point, the seated clientele in the high-ceilinged glass Victorian conservatory extension was not due to the obstructing pillars.

The police said that the killer could well have been waiting for their victim here but, although Margaret couldn't quite explain why, this didn't seem right to her.

It wasn't this woman's style.

David had told Mags how she'd jealously followed him even when they were married.

She had been closer than that.

Much closer.

Waiting to pounce.

*

Mags walked out past the neatly groomed, tree-lined path of the wooded area. David had walked this way after his lunch date with his new girlfriend; they'd parted to go their separate ways, agreeing to meet up later that evening.

Margaret headed down an adjacent path ending in a stretch of abandoned railway track, weaving through brambles and stinging nettles. It led to a small scrap metal yard. It was possible that, after killing her son, the killer didn't know exactly where she was going.

She'd left the scene of the crime and wandered before dropping the knife.

It was a hunch, and that was all it was, but it made sense if she were in "a daze" after her crime, as suggested at the trial.

Margaret continued down the nettled path. The grass felt bone hard, the sole of a foot wouldn't leave an impression, even when it was raining.

She came to a wire fence beside a seedy-looking bowling green.

Margaret had followed this route on Google Earth on her phone, sounding out her theory before coming out here, but Mags wanted to walk it on foot to satisfy her hunch.

A rotten fence behind an abandoned bowling green presented a gap to squeeze through into a narrow alleyway where red squiggles of graffiti stood out on brickwork as if the wall were bleeding.

On the other wall were racist slurs against Muslims, a swastika, and a few unreadable block letters in gaudy green and pink, creating a 3D effect that wouldn't be rivalling Banksy any time soon.

It read: Pakis Out!

Nice.

Another talentless dropout who could only desecrate and never build; hate and not love.

The ground in the alleyway strewn with litter, Margaret stepped on a rusty Coke can that had faded to a fleshy pink, almost turning her ankle on the bloody thing.

This neglected alleyway led to a small cul-de-sac with a dozen parked cars.

Mags paused for a moment to catch her breath, looking down a street leading to the cul-de-sac named St Clements.

She knocked on the first door of the house on the left-hand side of St Clements Close and worked her way up from there.

One month later ...

It's remarkable how much you can achieve in a week when you're sober and possess a drive like never before.

It's also remarkable how badly you can screw up a relationship with a sibling in just one week of living under their roof.

Little natural light illuminated the garage of Mags's rented new home – her makeshift office – as photo after photo served as wallpaper. She'd even covered over the solitary garage window. To come into this garage was to delve into the uncertain inner dimensions of a sliding obsession.

Her secret addiction.

Dominating the room, a classroom-sized whiteboard she'd bought on eBay. On it, in black marker pen, she'd scribbled fifteen or so bullet points making up a simple timeline for events in and around her son's death.

She'd been staying with her brother up until last week. It was a short-term move since she'd moved out of her old home and the memories it held.

It proved a lot more short-term than she'd planned.

Her younger brother, John, had let Mags take over his garage as her private den to work in, but having seen the transformation she'd instigated he'd had second thoughts.

It was freaking his kids out.

Leading to a stupid argument, one which resulted in Mags moving out altogether and renting the house she was currently residing. Luckily for her, there was plenty of property to rent around here since all the new developmental work last May. No one buying or even renting thanks to Brexit. Two days later, she was in her new place, doing what she wanted.

Her own woman again.

It was for the best, they agreed.

She couldn't complain, John wasn't a bad brother; he even helped her move the whiteboard along with the rest of her stuff into her new place.

Despite his concerned disapproval at her motivation for doing this with her spare time, she continued to work in the new garage.

Mags looked at the events each morning and evening with what she hoped were fresh eyes. She'd started to see an order, an obsessive order in the facts.

She'd thought last night about asking Heinrich over to look through the clues, but the urge died down as quickly as it came and common sense took over.

Heinrich would react the same way as her brother at the spectacle of all the maps, the photos, the statements and newspaper clippings decorating her garage walls. Besides, at this stage, the dedication here was likely something that only one mind could ever see.

Mags needed more time, and more progress before she could even think of bringing in Heinrich's dedicated eye and input to her theory.

Besides, Heinrich might try and talk her out of it with even more determination if he saw this, but she knew there were answers here in this garage.

Mags only had to keep going.

One month later ...

She couldn't even voice her son's name today. Her shrink told her that this was normal and that there'd be days like this ahead; lots of them.

Mags had seen an advert for insurance shysters on Sky Gold. It featured her – vivacious and angelic, the picture of health – the woman who'd butchered her son!

She continued smiling as if she were naive, sweet and innocent as she represented a firm who fleeced people for cash under false pretences. The type of pushy people who'd ring you up, having cross-checked your age in a database amongst other baby boomers. Mags lost her appetite for TV at that moment. It was just another way the world could hurt her.

Even though the 4K set was almost new, she gave it away to a charity shop and cancelled her subscription with Sky.

Mags wanted nothing to distract her from her purpose.

When you're a professional writer, it's easy to cancel plans with friends; she told them she was writing.

She felt so awful and detached from daily life that immersing herself in finding that elusive murder weapon was the only way she could go on. Considering new motivations for the killing, visualizing reopening the case, the one way she could go on living.

It was 10:30 a.m. on a Saturday and Mags, back from her weekly shop where she'd bought a powerful laptop, felt hope again. The computer in front of her boasted more RAM and hard-drive space and the latest generation quad-core processor so that she could upload files quicker and store more high-resolution photos.

The hard drive of her ancient MacBook Pro was almost full, with transcripts and interviews from the case. There wasn't a single file or document not related to her son's case on her old laptop.

With rising panic, Margaret remembered she'd invited Heinrich over for dinner next Tuesday; she'd have to resist the urge to show him the evidence vault in her garage.

Mags had an ulterior motive in asking him over. To persuade Heinrich, with all his wealth, to hire a private detective so that she could fill in some crucial timeline gaps on her whiteboard.

Looking at the empty schedule, it dawned on her how much this case was keeping her going.

It felt better than a case of vodka, which was what used to keep her going on her weekends not so long ago.

She missed her son and her old life of being a devoted mother.

She'd never feel like that again.

Mags had been driving on a dual carriageway last week when a feeling came over her; an alien feeling.

A sudden feeling that took her unawares. A feeling that she wished a car would swerve into her path and obliterate her in a head-on collision.

Margaret wished it would all be over in a second and an ending to all the pain.

One month later ...

It was Sunday and Mags had the day to herself yet again.

Sundays were the worst.

Sundays had always been a day for family, and she no longer had one.

Today her diet was out of the window as she demolished her second Danish in four bites chased with a Costa Latte from her Tassimo coffee maker.

Rebooting her laptop, she waited for the perfunctory operating system updates to complete. Mags looked at the mobile phone video footage someone had taken of the zoo on the afternoon of 29 October, only minutes before.

They'd posted it directly to Facebook.

Weeks later, someone had noted that this was around the same time that David was killed and made the police aware of its existence.

The proud parents are capturing their toothy six-year-old flying a kite. By accident, they also recorded the marquee and zoo café in the background. Mags watched her son emerge with his gorgeous new girlfriend as they ran for cover under the marquee.

The image both beautiful and painful at the same time.

She paused the video. David looked so happy, unaware that his life was about to be taken from him.

Mags stilled the footage and honed in on another person, without an umbrella. She was on the footpath running behind the marquee where David and his girlfriend were waiting for the heavy rain to stop.

She paused the camcorder footage again and zoomed in on a blurred face. She got to work on cleaning up the image with the ridiculously expensive new software she'd purchased online this morning.

The woman wasn't wearing make-up.

It's her.

And something else, something in her hand. The murder weapon perhaps?

Mags didn't know quite what she'd seen, but on a whim, she grabbed her car keys and headed out to the zoo.

This case was her life now. For everyone else, pursuing this frustrating case was soul-destroying.

For her, the detective work, no matter how fruitless, gave her a sense of inner peace and a will to go on living.

If it took all the free hours available to her to find those elusive answers, then so be it.

She will feel the pain that I am suffering, Mags swore to herself. *She will know that justice applies to all.*

Mags knew she needed something to go her way, a clue to spark some life into the case. She needed what most people need in life, a break. A little bit of luck as a sign so that she could turn things around.

Mags, a single mother most of her life, and a self-employed freelance screenwriter, knew you make it in this world through hard work and a dedicated attitude.

She had hoped that David's biological father, Heinrich, might help her this time; and not abandon her like he'd done, as a young man, when David was born.

But she wasn't going to rely on it.

She did feel that Heinrich shared her pain, and with that came the hope; Heinrich was a resourceful man.

Heinrich had always been able to make things happen that the average person could only dream of doing. That's why Mags – no one's fool, even as a young girl – had fallen for him.

He owed her this.

One month later ...

Mags arrived back from her Monday night support group, *Parents Grieving Together.*

It was a group dedicated to parents who'd lost their children to violence, hosted in an archaic, poorly heated community centre with paint peeling off its decaying walls. The place reeked of sweat and mothballs and was possibly an asbestos risk. The filtered coffee was lousy, but it was free and kept her warm, so Mags didn't complain. She brought a tin of M&S biscuits each week for the other support group members.

In her second week, she'd met a close friend at the group, Andy.

Andy (short for Andrea) had lost her only daughter Charlotte around the same time as Mags lost David. Charlotte had been given drugs at a music festival she'd attended to celebrate her upcoming twenty-first birthday, and had died in the back of an ambulance struggling to get out of a muddy field.

A boy, five years older than Charlotte, her wannabe boyfriend, had supplied her with the deadly pill. Giving it to her on a whim, and persuading her to "live a little", as irony would have it after she'd initially refused. He had previous for possession of a Class A drug as a minor.

A Polish mother spoke about her experience of her daughter taking an overdose. Her daughter became a recluse, after being sexually assaulted by a man in the car park of her workplace.

Again, no arrest; once again, the story of powerlessness.

The group founded by two women, Cathy and Ellen, Cathy had been married to an abusive man who'd caused her daughter to run off and never be heard from again. She'd found love again in the arms of a woman, her partner in life as well as this support group: Ellen.

Margaret suspected that Ellen was simply here for Cathy as she never spoke about her past or herself in general but asked intelligent questions whenever needed.

Ellen came up with the idea of writing labels on a wooden board – negative words people used about themselves, their attackers and their experiences – and then taking a sledgehammer to it. It was a group exercise in which everyone participated and became something of a ritual to let off steam.

Tonight they welcomed a newcomer, Ben, who'd unburdened himself. Ben had been suicidal himself after he'd found his son Danny hanging in his bedroom a month ago. Margaret felt sorry for single parent Ben in his ill-fitting charity shop clothes comprising of an academic's jacket with leather elbow patches, a faded floral shirt needing an iron and a pair of corduroy trousers. He provided the overall impression that he was off to a Seventies-themed fancy-dress party and not suffering another night of despair.

Ben described the events leading up to Danny's suicide. As he spoke, Ben couldn't meet the eyes of the others, as he gazed down at pointed shoes that looked a size too big for him.

Danny had been so enthused hours before, elated even, believing he was going on a date with a girl from his school. Ben saw the delighted posts his son had put on Facebook hours before his death. Danny had always found it hard to fit in and, being small for his age made him a target for bullies throughout his school life. The date turned out to be some cruel prank from teenagers in the year above that Ben couldn't understand; a cruel joke that ended in tragedy.

On the board, created to be destroyed, he'd written BETRAYAL in scruffy capital letters. He followed it up with EVIL PRANKSTERS, INSENSITIVE and BULLIES. About himself, he wrote WEAK, WIMPY, CLUELESS and FAILED PARENT.

When asked to pick out one word above all the rest, he'd picked out BULLIES.

"I failed him." Ben broke down. "Failed him as a father in the only way that counted. To be there for him."

Mags felt awful for Ben. She also felt anger grow inside her. There had been no convictions here either. Subsequently, Ben could only blame himself.

The familiar story.

After the others had written their words on his "board of shame", Ben took the most pleasure in destroying it. Laughing and wiping a tear from his cheek as he stomped on it before sitting down for a tea break in which Mags passed him the tin of M&S biscuits.

Mags heard Andy say to him, "Do you think prison time for them would help you? Because in the end, with Charlotte, I had to admit to myself that locking that boy up in an eight-by-six cell wasn't enough for me. I wanted him to suffer, to feel pain. That's why I had to let it go."

"You still want the confession though," Ben replied. "There's still the need to know every last detail, but you know you never will. Why they did it in the first place; why they were so cruel."

Mags, seated next to him, consoled him with a hug.

The support group established to draw empathy and positivity from the group, and Margaret was doing that, but not in the conventional way it had intended.

Each night, Margaret took copious notes as soon as she got home, scribbling facts and ideas into her notebook for an hour or two. She typed up those raw notes in the form of a teleplay on her new laptop.

Mags recreated the pain of their experience, fleshing it out on the page as best she could.

Applying her screenwriter skills to get justice for her son, Heinrich had been right. They had to stick to what they knew to get their justice. Conventional channels had failed them, as they had the others in her support group.

They had to get creative in their revenge.

One month later ...

Margaret felt alive again writing the script, but there was also a sadness mixed in as she finished the last page of it. Mags never felt more alive than when she was writing.

The script she'd produced was full of promise; finally providing an outlet for her rage.

The bitch was going to be scared out of her mind; that was for sure.

She had created the scariest possible scenario for someone hiding such a heinous crime.

She would experience the uncertainty David had suffered in his marriage, living in a house with a liar and a criminal who you could not escape. Unable to go to the police about it because he was a man.

Awake at night, afraid and unable to predict what would happen to him the following day. That was how he'd described it to Mags. She hated herself for not doing more at the time. But she wouldn't let David down now; she would make sure that this evil girl suffered in the same way. And her friend Andy had been right about that part. A prison sentence wasn't punishment enough for this psychopath, although Mags wanted that too. No, she had to be more creative than what the traditional criminal justice system served up as punishment.

This script would place her son's killer at the centre of the action at all times; her conscience eating away at her to confess with the others.

Margaret watched her son's killer for one last time on the news clip from YouTube. It had seven-point-three million views; an audience who wanted to know the truth. A market, as it were.

The truth never went out of fashion.

Nor did punishing the guilty.

And niche channels existed now, open to all. Ordinary people were producing content from their bedrooms and pulling in more viewers than traditional television networks.

Heinrich was starting to believe too. He had even managed to pull a few strings to get hold of the police file on their son's killer's stepfather. A detail Mags was keen to layer into her script for the shock factor, along with the dire stories she'd heard at her grieving parents' support meetings, providing substance as fleshed-out character backstories.

She forced herself to watch the news footage again. She had her hair in a ponytail and went make-up free so that she resembled a tearful child as she emerged from the courthouse victorious, her bolshie lawyer pushing the press out of the way to put her in the back of a taxi; whisked away to freedom.

And a new life.

A few weeks from now she'd be flown out by helicopter to an island.

An island of surprises and a house full of actors urging her to confess, standing to benefit financially from her doing so.

They wouldn't hold back in their roles. Mags's job to ensure the script gave them everything they needed, and she felt she'd achieved that.

Margaret couldn't wait to see the killer's face when she saw that board of shame she'd created especially for her. How she'd pick out her horrible label off the board, and appreciate the dire, dangerous company she was keeping.

No sooner had Mags finished one character she had yet another idea: a backstory of a twelve-year-old who'd killed his stepfather, which she'd read in the paper. These real-life incidents lent the script a darker undertone, as she started banging out the words like she was falling in love with writing all over again. She craved to live in this dark world where true justice was autonomous.

It was painful for her to be ripped from her laptop to go back to her bleak reality. She was Mags again in this world, the risk-taker she'd been as a young activist journalist writing her freelance pieces before she'd had an affair with Heinrich and given birth to David.

Above and beyond this, she wanted her son to rest in peace. And for the world to know that David was the one who'd suffered, not her.

As fate would have it, the moment she'd finished writing another disturbing character backstory, the phone rang.

It was Heinrich wanting to know how she was getting on; delighted to hear of her advanced progress. He'd put aside a staggering forty-five million pounds in a trust fund for David, and was promising to pour all of it into this project. Every last penny to make it work.

I'm a modern-day Count of Monte Cristo, Mags thought, *but I can't wait twenty-four years to exact my revenge.*

I'm too old and impatient for that.

When you get down to it, writing is all about motivation, and Mags had that like never before. Mags averted her eyes from her laptop screen for a moment to inspect a section of peeling paint on her office wall, reflecting that it resembled a small island.

This is really going to happen, she thought.

THE END

A Request from the Author

As you've reached the end of my novel, hopefully, that means you enjoyed it. It would mean a great deal to me if you would consider leaving a review on Amazon or Goodreads, or any other site of this nature.

Regardless, I would like to thank you for taking the time to read it.

If you enjoyed it, and are after another book with the same trope as *And Then There Were None*, I have written a novel called *To Die For*, which is also part of my *And Then There Were More* series.

I'm in the process of writing a third novel in the series, you can find out more about this project if you wish on my website andthentheweremore.co.uk.

N G Sanders

Printed in Great Britain
by Amazon

47672019R00208